3 Sleuths

2 Dogs

1 Murder

Maggie Pill

Gwendolyn Press
Port Huron, MI

CHAPTER ONE

Retta

It's hard to say which is worse: hearing that your gentleman friend has been arrested for murder, or learning that the victim was his wife.

I was browsing my favorite on-line shoe site when the news came. I'd just added an item to my cart, a darling pair of navy pumps with little pink bows at the heel, when a distinctive ringtone sounded. Reaching over, I touched the screen, and said, "Hey, Faye."

"Hi, Retta. Are you at home?"

"Yup, shopping from my living room, since we live two hours north of just about everywhere."

"Good." My sister's tone hinted at bad news. "Are you seeing a guy named Winston Darrow?"

I considered asking what concern that was of hers. My sisters leave me out of almost everything they do, and sometimes it hurts my feelings. A year ago they started a business without me—without even *telling* me. This year, because of storm damage to my second home in Florida, I was stuck in Michigan on the tenth of January. Any other winter, I'd have been drinking wine in the afternoons with my girlfriends in Deerfield Beach.

Since I had to stick around, I'd let my sisters know I was available to help the Smart Detective Agency (though I hate that name). I hadn't been invited to take part. In fact, Barbara Ann had told me in her usual brusque way that I'm hard to work with because I'm bossy.

So when Faye asked about Winston Darrow I thought, *Why should I share my private affairs with them?*

Still, it isn't Faye's fault. With her middle child issues, insecurities, and lack of self-confidence, she gets bullied by Barbara Ann. I've told Faye that Barbara is too stubborn to take good help when it's offered, but she just smiles.

Knowing Faye wouldn't ask about my social life if it wasn't important, I answered without being snippy. "Winston and I met at a thing and hit it off. We've gone out a few times."

Unlike my sisters, I have a social life, and I'd met Winston at a Republican fund-raising dinner a month earlier. While I'm not political, I do support candidates who support the police. My husband, a state police officer, was killed ten years ago in the line of duty. Since then, through efforts to get better body armor state-wide, I've run into most of the movers and shakers of Michigan's Lower Peninsula at one time or another.

As single attendees, Winston and I had ended up sitting together. He was good-looking and charming, though a little shallow. He'd said he was divorced, which is why the news Faye was about to dump on me was a double shock.

"Mr. Darrow called our office this morning. He's being questioned about his wife's murder, and he's afraid he'll be charged. He wants the agency to help."

I heard my voice go up a notch. "Winston is married? I mean, he was married?"

"I'm sorry, Retta. His wife died early Sunday morning. Barb didn't promise him we'd take the case or anything."

My mind went in a dozen directions. Winston was married. That was Shock #1. It was embarrassing to learn I'd been lied to. Barbara would snicker up her sleeve, Faye was obviously feeling sorry for me, and soon my friends would hear that I'd been taken in by a smooth-talker who was possibly a murderer. I thought of people who'd seen us together, imagining their reactions. My face began to burn. How dare he do this to me!

"I don't mean to pry," Faye said. "I just want a sense of what kind of person he is."

She didn't sound disapproving or judgmental. That's how Faye is, and I appreciated it. Barbara would no doubt have added, "What were you thinking?" or something like that.

Winston Darrow's handsome face came to mind. He was smart. He was funny. Apparently he was also a liar. But a murderer? I recalled him cringing once when I'd squashed a cricket with a rolled-up magazine. I couldn't see him killing anything, much less a living, breathing, still-attached wife. "Winston isn't the murdering type. I'd bet on that."

"Good to know." Faye's voice was low, and I guessed she was trying to keep Barbara from hearing. "I thought I should tell you, because you're bound to be dragged into it."

Another shock. "What do you mean?"

"According to Mr. Darrow, the police hinted he'd shot his wife in order to be free to marry you."

I shook my head vigorously, though she couldn't see it. "That's ridiculous. We never even mentioned marriage. And she was shot? Faye, Winston hates guns. It's one of the reasons I enjoyed his company—no long, boring stories about what he saw from his deer blind or what kind of rifle he picked up at the gun show last weekend."

"Well, he owned a gun, or his wife did, and it's missing."

"Which proves nothing unless that's what killed her." I was arguing Winston's case, which was odd in light of what he'd done.

I could almost see Faye raising a hand to calm me down. "If the police have a good case for domestic violence, we won't waste our time."

"It's not a waste." I sighed, irritated at both Winston and myself. "Winston isn't who I thought, but he's no murderer."

"He says he was with you Sunday night."

"Well, not *all* night, if that's what you're asking. He left around midnight." A series of painful images came to mind, people whispering behind their hands, hiding smug smiles. *He crawled out of Retta's bed, went back to his wife—and then shot her!*

"That doesn't help," Faye was saying. "Cops estimate the time of death was between eleven and two."

"So if he left my place at twelve, he had time to get home and kill her." I heard a sad little moan and realized it was me. "What are we going to do about this?"

"*You* aren't going to do anything," Faye said sternly. "You know Barb gets mad when you start giving advice."

"I never give advice, especially to Barbara I'm-Fine-on-My-Own Evans." Ideas gathered in my head as I spoke. "Tell her to call Rory Neuencamp and see what he knows. It's out of his jurisdiction, but cops talk to cops." That reminded me of something, and I asked, "Have Barbara and Rory started anything yet, or are they still avoiding each other like teenagers at a church mixer?"

"Um, they haven't gone out that I know of."

There's no pushing Barbara, but I resolved to say something to Rory the next time we met. It doesn't take a genius to see they're attracted to each other, but Barbara Ann would die in the desert before she'd ask anyone for a glass of water. And flirt? She doesn't know how!

I returned to the current problem. "Start checking divorce records in New Mexico. Winston told me he and his wife split three years ago."

Faye's reply sounded flat. "We'll do that, Retta."

"And keep me informed. Please," I added. Ending the call, I closed my iPad, too distracted to complete my purchase. I wandered the house for a while, letting Faye's news sink in. My dog Styx, asleep on his couch, raised his head as if to ask if we were going outside. I patted him, feeling soothed a little by contact with my best friend. "Not right now, baby." His head sank back to the couch, and he was snoring in seconds.

I must have mentioned my sisters' business at some point, so Winston had called their agency when trouble hit. Naturally he thought they'd help him prove his innocence for my sake.

Was he innocent?

Though angry he'd lied to me, I was pretty sure Winston Darrow wasn't capable of killing anyone. A couple of times he'd even joked about being a lover, not a fighter.

As someone who knew Winston well, I couldn't just sit around now that he was in trouble. Therefore the next question was clear: What should I do to help?

CHAPTER TWO

Barb

"So what did she say?"

Faye jumped a mile, and I chuckled to myself. She deserved a little scare for the covert call to Retta, but I'd known it would happen. Though tough when she needs to be, Faye is a softie who sometimes forgets that our baby sister drives us both insane with her meddling. Besides, this time she was correct. Retta was going to be named as the Other Woman in a murder investigation, so she had a right to know what we knew.

"He told her he's been divorced for three years." Faye's lip curled, betraying anger. "I'm betting this guy is a jerk."

"That doesn't make him a murderer," I replied. "Here's the odd thing, though. I did an online search for information on the Darrows, and there's next to nothing."

There's a lot to be learned about a person if you know where to look on the Internet, and the Smart Detective Agency has developed an impressive array of sources, thanks to Faye's office skills and my background as a lawyer. Checking my notes I read aloud, "Winston Darrow, born 1950, self-described entrepreneur. His wife Stacy has no job history. They're comfortable financially, own a home on a small lake between here and Gaylord, and have two vehicles: a Lexus and a Tundra. He's a member of the local Kiwanis Club, the Rotary, the

Republican Party, and the Friends of the Library, but he doesn't attend meetings. Instead he shows up at social events like dinners and receptions. Mrs. Darrow stays home a lot. She's a member of a dozen on-line groups, most focused on reading mysteries and collecting Carnival glass."

"Good reading choice." Cozy mysteries are Faye's favorites. "Did you finish the report on the missing money at the hardware store?"

"Yes," I replied. "They're going to handle the embezzlement quietly, but the owner says with what we gave him, he can demand repayment in exchange for a lesser sentence. He's happy with that."

"Good," Faye said. "That clears our schedule so we can spend some time with Retta's friend." She glanced at me then looked down at her keyboard. "Might Chief Neuencamp help?"

The suggestion had obviously come from Retta. While our local police chief could probably help, I was reluctant to ask. First, I didn't want Rory to think we expected him to do our work. In addition, I didn't want to appear to seek out his company. Our relationship was cordial, and though my sisters had insisted he'd take it a step farther, he hadn't. I told myself he was learning the rules of a new job in a new town, and he'd naturally keep professional distance between the Allport police and the city's only detective agency. What I didn't like to think was that Rory considered me only a business acquaintance.

"Let's do a little more on our own," I told Faye. "When I talk to the chief, I want to have my facts straight."

We spent the rest of the morning digging, and when we finished, we'd added a few bits. The Darrows had moved to

Michigan as newlyweds two years earlier from Taos, New Mexico. According to their marriage license, her maiden name was Stacy Kern, and she was fifteen years Winston's junior. Her parents, Alice (Duggan) and Charles Kern, were both listed as natives of Rutland, Vermont.

Stacy's lack of presence on social media—no Facebook, no Twitter, no Instagram—had me picturing a shy, plain girl who'd perhaps married a father figure. Winston had a Facebook page, and his timeline contained photos of him with a succession of different women. In each picture he looked confident and debonair while his companions looked startled, as people often do after multiple face-lifts.

The most recent photo was captioned WIN & STACY GOT MARRIED. The happy couple stood before a sprawling, red-brick courthouse, and when I set the cursor over it, TAOS, NEW MEXICO, came up. Unfortunately, the photographer hadn't timed the shot well, and the new Mrs. Darrow was digging in her purse for something. Though her face wasn't visible, Stacy had a knockout figure, revealed by a short, tight mini-dress, and a mass of dark hair. So much for shy and plain.

Had Winston Darrow murdered his wife in order to marry my sister Margaretta? She's an attractive woman, but as far as I'm concerned, Retta's charm fades each and every time she starts trying to run my life.

CHAPTER THREE

When Barb asked me to do the initial interview with Winston
Darrow, I took it as a sign she doesn't think of me as just the
office manager. I'd gathered intake information before, of
course, but this was only our second murder investigation.
Though the stakes were high, she trusted me to handle it.

Usually, I let Barb take the lead, bowing to her experience
with the legal system, but I try to do my part. Sometimes I take
the initiative, like when I handled Retta's stubbornness in the
matter of payment.

Retta wants to be part of the Smart Detective Agency, but
Barb refuses to make her a partner, citing her manipulative
ways. I'll admit, Retta likes things her way, and she's nosed in
several times already by sheer force of will. She really can be
helpful, (I swear she knows half the people in the state) which
makes it hard to leave her out completely. Barb's solution had
been to call Retta a consulting expert and pay her a fee.

After a while, though, I noticed that Retta never cashed our
checks. She didn't send them back or anything. They simply
remained outstanding. When I asked about it she got evasive,
claiming she forgot, but I suspected she was getting back at
Barb for leaving her out. It became my problem, since I do the
bookkeeping.

In the end I called her bank, got the routing numbers, and deposited the money directly into her account. That might not be possible everywhere, but in a small town it's doable. Retta could no longer "forget" to cash the checks, and I saved myself headaches Barb never even knew about.

Winston Darrow lived in Bonner County, thirty miles west of Allport as the crow flies. Since Bonner is mostly comprised of small lakes nestled among large forests, however, a direct route is nonexistent. Narrow country roads meander through touristy little villages, tracing lakeshores and skirting hills, so it took me an hour to get to the sheriff's office situated in Lawton. It was easy to find the county building once I got there, since it was by far the largest structure in town.

A cold wind pushed the door closed behind me with a bang that made everyone present look up. I introduced myself, ignoring the raised eyebrows at a woman of my age being a private investigator, and asked if I could see Winston Darrow. He was due in court for arraignment soon, and there was some discussion about whether he could have a visitor before he saw the judge. When nobody could think of a reason why he couldn't, I was shown into a bland room containing a table and three chairs with metal legs and one-piece plastic seats. A few minutes later a deputy brought our prospective client in.

Two decades ago, Darrow would have qualified as eye candy. He still didn't look bad: thick black hair with a touch of gray at the temples; a trim build, not athletic but hardly gone to seed; and large green eyes set into a fine-boned face. The favorable impression he might have made disappeared almost immediately when he stepped close, tilted his head down and to one side, and gave me a look meant to make me feel feminine and attractive. Instead I felt like backing out of the room.

"Mrs. Evans," he said in a mellow, low-pitched voice, "it's good of you to come so quickly." Taking my hand, he raised it slightly and I swear, only the look of warning on my face kept him from raising it to his lips.

Darrow's kind of charm never works on me. Stepping out of his personal space and re-possessing my hand, I said, "I'm Faye Burner, Barb's partner."

He smiled warmly to cover his mistake. "Mrs. Burner, sorry. Please call me Win."

He gazed into my eyes for that extra half-second men like him use to let a woman know she interests them, or to try to create that impression. I tried to maintain objectivity, but he hadn't gained a single point so far. Winston "Call me Win" brought words to my mind like *greaseball, sleazeball, egotist, lothario, scuz-bucket.* The list could have gone on.

Still, he'd just become a widower and might soon be a client, so I sat down on the hard chair and took out my notepad. "I'm sorry for your loss, Mr. Darrow. Please tell me what you can about your wife's death and I'll see if we can help."

"Win, please," he repeated. Sitting down opposite me, he glanced around the room. "Are the police listening?"

I shrugged. "They could be. This isn't a privileged conversation." Meeting his gaze, I asked, "Were you intending to tell me something you didn't tell them?"

"Of course not." He waved both hands dismissively. "I told them the truth, same as I'm going to tell you."

He was smooth, but I noted fraying at the edges of his persona. His un-shaven beard was grayer than his hair, betraying his age. His clothes were rumpled, and his eyes were slightly glassy. Maybe he was grieving. With visible effort, he pulled himself together and began his story.

"I was with Retta Stilson—your sister—Saturday night until about twelve. After we had dinner at that new Mediterranean restaurant, she invited me back to her place. She'd made a pie, and she said she'd never eat it all by herself." He tried to look innocent. I tried to look like I didn't care what he and my sister did after eating pie.

"When I left Retta's it was storming, and the east-west roads had drifted badly. The trip took longer than usual, white-knuckles all the way."

"What time did you get home?" I almost added "to your wife."

"About one-thirty. Everything was white, and I couldn't see the driveway posts. When I turned in, one wheel went off into the ditch. I tried to back out, but I just made things worse. The car was off the road far enough that it wasn't a hazard, so I left it there, figuring I'd call someone with a tractor in the morning. The house was dark, and my hands and feet were freezing from trying to push the car." He looked down. "I didn't look in on Stacy, just went to my own room and took a hot shower."

"You had separate rooms?"

He licked his lips. "Stacy likes—liked her privacy, and we had plenty of space." Darrow's voice dropped a little. "She'd lost interest in pretty much anything that had to do with me."

"Was that because you went around telling other women you were divorced?"

He tried for anger, but his reply sounded defensive. "We might as well have been."

"You stayed because she had money?" It was a guess, but why else would a charmer like Darrow stick with a woman who ignored him?

It looked for a few seconds like he might cry, but after a choky little cough he said, "I'd have been a good husband if Stacy had been interested in being a wife."

I rolled my eyes. Every bar in the world has at least one guy leaning on his elbows and moaning, "My wife doesn't understand me." To be fair, there are women saying the same thing about their husbands.

"Do you think she'd found someone else?"

He huffed in denial. "I don't see how. She never went anywhere."

I leaned back, and the chair made an ominous creak. "Where did you meet?"

Winston also leaned back, unconsciously mirroring my action. "In New Mexico, in one of those artsy areas in Taos. I was having lunch at an outdoor café when Stacy came in. The place was crowded, she asked if we could share a table, and we got to talking. She'd just moved from Delaware. Her husband died, and she decided to start a new life somewhere else."

"Delaware." As I wrote it down, I thought I recalled Barb mentioning Vermont, but I could check that later. "How did her husband die?"

"Car accident, she said. Anyway, we hit it off, and I asked her out to dinner. From there on things went well, and it wasn't long before we decided to get married."

"How long?" I asked.

"Three weeks." He looked embarrassed, and I thought I knew why.

"By that time you'd figured out she was well off."

Leaning forward, he stretched his arms across the table toward me. "Just because a guy knows something like that doesn't mean—"

"He's a gigolo?" I finished.

Win tapped the table in rebuttal. "I liked Stacy. She was fun, she was gorgeous—"

"She was a lot younger than you. How'd you pull that off, Mr. Darrow?"

"Win," he corrected automatically. He shook his head like a kid who doesn't want to take his medicine. "She said we made a great couple. That was before she—" Looking at his hands, he put one over the other as if to hide the wrinkled skin. "She lost interest."

"Did she make you sign a pre-nup?"

"Um, no." He looked uncomfortable. "She kind of thought I had money too."

"Wonder where she got that idea." Win looked away, and I guessed it was time to back off a little. "Okay. Tell me about your background."

He looked away, like my sons used to do when I asked where they'd gone the night before. Win wasn't going to tell the truth he'd promised earlier.

"I grew up in the San Joaquin Valley, worked in the movie industry as a kid—commercials, a few parts on sitcoms and once in a movie. My parents were pretty well off, but bad investments Dad made wiped out everything. He died of a heart attack when

I was eighteen, and Mom went a month later, leaving me nothing but funeral bills and memories." His tone was sad, but the story sounded rehearsed, as if he always told it the same way.

"No siblings?"

He smiled modestly. "Mom always said I was enough of a blessing."

"What did you do after they died?"

His lower lip jutted briefly. "I did a little of everything, commercials, bit parts, some editing, and a stint as a first assistant on one of the daytime dramas."

"Any other marriages?"

"None." He went on in the same practiced tone. "A few years ago I got tired of it—all of it. I walked away from the Hollywood scene."

"And went to New Mexico."

"Yes. An old friend there invited me to stay in her guest house until I decided what I wanted to do." He pulled at his collar in an unconscious grooming gesture. "She was very kind."

As I took notes, I looked for items that could be researched and proven. Win might or might have had well-to-do parents, might or might not be from California, might or might not have worked in Hollywood. Barb had found he listed himself as an entrepreneur. I guessed that meant, *I'll see who I can find to support me.*

"Stacy didn't mind that you really weren't wealthy?"

"She said it didn't matter."

"So you were happily married in Taos."

"Yes—well, no. As soon as we were married she said she'd found this great place in Michigan." He grimaced. "I've never been much for winter, but Stacy promised we'd look for a second home somewhere warmer once we got settled."

"So you moved north."

He gave a dry chuckle. "To the friggin' boondocks. Not one real city in the whole county."

"But your wife liked it here?"

He spread his hands. "There wasn't any more talk of getting a second place, that's for sure. She settled into that house like it was the last place on earth."

"She didn't go out?"

"Sure she did." His tone turned sarcastic. "She went out to the barn to see her horses. She went out to the woods to ski. She went out to the lakeshore to think. Everything else came to her. I got the groceries. I took the cars in for service."

"You did everything?" I was wondering if Stacy had simply wanted a cheap housekeeper.

"Well, she did the banking," he replied, "but most stuff that meant going where there were people was up to me."

Win's wife hadn't trusted him with her money. Go figure.

"So you started going places where no one knew you, meeting women and telling them you were single."

He turned up the charm again. "Mrs. Burner, I don't claim to be a saint, but I'm no monk, either. Stacy didn't sleep with me, she didn't talk to me—hell, there were times I don't even think she saw me." He picked at a fingernail. "She should have just hired a personal assistant. It would have been a lot kinder."

I sighed. "Tell me what happened Sunday morning."

Win licked his lips. "I woke up around nine, had a bowl of cereal, and watched a little of the morning news. When I realized I hadn't heard Stacy moving around, I knocked on her door. There was no answer, so I looked in. The bed was made, the computer was on, and there was a full glass of Mountain Dew sitting on the desk, like she'd sat down then got up again.

"I started looking, but she wasn't in the house or the garage. I was about to check the barn when I noticed an odd bump under the snow on the deck out front. I went out there, and—" There was real emotion in his voice now. "—I knew it was bad. I bent down and—" His voice caught but he swallowed and continued. "It was Stacy, buried in snow." He looked up at me. "Her head—I never saw anything like that before. I never—"

When I realized he wasn't going to finish I asked, "Why did the police arrest you?"

The sneaky look returned to his eyes. "I don't know. I swear to you, Mrs. Burner, I did not kill my wife. Why would I? I mean, I had to ask her for money, but she never said no. Stacy didn't like to travel, but she let me go whenever I wanted. I had no reason to kill her. None."

Darrow's claim of innocence got a laugh from the Bonner County sheriff when I repeated it to him a few minutes later. A sun-burned, raw-boned man, Wade Idalski seemed amused that a private investigator was asking about his case. Though he didn't pat me on the head and tell me I should go back to the kitchen, he was amused by my assumption that anything Win Darrow had told me was the truth.

"If she let him live as he wanted on her money," I argued, "why would he kill her?"

Sheriff Idalski folded his arms. "It's early in the investigation, ma'am, so I can only tell you the basics. Mrs. Darrow was shot at close range with a pistol, possibly a .38 that's missing from the home. In most homicides, the motive is either emotional or financial. We believe both motives are in play here."

I started for home, satisfied we had enough to decide whether to take the case. I'd have leaned toward a *no* vote if not for Retta's involvement. If we took the case we could protect her reputation, making sure her innocence in Stacy Darrow's death was established.

The day was bright, and the snow glistened, making sunglasses a necessity. As I navigated the twisty, snow-covered roads around the lakes, I appreciated my recently-acquired vehicle. When the Smart Detective Agency began making a small profit, I'd upgraded my ride to a new-to-me 2010 Ford Escape. It was quiet, held the road well, and was an attractive shade of green. I liked its roominess after years of driving cars that were too small, too low, and all too likely not to start when I turned the key.

Once I left the lake shore, large tracts of wooded land took over, with only a few cleared fields here and there. They were buried in snow, but corn stalks, stumps, and rock piles interrupted the otherwise solid blanket of white.

Five miles out, something lay in the road. At first I thought it was a bag of garbage someone had tossed from a car window, rumpled black with spots of white. When it moved, I realized it wasn't trash. Checking the rear-view mirror, I pulled the car close to the banked snow and turned on my flashers. There wasn't much room, but I had to see what living thing lay exposed to cold and danger.

It was a middle-sized dog of mixed breed. His curly hair was matted with ice; his eyes were large but dimmed with suffering. As I approached, he raised his head slightly and made a sound that would have been a growl if it had any strength behind it.

"Hey, buddy. Hey, boy. What are you doing out here?"

I looked around. No houses in sight, nothing moving. There weren't many inhabited places along this stretch, just boarded up summer homes and cabins.

The dog kicked his front leg weakly. "Are you hurt, buddy? Can I look?"

Ever so slowly, I stretched out a hand toward him. Again he growled, but I spoke softly, crooning encouragement. I let him sniff my hand and waited until he relaxed a little. Next I touched the spot behind his ear where every dog in the world likes to be scratched. Though still tense, he let me rub the spot. Talking in a soft voice, I moved my hand to his head, petting and scratching. He might not have allowed it if he'd been well, but he wasn't. Gradually he relaxed a little and I moved my hand to his body, probing gently.

His back seemed okay, as did his front legs, but he flinched when I touched the right back one. When I found a distinct break in the bone, the dog let out a yip of pain and nipped at me. It was a reflex, and once I let go, he seemed penitent. "Sorry, buddy. I don't mean to hurt you."

A car passed, and the driver frowned a warning. He had a point. It was a terrible place to stop in the road. Sitting back on my heels, I took stock. The dog was malnourished, possibly abused, hurt, and hostile. What was I going to do with him?

Going to my car, I got an old fuzzy blanket kept there for emergencies. "You aren't going to like this, buddy," I told the dog when I returned, "but it's got to happen."

Setting the blanket on the ground between us, I anchored one edge with my knees. The other edge I planted behind the dog then quickly pulled it toward me, sliding the fabric under him. Once the two edges met I rolled them together, encasing the dog tightly inside. The phrase "doggie bag" came to mind.

My action kept him from biting me, but that didn't mean the dog stopped trying. Holding the front edge with my knees, I rolled the blanket's side edges up until he could hardly move at all. He gave up struggling, but his hopeless whine almost broke my heart. I wished I could let him know that my intentions for him were all good.

Speaking soft words of encouragement, I picked the dog up, carefully centering his weight on my arms. He yelped; the broken leg had to hurt. When I got him to the car, I set him gently on the back seat and tucked the blanket ends tightly into the seat cushions. A healthy animal would have easily escaped, but this one was too weak. With a sigh of resignation, he slumped against the seat, accepting whatever happened next.

Climbing into the front, I headed for Allport and the nearest veterinarian.

CHAPTER FOUR

Retta

I couldn't settle down after Faye's call, though I had plenty to do. The Allport Ice Festival was a few weeks away, and I still had at least a dozen businesses to contact for donations. Our alumni association was having its annual Lady Slipper Night on the 25th, and I had volunteered to organize the program. I'd baked a cake that morning (I love how baking makes the house smell.) and it was ready to be frosted. My daughter and her kids were coming for winter break, and I planned to order new curtains and bedspreads for their rooms. None of it got done as I wondered how I'd been so wrong about Winston Darrow.

I hadn't lied to Faye. Winston was not my Mr. Right, not even close, but he was witty and debonair. He'd traveled. He'd seen Paris—the city, not the Vegas hotel. He danced well. He spoke a little Spanish, and he didn't think Pablo Picasso was a resort in Mexico. In short, he'd been pleasant company, different from other men I knew.

That said, dating a married man is a violation of my personal code of conduct. A woman who takes a man from his wife gets a hound who'll soon be on a new scent.

Trying to remember what he'd said the night we met, I imagined Winston's voice in my mind: "My wife and I divorced because we didn't have the same interests anymore." Had he used the word *divorced*? I thought he had, but he might have said "split." Had I assumed the marriage was dissolved? If so, I'd proved that it's true what they say about assuming.

Still, Winston had cultivated the idea there was no one else at home, and I realized there was a good reason why he'd never invited me to his place. That meant he was a hound, but was he a murdering hound?

I couldn't see it. For one thing, he was a little wimpy, as I'd admitted to Faye. Though I'd told myself it didn't matter, Winston cared more about how well his suit jacket fit than how well his car ran. Everything he owned was turned over to experts: his A/C, his lawn, his broken treadmill. He had no idea how to turn on an electric drill, much less repair a loose board on the deck of his house.

By comparison, my Don had been able to fix anything, from my broken hair dryer to our furnace. In my mind that was what a man should be like, so despite Winston's charm, I'd never seen him as husband material.

Don was gone forever, killed by a drug-crazed addict too high to realize what he was doing. I wished for another man like Don, but so far I'd only met men like Winston. Men like him were easy to find. Men like Don, not so much.

That thought brought the tears that had threatened since the news came. I missed Don, who'd been the love of my life, and learning about Winston's lies made me feel like a stupid, desperate woman.

After a while, I wiped my eyes with a tissue and pushed aside wishes there's no use dwelling on. Knowing Faye and Barbara needed all the information they could get, I dug out a pad of paper and wrote down everything Winston had told me about his background.

RAISED IN CALIFORNIA
MOVED TO TAOS, NM
CAME TO MI APRIL, 2012
WORKED IN MOVIE INDUSTRY UNTIL (?) A FEW YEARS AGO

I stopped, staring at the pink three-by-five inch scratch pad. Was that all I knew about Winston? When we were out together, he'd talked, but it had been mostly about the exotic places he'd visited. Now that I thought about it, he'd answered direct questions about his past with a few glib sentences and moved on to something else. It hadn't seemed odd at the time, but now it was downright suspicious.

CHAPTER FIVE

Barb

Faye came back to the office with news that was not completely welcome. "Barb," she said breathlessly as she closed the office door behind her, "I found a dog on the road. He's hurt, and the vet is working on him now. I'd like to keep him if no one claims him." She bit her bottom lip. "Is that okay with you?"

I tried to maintain a pleasant expression. While I have nothing against animals, I don't relate well to beings with no higher thinking skills. In my experience, dogs either jump on you to demonstrate affection or try to eat you to demonstrate dominance. I'm not thrilled with either.

On the other hand, my home was now Faye's home. When we started the detective agency, I'd invited her and her mostly-disabled husband Dale to move into the downstairs of my rambling house near Allport's business district. There was plenty of room for me upstairs, and the main floor had comfortable living space for them in addition to the two formal parlors at the front we now used as offices.

Having spent her adult life in a series of cramped and unlovely rental homes and apartments, Faye fell in love with the house's numerous windows, ten-inch mop-boards, and nine-foot ceilings. She also loved the back yard and spent winter evenings drawing diagrams of the lovely and aromatic flowers she planned to plant when spring came. I figured if she kept the dog, its house could take up a corner of her garden plot.

"Faye, you live here," I said. "You don't need my permission to get a pet."

The look on her face was worth giving up a tiny piece of yard. "Wait till you see him! He's only about fifteen pounds, but he'll put on weight once we get him home and feed him right." She bit her lip again, this time in thought. "I wonder if I kept the dog bed I had for Sheba. It might fit in the corner of my bedroom where the bookcases meet."

Before I could speak again, she headed off to find it. Not only had she not told me about the Darrow interview, but apparently we were going to have a dog that lived inside.

Once she found the dog bed Faye returned and, wiping hair from her clothes, recounted her meeting with Darrow. When she repeated what the sheriff told her afterward, words like *liar* and *slime-ball* made it clear she didn't like our client much.

"Okay," I said when she finished. "He's no hero, but is it possible he killed his wife?"

She hesitated, rubbing her neck absently. "I can't picture the guy putting a gun to someone's head and pulling the trigger, but strange things happen between husbands and wives. It's just that—well, you know."

I knew. She felt compelled to take the case for Retta's sake, and so did I. Baby Sister had been fed a line by a man with few, maybe no morals, and we knew how embarrassed she must be. It seemed disloyal to discuss her being taken in by a handsome face, however true it might be, so "you know" was as far as either of us would go.

"So we look into this?" I asked.

"Yes, at least that's my vote."

"Agreed. And we can't leave Retta out this time."

"No." Faye sounded relieved.

"Will you call and update her?" I glanced at my watch. "I have to go out for an hour or so."

"Okay, but then I visit The Meadows."

"What's she done now?"

Faye's mother-in-law, ninety years old and senile when she chooses to be, has become Faye's responsibility due to Dale's weakened condition and the rest of the family's disinterest. Having met the old bat a few times, I admire the patience of those who have to deal with her, especially Faye, who seldom does anything the old lady approves of.

"She filed complaints about the food again, this time at the state level."

"I thought you took her phone away."

Faye shrugged. "She borrowed one from some dewy-eyed newbie. You know how convincing she can be." Dropping her phone into her purse she asked, "Where are you headed?"

"To find out exactly what they've got on Darrow. Rory might be willing to ask the sheriff for information he won't tell us."

In order to keep our relationship businesslike, I'd always called to make an appointment before visiting Rory Neuencamp's office. Not only is it unprofessional to drop in, it's unrealistic to expect the head of a mid-sized police force to have free time whenever he chooses. Still, if nothing big was happening, I thought the chief would give me ten minutes.

Once a city cop, Rory had looked for something less stressful after twenty-five years on the Chicago police force. Allport was perfect for a man tired of the big city but still capable of doing the job. Our town kept him busier than he'd expected, but I thought he was pleased to have his own department.

Once he'd told me in passing that he liked to stop around three o'clock and take what he called a personal break. "Mornings are rushed," he'd said, "catching up, getting things done. Lots of times lunch is business, and just before shift ends some deadline always seems to pop up. But around three o'clock it gets pretty quiet. If I can, I put my feet up for a while." He'd grinned as he added, "At fifty-plus hours a week, I deserve it."

It was just a few minutes before three, and I figured Rory wouldn't mind the interruption if I brought some of Faye's peanut butter cookies along. Everybody loves Faye's cookies, and Rory is a man who likes his sweets.

Janet, the woman at the front desk, said the chief would see me almost at the same instant that Rory came out to welcome me himself. Leading the way into his office, he offered coffee or tea. I chose the latter, knowing he liked tea in the afternoon. Like a true Irishman (on his mother's side; his father was mostly Native American Anishinabe), he kept a small set-up in one corner, with real tea leaves in a rectangular tin, a china pot, and a one-burner unit with a kettle already heating water. Checking the temperature by touching the kettle lightly, Rory poured water over the loose leaves in the pot and set it down to brew. While we waited, I set the cookie plate on the desk between us.

After precisely four minutes, he poured tea into our mugs, added cream to his from a small carton on the tray, and took two cookies, setting them on his napkin with obvious anticipation. As we sipped carefully, he caught me up on the day's events, speaking candidly of the city commission's short-sightedness and the planning commission's mistaken belief that the citizenry wanted a parking ramp downtown. Once we'd hashed that out he asked, "What are you up to, Barb?"

I checked my watch with a grin. "Is break time over?"

He raised a brow. "This isn't a social call, then?"

My hands got fidgety. "I don't want to take advantage of our friendship, um, our acquaintance—"

"Barb," Rory interrupted, "You're not the kind of person who'd take advantage of me." Picking up his mug, he added, "Not that I'd mind."

Since I often have trouble deciding how to take Rory's comments, I ignored that one. "We got a case this morning, and I wondered if you know anything about it." I told him about the murder and Darrow's arrest.

"I heard it on the news, like everybody else," he said when I finished. "Let me see what I can find out." Turning to the phone, he hit a number and waited. "Sheriff Idalski, please. This is Chief Neuencamp over in Allport." After a short wait he said, "Wade? How are things?" He listened for a while before saying, "I understand you have a murder suspect in custody." ... "Oh, is that right? Well, can you answer some questions for me? Rumor says the guy was involved with a woman here in Allport, and I'd like to stay informed." He listened for a longer time, taking notes and responding with grunts and "um-hums." Finally he thanked the sheriff and ended the call.

Raising my brows, I asked a tacit question.

"It isn't pretty," Rory said, taking a sip of tea. "First, the guy's wife was apparently planning to leave him. They found two packed suitcases under the bed and a one-way ticket to La Paz. The sheriff thinks she meant to visit the bank Monday morning, get her money, and leave."

"They think she heard about Retta so he killed her."

"Not intentionally. Idalski thinks they fought when he realized she was leaving."

"So second degree, maybe manslaughter if she's the one who got the gun out."

Rory set his cup down on the desk. "Another thing: Darrow didn't call the police."

I almost spilled tea in my lap. "What?"

"Their housekeeper arrived around 8:30 a.m., saw one car in the ditch near the end of the driveway and the other one gone. She didn't find anybody in the house but noticed footprints in the snow on the back porch. She went out to investigate, and thirty seconds later she was calling the police, screaming, "He killed her! He killed her!""

I sensed there was more. "What else?"

"Sheriff Idalski has seen Darrow around, and he'd formed an opinion of your client. When the news came in, Wade immediately sent a deputy to the bank. Shortly after 9:00 a.m. he caught Darrow withdrawing all the funds from the only account he had access to." He rubbed his chin. "By the way, there's no will, so he gets everything—unless he killed her."

I sighed. "Retta says Darrow wouldn't know which end of a gun to hold onto. Faye distrusts him but doesn't think he's the murdering type."

"If there is a type." The chair squeaked as he shifted position. "What's your take on it?"

I felt a little thrill at the genuine interest in Rory's voice. "If he killed her, it seems to me he'd have run."

Rory shrugged to indicate that was a possible but not telling argument. I moved to my next point. "The con men I've met use charm to solve their problems, not violence." As an assistant D.A., I'd seen my share of criminal types.

"That's true," Rory replied, "but you and I know anyone can become violent if the circumstances are right."

"Agreed. But if a con man planned a murder, wouldn't he either figure out a way to disappear or come up with a method that didn't leave him on the hook for the crime?"

"Maybe he didn't plan it. If she was about to leave him, he might have panicked." Rory wasn't dismissing my idea. He was playing devil's advocate.

"But why was she leaving?" I asked. "Darrow claims Stacy insisted on coming to Michigan. She loved the house; she loved her horses and the lake and all that. If she was tired of his philandering, why didn't she kick him out?"

He tilted his head to one side. "Afraid he'd get a chunk of her money in the divorce?"

"That's possible, I guess." I thought of something else. "Darrow travelled a lot. Maybe Stacy had a lover, and he killed her."

"And arranged for the husband to take the blame."

I nodded. "If Stacy was about to leave Michigan, something about her situation had changed."

He sighed. "I'm on the outside looking in, but your logic works for me. Most con men I've known would have offered her the moon rather than chasing her around with a gun." He drank the last of his tea, adding, "And if Darrow's charm didn't work, I agree with you. He'd make it look like an accident."

Faye

"Their eggs taste like crap."

I sighed, looking at my mother-in-law's pinched face. Apparently she'd misplaced her teeth again, so her lips folded inward, tight with disapproval. She was dressed in blue polyester pants and a purple tee-shirt that said I LOVE THE MACKINAC BRIDGE, and she wore soft-soled shoes with Velcro closures. She considers it a point of pride to rise each morning, make her bed, wash, and make herself "presentable," though these days it requires a lot of help from the staff. Her outfit always includes jewelry in the form of Mardi Gras beads the facility gives out as Bingo prizes. When she's in a good mood she often offers me a necklace, often with the admonition that I need to "pretty up a little." Beads clicked as she shoved the tray away.

Wincing at the waste of food I said, "Last week you said scramble eggs are the only food they make right."

"No, I didn't."

I opened my mouth to argue, but experience made me close it. "Harriet, you can't call the state because your eggs were rubbery."

"I did it, didn't I?"

Another sigh, this time from the dietician, who stood behind my mother-in-law, her mouth a parody of a smile.

"Mrs. Berrien is going to see you get whatever you want for lunch. How will that be?"

Mrs. Berrien and I both knew Harriet would take two bites of anything they offered and claim she was full. How she's lived the last few years on the tiny amount she eats is anybody's guess. Dale says she only eats in order to find something to complain about. The food is cold. It's salty. It's tasteless. Most often it's "crap," except when it isn't, which happens sometimes. There's no way to predict her approval or disapproval.

We all need something to live for, and my mother-in-law lives to complain. It hadn't been that way when she was still able to get around. Back then she went to garage sales, had coffee with her friends, and gambled a little at the casino. When she broke a hip and became unable to walk, she turned into a full-time grump. Her mind isn't always sharp, so there are times we aren't even sure what the complaints are about. Other times, though, she's as clear as a bell. Her unhappiness makes Dale a nervous wreck, so I run interference, trying to keep her from unloading on him.

The dietician spoke in a voice as fake as her smile. "We're going to see you get our best, Mrs. Burner. We appreciate the chance to improve our service."

Harriet waved a hand that looked like someone had pounded it with a hammer. "Sure, sure. Help me into bed. I want to take a nap before they bring in my crap lunch."

Mrs. Berrien, certified in food but not in patient re-positioning, backed out the door with a horrified look on her face. "I'll send someone down." Her shoes squeaked a little as she hurried way with quick steps, eager to be somewhere else.

"Didn't she hear me?" Harriet has no concept of job descriptions and expects whoever is nearby to do as she wants. Aide, doctor, or visiting pastor, anyone in sight might be ordered to take her to the toilet or fetch her some Boost. Worse, she assumes everyone at The Meadows is a health care expert, which has led to some interesting situations. For example, on the advice of "the nurse," she decided a while back that she'd do better without pills that "messed up" her mind." That "nurse" had actually been a janitor with a mouth too big for her own good. Her advice resulted in a week-long crying jag for Harriet, a letter of reprimand in the janitor's personnel file, and a lot of headaches for me.

Harriet glared. "Will you get me into bed or not?"

"We're supposed to have help," I responded.

"So what was that fat woman? Chopped liver?"

Luckily, I didn't have to explain. An aide slipped into the room and began maneuvering Harriet's wheelchair into place. "We'll get you back in bed in a jiffy, Mrs. B," she said. I admired her cheerful demeanor despite dealing with problems like Harriet all day every day. Patting my mother-in-law's arm, she said, "You've got time for a little snooze before lunch."

"I'm going to have scrambled eggs," Harriet said, smiling up at her. "The cook in your restaurant makes really good ones."

When I returned to the office, a man was stepping onto the front porch. Instead of going in the back door, I parked in the narrow driveway and hurried up the steps to let him in.

"Sorry," I apologized. "We have a lot going on today, and I had to go out for a while."

"I see." His tone said he couldn't have cared less. He was a stranger, probably from someplace where closing an office to run errands was considered unprofessional. He stepped inside and did a quick turn of the outer office, his shoes clicking on the wood floor as he made an obviously judgmental appraisal.

His cold manner and the thought that we'd made a poor first impression made me nervous. Taking off my coat, I hurriedly slid my purse into a desk drawer and kicked off my boots, babbling a little to fill the space. "It's been one of those days. My mother-in-law needed me, and my dog is at the vet. He was hit by a car." The words *my dog* brought a tiny twinge of warmth. I hadn't realized how much I missed having a dog, but Buddy's presence already made life seem better. Reminding myself that he might belong to someone, I resolved to put a notice in the paper that afternoon.

Returning to the present, I focused on my guest in a businesslike manner. Well-dressed and perfectly groomed, he was at least ten years my junior with wavy, dark-brown hair, deep-set brown eyes, and a clean-shaven jaw except for a narrow strip that ran vertically from lower lip to jaw line. He wasn't a bad-looking man, but his face was blank, as if he only allowed emotion to show when he chose. His eyes were flat, like the tunnels Wile E. Coyote used to paint on a cliff face.

A quick glance confirmed my impression he was from somewhere else. Though his clothes looked expensive, he wasn't dressed warmly enough for a Michigan winter. The well-cut leather jacket was too light. His expensive-looking loafers were stained with salt, and he had no hat, gloves, or scarf. Definitely a tourist, probably a first timer.

"What can we do for you?" I gestured toward a chair as I sat down at my desk.

He peered at the chair before sitting as if to assure it was clean. "I am Maximilian Basca, and I have a proposal for your employer." He shifted the chair to a spot that suited him. "I believe she's taken the Darrow case."

Miffed to be taken as only a receptionist, I said, "My partner and I can't discuss client business, Mr. Basca."

His gaze turned more focused. "You don't need to tell me anything, Ms.—" He glanced at the nameplate on my desk. "—Ms. Burner. If you hear me out, your advantage will become clear."

It felt like I was being manipulated, but I remained polite. "Then I will listen."

He touched the patch of hair at his lip. "Your client took some items that belong to me. I want them back."

My expression remained impassive, but my mind began working overtime, considering new possibilities in the death of Stacy Darrow. "What items?"

A look put me in my place. "All you need to know is that if you help me, you will receive a reward."

I felt my eyebrows rise. "And what would we do to earn this reward?"

He raised his palms, indicating a piddling amount of effort. "Take a proposal to Darrow."

"A proposal?"

Basca shifted again in his chair, and the image of a tiger flexing its shoulders before lunging at prey rose in my mind.

"Your client is in a great deal of trouble. I can help, but I require a sign of good faith from him." Taking a small, unpadded mailer from his jacket pocket, he set it on the desktop. "Tell him to write down the location of my property and seal it in this envelope." He smiled a tiger's smile. "I leave it to you to avoid the local sheriff as you do this. Bring the envelope to me, and I will send someone to retrieve my property. Once I have it, the police will find evidence that Darrow did not kill his wife." He paused before adding, "At that time, I will pay you a finder's fee of one thousand dollars."

"If something was stolen from you, Mr. Basca, why haven't you gone to the police?"

He dismissed the question with a smile. "Who can say when I'll get my property back if they are involved?"

"It sounds like you don't want them to know about it."

His gaze turned cold. "Your concern should be returning stolen property to its rightful owner."

Doubtful about the "rightful owner" part, I asked, "How would you prove Darrow is innocent?"

A gentle shrug. "I have helped the police see things differently in the past." He returned to his point. "You will save your client from prosecution and at the same time earn for yourselves a substantial amount of money. I ask you, where is the disadvantage to that?"

I was trying to figure that out, but I wasn't tempted to take the guy's offer. He gave me a huge case of the creeps. Some of what he said might be true, but how much? A sickening thought hit me. Had Basca killed Stacy Darrow to make Winston give up whatever it was he'd stolen?

Basca stroked the soul patch again. "Will you do this?"

"No."

He seemed surprised. "Perhaps you don't understand."

"Oh, I understand. You're asking us to be complicit in a criminal exchange."

Touching his jacket pocket he said, "I can offer two thousand dollars." The smile remained in place, but his eyes were hard as granite. "Do not press for more."

"*No* was my answer, Mr. Basca, not a step in negotiations."

His nostrils flared at my tone, but then, I didn't like him, either. Rising, he zipped the leather jacket and fastened the bottom and top with quick, sharp snaps. "I suggest you convey my proposal to your partner. She might be more experienced in practical matters."

"I doubt she'll be any more willing than I, but I assure you, she'll hear about your visit."

With an angry frown he left, closing the door more firmly than necessary. I watched him go, thinking of things I should have said. The main one was, "I'm calling the police."

CHAPTER SEVEN

Barb

When I left Rory's office, I punched the address for Winston Darrow's house into my GPS. They'd charged him with failure to report a murder and released him, but the sheriff told Rory he'd almost certainly face more charges as the investigation proceeded. Darrow had hired a local attorney with a decent reputation, Byron Glass. If the Darrow assets weren't already frozen they soon would be, but Glass was apparently willing to work on spec.

The sky was gray, but Michigan winters have multiple shades of gray. Today's tone was steely and flat, filtering the sun's light to a somber glow that said *It's January. Get used to it, because there's still a long way to go.*

Darrow lived a few miles east of Lawton, on Morning Glory Lane, which meant I had to navigate an irritating succession of smaller and smaller roads without one straight mile the whole way. At this point in the winter, four-foot snow banks lined the way, narrowing the roads until it felt like I was on a luge run.

Caving to the demands of Michigan winters, I'd bought an SUV and stored my beloved '57 Chevy to protect it from salt, sand, and snow damage. The Ford Edge kept me firmly on the road, but the drive was dull under the black-gray-white landscape people of the Midwest are used to in January. Following the GPS directions, I turned onto the lane where no morning glories would be seen for months.

Rural with a capital *R,* the Darrow home was the perfect place for someone who wanted to get away from it all. Unlike the closely nestled cottages I'd pass along the way, the house was set apart from others by some distance. It was situated on the far side of a small lake, so I was able to see it for over a mile before I actually arrived. The ground floor, lined with glass doors, had a cantilevered deck overlooking the lake. Above it, the second floor had its own deck, also fronted with glass. Above that was a sharply slanted roof of cedar shakes, its various peaks signaling rooms with many different views. A manor house for the gentry of Bonner County.

I rang the bell, and Darrow answered with a glass of wine in hand. When I'd called to say I was coming, he hadn't responded until I identified myself. He knew enough to screen his calls, but it was only a matter of time until the press showed up on his doorstep.

"Mrs. Evans? Please, come in." He glanced across the lake, checking the road for traffic before closing the door after us. "Would you like a glass of wine?"

"No," I said brusquely. "I'm here to give you a second and final shot at telling us the truth!"

He peered into his glass. "I never lied to Mrs. Burner."

"But you failed to tell her some important things."

Darrow set the glass down on a marble-topped end table, making a sharp clink. "I thought if you found who killed Stacy it wouldn't matter that I left some things out."

"It doesn't work like that." I glanced at the deck, visible through French doors over Darrow's shoulder. "She was leaving you."

He gestured angrily. "I don't believe that."

"You told Faye your marriage was less than idyllic."

"Well, yes, but Stacy liked things the way they were." He folded his arms around his ribs, as if he'd caught a chill. "She liked it here."

"In Michigan?"

"In this house out in the middle of nowhere." He glanced around, obviously unable to comprehend his wife's choices. "No friends, no culture, no summer—not what I call summer. She had her computer and her horses. That made her happy."

I heard a note in his voice. "You're not a horse person."

He waved toward the barn dismissively. "They don't like me. The stupid red one always tries to bite me if I get too close. One time—"

Uninterested in livestock stories, I asked, "If Stacy didn't intend to leave, why did she buy an airline ticket?"

"No idea." He rubbed his chin. "Just a few weeks ago she told me this was the best life she could hope for. That doesn't sound like she planned to leave, does it?"

It didn't sound particularly positive, either. The best one could "hope for" wasn't the best that could be. I went on to the other lie. "You went to the bank instead of calling the police."

Darrow raised a palm as if that was easy to answer. "I had to get the cash I had access to before the cops froze everything."

He tilted his head to one side in a pose he apparently thought was appealing. "It's not like an hour was going to change anything."

The death of a loved one—or in this case, a liked one, can create strange behavior. A friend once told me that when she learned her husband been killed in an accident, her first thought was, "I have twenty-two dollars in my purse." Though Darrow's story was plausible in that light, I'd already figured out that in this case there was truth and there was Win-spin.

Picking up his glass, Darrow took a hefty swig. I watched as he wiped his lips delicately with a knuckle. Despite my objections to Retta's pushiness and her obsession with social status, I consider her a pretty good judge of character. She admitted Winston was shallow, but she insisted he wasn't a killer, and honestly, he didn't seem like one to me, either.

"Did you and your wife get along, Mr. Darrow?"

He thought about that. "It sounds weird, but we did. I didn't like living in this cultural vacuum, but when I got bored, Stacy would just say, 'Go someplace warm for a week or two!'"

"She paid?"

"Always."

"But she had no interest in going along."

"She said I'd earned it." Darrow gestured vaguely toward the kitchen. "Before I left, I'd make meals and freeze them." He chuckled dryly. "I put notes on them: THAW FOR THREE HOURS. COOK AT 350 FOR THIRTY MINUTES. The most food preparation Stacy ever did was filling the coffeemaker with water. We were different, but we did okay together." His eyes teared up, and I turned away to give him a minute.

Darrow seemed truthful, at least at that moment, and I wondered what kind of woman his wife had been. Glancing out the windows, I concluded she'd sought solitude in this very rural setting. What had she thought of her philandering husband? Who aside from him might have wanted to chase her through her house, onto the deck, and shoot her dead? Had she been afraid of someone?

I turned to Darrow again. "You traveled while your wife stayed home alone, and she was fine with that."

"Right."

"And when you flirted with other women, was she okay with that, too?"

He put out both hands in a plea for understanding. "Would she leave over a few dinners with Retta when she didn't object to me taking river cruises in Europe and month-long trips to the temples of Vietnam?"

He was correct. A wife who encourages her husband to go off on his own might expect he'll find more than beautiful vistas along the way. If she was upset he'd found a woman close to home, why not demand he end it? Those who allow extramarital affairs often set conditions like "not in the neighborhood" or "not among our friends." Darrow probably would have complied, being fond of Stacy and more than fond of her money.

I took Darrow through his story again, this time following as he recreated his movements. I spent a few minutes in Stacy's room, but nothing struck me as unusual. Loaded bookshelves, a computer, a queen-sized bed. Neat but not obsessively so. I ran a finger lightly over a row of books, recognizing some authors Faye liked.

As Win acted out what he'd done, I listened for false notes, but he seemed to be telling what happened as he remembered it. I heard real distress in his voice when he came to the part about finding Stacy's body. As far as I could discern, it was a truthful account. What was he leaving out?

When I could think of nothing else to ask, we returned to the living room. I picked up my coat, which Darrow took and held for me. "The press will be here soon," I warned as I buttoned up. "You should close the blinds."

He glanced out the window again. "Glass says they'll interview anyone who ever spoke to Stacy or me."

I nodded agreement. "People who aren't even sure what you look like will gladly offer their opinions of you, your wife, and the way you treat your horses."

He moaned softly, and I felt a little sorry for him. Until they've been hounded by the press, few understand how intrusive it is. "Stay low for a day or two," I advised. "We'll see what we can find out. Oh, and let Glass know we're working for you."

"Already did," he said. "I appreciate you coming out here, and Mrs. Burner was really nice." His mouth drooped. "She's the only person so far that said she was sorry for my loss."

That was Faye. Though she didn't particularly like Darrow, she'd still had the decency to offer condolences while everyone else, including me, had ignored a human being who might—just might—be shocked and grieved by his wife's death.

I arrived home to find the CLOSED FOR 20 MINUTES sign on the front door. Knowing Dale seldom went far, I walked through the house and out the back door. While Faye laid claim to the yard, her husband had taken over a garage too small to be of much use for modern vehicles. I'd had a carport built and stored my Chevy in a shed just out of town, leaving him the eight-by-eight structure for a workshop. He'd installed a small pellet stove and now spent his days out there, repairing small engines for neighbors, family, and friends.

Peering in the window, I knocked once then entered. Dale was at the back, bent over a snow-blower. Once a strong guy who operated an impressive array of forestry equipment, Dale was left with brain damage when a tree branch—a much-dreaded "widow-maker"—fell on him. He has to wear dark glasses all the time, and in the workshop he uses earmuffs to deaden sound. He managed to keep his sense of humor, which I appreciate.

Though he didn't hear me knock, Dale looked up at the flash of light as the door opened. "Hey, Barb," he said, removing the muffs. The space heater wasn't very efficient, and the room was nippy. He wore gloves, which no doubt interfered with his work. I wondered if there was a way I could provide a better heater without insulting his pride.

"Where's Faye?" I kept my voice low. High pitched noises are hard on him, which is why he spends as little time as possible with either his mother or Retta.

"She went to get the dog. Vet said he can come home."

The dog. Home. We had a case, and Faye's mind was on the dog. "Okay, thanks."

As I entered through the back, I heard steps at the front. Hurrying forward, I found Retta on the porch. She wore a blue coat over a soft sweater of emerald green that set off her honey-blond hair, leggings I wouldn't have attempted in my twenties, and stunning jewelry in gold and tiger eye. Despite the fact that she lives out in the country, Retta gets up every day, showers, fixes her hair and make-up, and puts on pretty clothes, just in case.

Honestly, I don't get it.

I unlocked the door, and after tapping her toes on the frame to shake off the snow, she came in. "Hi, Barbara."

"Hi." Closing the door behind her, I shrugged off my coat and hung it on the hall tree. When I turned toward Retta, she reached out and straightened the collar of my shirt, pressing it with her hand until it laid the way she wanted it to. She didn't notice my annoyance, or if she did, she ignored it.

"Where's Faye?"

"She went to get her new dog."

"A dog?" Retta's face lit. "What kind did she get?"

"I haven't seen it yet, but I gather it's a mutt."

The light dimmed. "She's adopting a stray?"

"It has a broken leg."

"So she'll take it to the Humane Society now?"

"I think she plans to keep it if no one claims it."

Retta touched the side of her face as if to assure herself this wasn't a dream. "If I'd known she wanted a dog, I'd have helped her find one."

"She wasn't *looking* for a dog. This one was hit by a car, and she couldn't leave it lying in the road."

"But a stray?" She shuddered. "It might have a mean disposition or a personality quirk or some nasty disease."

Shaking a finger at me she advised, "You need to find out what kind of dog she's bringing into your home."

I had an unusual feeling of warmth for Retta. Reluctant about having a dog around, I'd been feeling guilty. Now I could console myself with the thought that at least I'm not a canine snob like Baby Sister.

Dropping the topic of dogs, I filled Retta in on what we'd learned about Darrow. She asked intelligent questions from time to time, but mostly she listened, which was refreshing. When I told her the extent of his lies, she didn't seem hurt, just irritated.

When I finished, she asked, "Should I go talk to him?"

"There's nothing you can do for him right now, and he can do you tons of damage."

"But I'm not one to desert a friend in need."

"A friend, Retta? He's lied to you for months."

"I know." She ran a hand over her hair. "It was hard to accept, but I get it now. Faye says he and his wife had separate lives, so he *felt* like he was single, you know?"

Oh, the deceptions we allow ourselves! Already leaning toward forgiveness, Retta had decided to "be there" for Winston, a term I despise as unspecific and maudlin. There was one thing that might stop her, and that was the bald truth. "Do as you like, but if you go—" I gestured a banner headline. "*Hero Cop's Wife Tied to Murderer.*"

"I didn't think about them pulling Don into it." Her nose wrinkled. "What can I do, then?"

This was also refreshing: Retta asking for advice from the sister she considers dowdy and hopelessly out-of-touch. I did, of course, have decades of experience dealing with crime and the

media. "You might call a reporter you trust and offer an exclusive interview. You knew Darrow as a friend, you and he shared an interest in...something boring, like philately."
Leaning back in my chair I asked, "Did anyone ever see the two of you being affectionate?"

She thought about it. "I don't think so."

"Good. Without saying you weren't having sex, try to give the impression you weren't."

She raised perfectly-shaped brows. "How do you know we were?"

I chuckled. "I'm a single girl, too, Retta. I suppose when an attractive man comes along, we both make the same choice."

CHAPTER EIGHT

Faye

When the vet called to say I could bring Buddy home, I locked the front door again and went to get him. I'd already prepared a spot in our bedroom that was comfortable and stocked with toys, and I was anxious to see him snuggled in and content.

I put my unsettling encounter with Basca aside as I drove. If I called the police, there wasn't much I could tell them. He hadn't actually asked me to do anything illegal, and Basca's claim that our client stole from him would only make Win Darrow's situation worse. Once Barb and I talked it over, we'd decide what to do about Basca's visit.

My dog (well, almost mine) was awake when I arrived, and he peered at me groggily from a cage in a remote corner of the animal dormitory.

"The break went together well," the vet said, "no pins or staples needed. Keep him off the leg as much as you can and bring him back on Friday."

She guessed his age at just under a year, which she warned meant he might still have the urge to chew. I'd bought toys for that, hoping they'd keep him from destroying my things—and more importantly, Barb's.

As we talked, the dog watched with large, black-button eyes. When I moved to pet him Dr. Camp warned, "Be careful. He's tried to take my hand off twice."

The look he gave me seemed neutral. He didn't growl when I put out a hand and let him sniff it through the metal grate. As if to counter the vet's claim, he licked my thumb once.

"Ready to go home, Bud?" I asked, opening the cage. His answer was a sigh I interpreted as approval. I picked him up, supporting the broken leg with one hand. Dr. Camp opened the carrier gate, and I set him inside. Buddy made no objection. When I stopped at the desk to pay the bill, he was quiet, despite a cat and two other dogs within a few feet. I had a feeling it wasn't his usual way, but I took it as a sign he felt safe with me.

At home I went in through the back door, carrying Buddy to our bedroom, where I set the carrier beside the bed I'd prepared for him. Getting a bowl of water, I put it inside the carrier in case the anesthetic had made him thirsty. "You aren't supposed to move around for a while," I explained, "so I have to leave you in jail for now."

He didn't complain, and I thought he realized he needed time to recuperate. It seemed he was also beginning to trust me, to believe my actions were in his best interests.

I could hear Barb and Retta talking in the office, so once Buddy settled his head on his paws and closed his eyes, I joined them. Barb asked politely about the dog's condition, and I updated them. "He was such a good boy," I finished. "He didn't bark once, all the way home."

"What's his name going to be?"

"Buddy, I guess. It's what I've been calling him."

"Oh." Retta's smile was a shade too bright, like it always is when someone says something she thinks is dumb. "A better name will come to you once you get to know him."

Without agreeing or disagreeing, I told them about Max Basca's visit. "Winston is more than a lady's man," I said in conclusion. "He's apparently a thief as well."

"That still doesn't make him a murderer," Retta replied. "Maybe this Basca killed Stacy in an attempt to get back whatever he's looking for."

"As a warning to Darrow." Barb traced her bottom lip with a finger.

"Pretty extreme," I commented. "Why kill the wife?"

"Maybe she tried to run away," Retta said.

Barb looked doubtful. "Then why didn't Basca wait for Darrow and make him give his property back?"

"You're right." Retta sounded disappointed. "If he was willing to kill, he wouldn't just walk away without it."

"What do we do about Basca?" I asked, looking to Barb. "Do I tell the sheriff about him?"

"He's got Darrow for murder," she replied. "I doubt he'll investigate a claim of stolen property when the owner inquired about it through the back door."

"He should if it suggests other possibilities for Mrs. Darrow's death," Retta argued.

Turning her chair toward the computer screen, Barb said, "This is something from Darrow's past, something he thought he'd escaped." Tapping at the keys, she added, "A thief and a con man—he probably has a history with the justice system."

"Maybe Retta could use her contacts with the state police to get information on the Darrows or Max Basca," I suggested. "Now, he's a man I'll bet has a criminal record."

Turning to Retta, Barb asked, "Do you think you could get us some help from the state police?"

Retta's pause revealed surprise at a request from Barb. "Um, sure. I'll make some calls." She rose to go, sliding on a bright blue coat that looked darling on her but would have made me look like a Smurf. "I'll call in the morning to let you know what I find out."

After she left I said, "It's good you let Retta help. I'm sure she's freaking out over this."

Barb shrugged, still typing. "She's in until the first time she tells me what to do. Then she's just another woman who got taken by a smooth-talking lady-killer."

CHAPTER NINE

Barb

The next day was my morning to have breakfast with Faye and Dale. My sister loves feeding people, and she insists I need home-cooked food periodically in order to be healthy. (She often adds that thawing Chang-La boxes of stir-fried shrimp in the microwave doesn't count as home-cooked.) To please her, I join them for one breakfast, one lunch, and one dinner each week.

Dale was quieter than usual, but the cause wasn't clear until the new dog limped into the room. Seeing me, it gave a decidedly unfriendly snarl, and Faye said quickly, "Buddy, behave!"

The dog and I examined each other while I tried to think of something nice to say.

He was a mess. Undernourished, of course, but I didn't see much potential for improvement after proper feeding. He was simply a homely dog, and if dogs have facial expressions, his was ugly. Nevertheless, I fussed a little to please Faye, ignoring his growls as I commented on his bright future once he got some meat on his bones. Inside my head I was hoping someone would claim him. Soon.

Dale didn't get any better treatment than I did. He was helping Faye prepare breakfast, setting dishes, silverware, and ingredients she might need at her elbow. The dog bared his teeth and growled each time Dale passed, until Faye finally turned and pointed to the door. "Buddy! Go!"

Head low, the dog left the room. An odd *tick-tick-tick-thump* sounded on the wood floor then stopped abruptly.

Dale muttered something. I only heard the word *night,* but Faye got the message. "He'll settle in after a few days, Dale." She spooned perfect hash browns onto a plate. "He just needs to get used to everyone."

"Is there a story here?" I asked.

Dale looked to Faye, who sighed heavily. "Last night Buddy decided Dale wasn't allowed in our room."

I bit back the smile that threatened. "Really."

"Came right at me," Dale said resentfully. "Left me standing outside my own bedroom door in my underwear." He set a half gallon of milk near Faye. She glanced at it, and when he turned away, put it back in the fridge.

"Tonight we'll make sure you're in there first," she told Dale, "so he knows you belong."

"I have to have the dog's permission to go to bed?"

"He'll get used to you." She patted Dale's shoulder. "I want the two of you to get along."

He folded, as he always does when Faye really wants something. "We'll work it out." He glanced down the hall. "As long as he's willing to meet me halfway."

I smiled to myself at their exchange, but my smile turned to horror when the dog reappeared, carrying my left boot in his mouth.

Hurrying forward, Faye took the boot from him and gave it to me. "Bad dog!" To me she said, "I'm sorry, Barb."

"It's okay," I assured her. "I shouldn't have left them by the door." Forcing a casual tone I added, "He didn't hurt a thing."

That wasn't exactly true. The boot had a set of small, round punctures near the top. Reminding myself Faye's happiness was worth more than footwear, I put my thumb over the holes and said, "A little damp, that's all."

Relief showed on her face. "I'll watch him," she promised. "He's really smart, so it won't take him long to learn what he can have and what he can't."

"Yes," I agreed. "Now let's eat before our food gets cold."

By 8:30 we were at our desks, researching the case. Neither of us found any trace of Max Basca. He'd lied. No big surprise.

When her phone rang, Faye dug in her purse for at least thirty seconds, found it, and answered. I could tell it was Retta, and Faye's brief responses meant she was doing a lot of talking. Not unusual.

As she ended the call, Faye's expression was half-irritated and half amused. "It seems the state police are aware of Retta's relationship with Win Darrow. She was told politely but firmly that they won't be sharing information with her."

"She's seriously ticked off, I bet."

"Um, that would be a yes."

"It's disappointing, but I can't say I'm surprised. Maybe Rory—" As if on cue the office phone rang, and APD appeared on the caller ID.

"Smart Detective Agency." Faye said. "Good morning, chief. She's right here." She turned in her chair. "For you."

Still taking notes, I picked up the phone. "Rory."

"Good morning, Barb. I have information for you."

"On my case?"

"Yeah."

I tapped my pen on the desk. "I didn't mean for you to spend your time doing my work."

"So you'll owe me. If I ask a question and get an answer, it saves you having to dig and plead and wait until some cop feels like responding."

"We're grateful for the help."

I heard Rory's chair squeak as he moved. "Idalski's even more certain today that he's got the right guy. It seems the real Winston Darrow died in the 1950s at five years of age."

"What?"

"Yup. Years after the little guy passed away he re-appeared, alive and well in Columbia, South Carolina." He supplied specifics, reading from a print-out as I took notes. "Since Winston re-animated he's moved around pretty regularly, but he ended up here."

I got disgusted at Winston—or whoever he was—all over again. "Identity theft."

"I asked Wade to send over what they found," Rory said. "When I get it, I'll send it to you."

"Is that legal?"

He chuckled again. "Legal, but not politically correct, so let's keep it among the four of us."

Call me crazy, but I was pleased he didn't say "*between* the four of us" as many would. My little grammar-glow faded as his meaning registered. "The four of us?"

"You, me, Faye, and Retta, right? I hope they know how to keep a secret." I felt a shift in Rory's mental gears as he asked, "*Now* do you think Darrow-who-isn't-Darrow killed his wife?"

"There's been an interesting development." I told him about Faye's visitor and his demand that we convince Darrow to turn over something he'd stolen.

"If the theft story is true," I finished, "this Max Basca might have killed Stacy in reprisal. Winston's false identity lends some credence to that possibility."

"Do you think she was aware of it?" he asked.

"Hard to say with how little we know about her."

"If I get time, I'll see what I can dig up."

"Thanks, Rory. Again, I appreciate it."

His tone changed. "Then pay me back."

"How?"

"Have dinner with me tonight."

I felt what Retta's romance novelists would call a *frisson*. After months of casual acquaintance, Rory was asking me out. "Are you sure that's a good idea?"

He let out a puff of breath. "I've been a good boy for months, friendly to everybody in town but not too friendly with anybody. All that time I've been wishing you and I could have a second dinner together." His tone turned teasing. "The first time, other things got in the way."

Like murder and attempted murder, I thought, but what I said was, "What will people say about the chief of police dating the local lady detective?"

"I guess they'll say whatever they want to."

With a sniff—a very ladylike one—I said, "I can tell you didn't grow up in a small town."

"You're avoiding the question, Barb. Dinner?"

I chewed on my bottom lip. "Could we go out of town?"

There was a grin in his voice as his accent turned heavily Irish. "It's ashamed of me y'are."

"Not ashamed, just cautious." I looked through the office doorway, where my sister was pretending to work at her computer and trying to hide a smile. "We work hard to make people take this agency seriously, Rory. If you and I start something, they'll say—" I stopped, embarrassed.

"That you're sleeping with me to get information, like Belle Boyd or Mata Hari?"

"It's more likely they'll say you solve the cases while we take the clients' money."

"Tell you what," he said after a brief pause. "We'll keep it between us this time. If things don't work out, we go back to being business acquaintances. If—if we become a thing, they'll have to say what they say. Is that fair?"

"I guess so." The smile Faye had been suppressing turned to a look of amused irritation, but she'd been married for thirty years and had no idea how much interest people take in such things. A woman who's single after forty is presumed to be a lesbian, but if it turns out she isn't, then she must be absolutely desperate for the attention of a man.

"Must we travel in separate vehicles to some faraway trysting place?" Rory asked, still laying on the Irish accent.

My sense of humor overcame my sense of decorum. "Let's leave after five. It'll be dark enough no one will recognize you."

"Pick you up at five-thirty. I'll call if something comes up between now and then."

When I ended the call, Faye sang, "You have a date with the chee-eef."

I tried for nonchalance, but inside I was giddy. Things he'd said replayed in my head, and emotions I'd repressed for months bubbled in my chest. Things had changed with a simple invitation: *Have dinner with me tonight.*

"It's just dinner," I said as much to myself as to Faye. "We'll see if it leads anywhere."

"Let's hope it does." She took a bite of the doughnut that served as her brunch. "You've been alone too long."

Unwilling to argue and unable to disagree, I returned to the case. "Our Mr. Darrow is not who he says." Her eyes widened as I explained. "We need to find out who he was before he turned into Winston Darrow."

"When was that?"

I consulted the notes I'd taken. "November 10, 1982."

"No Internet then. Hope the records were scanned in."

We spent the better part of three hours making calls, consulting on-line records, and trying to piece information together. The real Winston Darrow had indeed died as a child in South Carolina. In the fall of 1982, someone had come in requesting a replacement birth certificate. We were pretty sure that had been our client.

I suggested Faye email the Facebook photo labeled WINSTON GOT MARRIED to the high schools in the area to see if someone recognized him. "That's a faint hope all these years later," she said, picking up the phone. "I have a better idea."

"Whom are you calling?"

"The guy who knows who Winston Darrow really is," she answered. "Winston Darrow."

"Mr. Darrow," she said a few seconds later, "this is Faye Burner from the Smart Detective Agency. You need to pick up." In only a few seconds there was a response. "Where are you? ... I was afraid of that. We'll meet you there." Ending the call, she told me, "He's on his way to the sheriff's office with his lawyer."

Opening her desk drawer, she took out her scruffy denim purse and shook it, listening for the jingle that revealed where her car keys had settled. "Since he isn't who he says he is, the judge revoked his bail. Our Mr. X is considered a flight risk, and now the charge will be murder."

CHAPTER TEN

Faye

To protect Dale's ankles I shut Buddy in the bedroom, promising him it wouldn't be for long. When Barb and I got to the jail, Darrow's lawyer, Mr. Glass, introduced himself with chilly reserve. A cautious type who smelled of fruity hair products, Glass made us promise we'd treat what his client said as privileged information. Even after we agreed, there was discussion of generalities and what-ifs before Darrow—who again asked that we call him Win—was finally allowed to tell his story.

"The name I started life with is Walter Dubey, and you can imagine the teasing that came along with that name. I come from a small town in South Carolina where I was nobody special: not smart, not athletic, and according to my teachers, not very ambitious." He smiled disarmingly, but when no one smiled in return, he cleared his throat and went on. "After high school, I went to work in the little factory where everybody who didn't go to college ended up. It was an okay place, you know? A decent living.

"The one thing I was good at was getting women, and it took me a while to see that I'm better at it than most guys.

There was this ritzy girls' college in the next town, and my buddies and I used to go there on weekends and pick up rich girls wanting a good time. After while I realized the guys brought me along because the girls liked me. They didn't mind getting the leftovers, you know?"

Barb shifted impatiently in her chair. Winston got the message and sped up his tale.

"I was pretty happy with life, I guess, but then in 1979 the factory closed down, and I lost my job. I'd been dating this girl named Chandra for a few months, and when I told her, she just laughed like it was nothing. 'No problem," she said. "'You can be my boy-toy.'"

Darrow—Win— set his hands on the table before him, and I noticed that the nails appeared to be professionally cared for. *Where does a man in northern Lower Michigan go for a manicure?* I wondered.

I returned my focus to the story when Barb said, "This woman offered to support you?"

"Yes. At first I thought she was joking."

"But she wasn't."

Darrow wore a heavy gold wedding ring, and he began turning it on his finger as he spoke. "She told her parents I was tutoring her in finance. They were so desperate to see her get passing grades, they never questioned it." He sounded surprised at the turn his life had taken, even years later. "I moved in with her, and when she graduated that spring, we moved to Columbia, to a nice apartment her parents paid for. Chandra went to work at her daddy's PR firm, and I did stuff for her."

"Stuff?"

"Took her clothes to the dry cleaners, drove her to work and picked her up so she didn't have to deal with traffic and pay parking fees. I made her life easier."

"Her parents didn't object to you...being around?"

Win's smile turned bitter. "They weren't thrilled their little girl lived with a guy whose dad was a short-order cook, but they knew I was good for Chandra." He turned the ring again. "Her dad made it pretty clear that I was expected to earn my way by keeping her out of trouble."

Barb made a shrewd guess. "She was abusing drugs."

"And more. Chandra was a mess, and my job was to get her out the back door when trouble came in the front." His fingers tiptoed across the table in a parody of escape.

"Basically you got room and board in exchange for babysitting a young woman who refused to grow up."

Win took offense at Barb's tone. "You're not going to try to tell me that women don't do the same thing."

"*Some* do." Barb raised a hand, indicating she wouldn't argue his decision. "You had a woman willing to support you. What happened to that cozy arrangement?"

Win glared at her for a second before going on. "After three years, Chandra met a guy who partied *with* her instead of trying to keep her straight. One days she said I was a drag, a party pooper, and she wanted me gone." He sighed deeply at the memory, but a smile—actually more of a smirk—appeared when he added, "By that time, the other women in her circle had seen how good I was to her."

"And some of them wanted the same thing." Barb's tone said she could hardly believe it.

Win's expression was smug. "When she tossed me out, one of her friends stepped in—" He stopped, apparently trying to remember the name. "—Paula."

"She offered to support you?"

Win was patient with our disbelief. "These women mostly meet men who are as spoiled and self-centered as they are. What they want, at least at some point in their lives, is a guy who treats them like a goddess."

"A guy like you."

"Exactly." He squirmed a little in his chair. "It went on like that. When one woman lost interest, there was always another one eager to get the Walter treatment."

"This sounds like a daytime serial," I objected.

Win's lips tightened. "I treat them right, and they're grateful."

"If they're rich enough."

"Know what?" His tone was angry, and he rapped his knuckles on the tabletop. "It's true what they say. It really is as easy to love a rich person as it is to love a poor one."

Barb stepped in before I could argue. "Okay. So when did you become Winston, and why?"

His smile turned rueful. "After my thirtieth birthday, pickings in the Carolinas started getting thin. I'd been thinking about a career in the movies, so I planned a move to the West Coast. In order to break in out there, I decided to dump Walter Dubey and become somebody better."

"How'd you manage that?"

Glass shifted nervously in his chair, but Winston seemed eager to tell. "First, I went to the county where I was born and looked up the birth certificate of a neighborhood kid who'd died in an accident just after we started kindergarten. All of us kids talked about it for weeks, trying to understand what *dead* meant, you know?"

"The boy's name was Winston Darrow."

"Great name, right?" When no one answered, he went on. "I don't know how it works now, but back then, the records were accessible to everybody. You went in, told them you were researching your family tree, and they let you go back and find what you needed. I found Winston in the book and read everything they had about him.

"Once I had it memorized, I left the office and waited until the clerk who'd waited on me went to lunch. When she left, I went back in and told the new clerk that my house had burned down two nights before. I made it a great story, telling how I lost everything I had when I ran out in just my boxers."

"Unbelievable," I muttered, but we were all listening.

"The second clerk was young, cute, and sympathetic. She went and got Winston's birth certificate out and quizzed me on what it said. When I had all the right answers, she decided I must really be him. For a few bucks I got a certified copy."

Darrow paused, but we were waiting for more, so he said, "After that it got easier. I applied for a driver's license, saying I was raised in the city and never needed one before. I had to take the tests, but that was easy.' He spread his hands out on the table before him. "With a driver's license and a birth certificate, you can get everything else you need."

Glass cleared his throat. "So to be clear, you changed your identity, but you had no intent to defraud anyone."

"That's right," Winston replied. "I just wanted to be someone with a little class, you know? And it worked. Winston got a Social Security card and a degree from Stanford—at least he had a diploma that said that. After a few years he applied for a passport. They don't check back as far as you might think—at least they didn't before 9-11. Credit cards are easy."

"Did 'Winston' ever work?" Barb made quotation marks in the air with her hands.

He looked offended. "Of course. But not in front of the camera. That's every bit as hard to break into as they tell you. I worked as an assistant to the assistant on a couple of movies and TV shows, and I spent some time with a big talent agency."

"As an agent?"

He gave me a look, and I blushed at my naïve guess. "As a gofer, though they're called personal assistants today. I ran errands, arranged schedules, and even played surrogate dad to one agent's kids. The things I'd done for my ladies served well in an industry full of people too busy to live their own lives."

"But you went back to your 'ladies' eventually."

Win shrugged. "Hollywood was okay, but the acting career I hoped for never materialized. My jobs there helped me pick up convincing little touches for Winston's background, though: letterhead stationery from some well-known studios and polo shirts with impressive logos." He swatted Glass playfully. "Once I even gave myself an award for administrative excellence. But my real talent was making women happy, one at a time."

"And there were women everywhere out there." Glass looked surprised at the sound of his own voice, but he was as interested as Barb and I were.

"Yes. Hollywood is full of ladies who need emotional and social support." His brow furrowed. "In the '80s I had a long-term relationship I hoped would be permanent. A mature actress whose name I won't mention wanted a man in her house but not in her bed, if you get what I mean."

"A lesbian."

"You'd be surprised how hard they tried back then to keep that private. We did well together for a long time, but things changed, and her secret became less important."

"So you were out again."

"I gave her nine good years." His tone was aggrieved, but he ran both hands through his hair and went on. "I got past it, though. A good reputation goes a long way."

"Why did you leave California?"

"Because of—" He thought for a second, again trying to call up a name. "—Bridget. She was twenty years older, but she had a great vacation home in Taos. After I'd given her three good years, I noticed Bridget flirting with the guy who was ghost-writing her memoirs." He snorted. "He was about twenty-two, much too young to appreciate her, but he had a great body and really, really white teeth."

Win paused, possibly picturing the guy who'd replaced him. "It was unexpected, so I didn't have anyone lined up."

"And you weren't getting younger," Barb commented.

Unconsciously, he touched his neck where the skin had begun to sag. "I have good genes, but no one's discovered the Fountain of Youth yet."

I recalled a friend's comment: "One day you slip on your coat and your mother's hand comes out the sleeve." For most, getting old was regrettable but inevitable. For a guy who'd spent his life being attractive and attentive, the fading of physical charms must have been terrifying.

His smile tinged with sadness, Win said, "I was used to my girls moving on, but this time it made me uneasy. I was sixty years old, and I had nothing of my own. I needed to find stability for my old age."

"You needed to get married, preferably to someone who didn't mind the fact that you had no money."

He made an irritated gesture. "Marriage is hard these days with all the pre-nups and background checks."

"So inconsiderate!" Barb rolled her eyes.

Win's lips quivered at her lack of sympathy. "Anyway, Taos is an amazing place to meet people, so I stayed, trusting my luck. One day I was sitting in a café, looking dignified but possibly available, when Stacy came in. She was stunning. I thought about making a move, but I'd been finding my charms worked better with cougars than tigresses, if you know what I mean."

"We know." Barb's voice betrayed impatience.

He ignored her, caught up in his story. "Anyway, her smile left no doubt she was interested. Needless to say, when she asked if she could join me, I was thrilled."

"You didn't lie about that? She came on to you?"

Winston clicked his tongue in irritation. "I told you. Women like me."

"*Some* women," Barb corrected. "You were—what, sixty years old? She was a lot younger. You didn't suspect she was playing your own game on you?"

He smiled at her naiveté. "Of course. I checked her out right away. She had a condo at the St. Bernard." Looking embarrassed, he added, "I was at Motel 6, but I managed to give her the impression I was at El Monte Sagrado."

Barb made another "keep talking" gesture. "So the relationship blossomed."

"It did. I took her to dinner, we ended up talking until late. She invited me back to her place." He raised his hands as if helpless to stop the train of love. "I never left."

"Stacy was looking for a husband?"

His brow furrowed. "She said she was looking to settle down somewhere quiet. I was thinking the south of France, but next thing I knew we'd bought a house in Michigan." His ebullience dimmed a little. "Where she was perfectly happy to stay twenty-four seven."

"And where she started ignoring you."

Darrow nodded glumly. "She was eager to get married, but she wasn't that thrilled with being a wife."

"Maybe sex wasn't meant to be part of it." Glass suggested.

Darrow looked offended. "I can promise you, it was not bad sex that led to separate bedrooms." He paused, possibly considering citing Retta as proof of his prowess. He must have decided against it. "When I tried to talk to her about it, Stacy said I was the kind of husband she wanted." Looking away he said firmly, "She told me, 'You're exactly the man I need.'"

I looked to Barb, who raised her brows. Though Darrow's story sounded strange, his demeanor was honest. He thought the story was true, whether it was or not.

"A man came to our office yesterday claiming you stole from him," Barb said. "He wants his property back."

Win seemed genuinely surprised. "Me? I've never stolen anything."

"Maybe you thought you deserved something one of your lady friends had. A painting, some jewelry, a family heirloom?"

"Nothing." His tone was firm.

"Sometimes a person doesn't understand the law completely. Even if you didn't break into a person's home and take things out of his safe, theft might still be the charge, especially if fraud is involved. Fraud is presenting yourself as something you're not, and it can be—"

Win interrupted her. "I only ever took things my ladies bought for me, like clothes."

"How about Stacy?" I asked. "Did she bring anything of value when you moved north?"

He chewed his bottom lip. "I can't think of anything. She only cared about her horses, which she bought up here, her computer, and her books."

"Are any of the books rare copies?" I asked.

He shrugged. "Just mysteries, far as I can tell."

"I saw them at the house," Barb agreed. "Paperbacks, pretty usual stuff."

"Stacy kept every book she ever read," he said with the uncomprehending air of a non-reader.

"Are the book still there?" I asked.

"I guess so."

"Would you mind if we went to your house and looked through them?" I was thinking there might be something hidden in one of the books, cash or stock certificates.

"Go ahead. The police have been all through the place, probably twice by now. I doubt they looked very hard at the books." He turned a palm upright, adding, "I mean, nobody ever got killed for a book, right?"

CHAPTER ELEVEN

Barb

My evening with Rory was the nicest I'd had in ages. He picked me up promptly at five-thirty, and from the soapy fragrance in his car I could tell he'd showered between work and his arrival. I was dressed in the fourth outfit I'd tried on, and I'd applied a tiny bit of blush and lipstick.

We headed for Arbor, a lovely resort in the pine woods of central Michigan. On the way, I told him about Winston's most recent revelations. He recommended we pass the information on to Sheriff Idalski and the state police, who were helping with the investigation.

"Ron Glass was there," I said. "He was eager to tell them, since it casts doubt on Darrow as Stacy's killer. Idalski will probably call for details tomorrow morning."

"It certainly makes all this more interesting."

"Isn't that the truth."

By tacit consent we left business at the restaurant door to better enjoy the ambiance and each other's company. The Arbor was as nice as I'd heard, the food delicious, and we were far enough from Allport we weren't likely to see anyone we knew.

Rory was a wonderful dinner companion. He talked, he listened, and he seemed to be having a good time. In the unhurried atmosphere, we drifted from topic to topic in a natural fashion. He chuckled when I described Faye's new dog and his proprietary attitude toward her. I learned he favored the White Sox, significant tax reform, and parents who didn't say things like "Now, Timmy, we talked about this before we left home."

"Do you have children?" I asked after I'd told him about Faye's three and Retta's two.

He nodded. "A daughter at Ball State. Jessica." He grinned. "No pictures. I didn't want to bore you on our first real date."

"I'll be happy to look at them next time."

"Then we have to make sure there's a next time," he said lightly, taking up the after-dinner menu. "Dessert? Since we've gone this far, we might as well have it all."

We drove home in contented silence, and I realized I hadn't felt this way in a long time.

At my age I've figured out that fretting about the future is useless. When a person's life is half over, it's time to enjoy present happiness and put tomorrow where it belongs, in an unknown, unknowable future. I thought I might be falling in love with Rory, but what that meant for us, I couldn't imagine.

Like the men of our generation were taught, Rory walked me to my front door. When he kissed me good-night, gently but firmly, I responded warmly. Rory was as good at kissing as he seemed to be at everything else.

After he left, I didn't feel ready for sleep. Things we'd said ran through my mind, times I made him laugh, things he told me about his past. Wide awake, I decided to finish a Correction Event I'd been considering.

Secretly but regularly, I do little things to fix the grammatical errors rampant in our community. People are careless with apostrophes, sloppy about spelling, and woefully unaware of correct word usage, especially homophones. In my car I keep a bag of supplies, including black clothing for night-time work, paints and brushes, flashlights, and other tools for fixing painted signs that have errors. Of course there are plenty of errors in printed material, too, and I'd run into one recently that screamed to be corrected.

From my nightstand I took out a newsmagazine that had come in the mail earlier that week. I'd already circled four irritating errors with red marker. Booting the computer, I listed them in order:

1. First line, 2nd paragraph: *affect*, not *effect*. Prices can't "effect" tourism. If you can't keep them straight, I suggest you use a different word.
2. The *1990s* or the *'90s*, not "the 1990's." They don't own anything.
3. *He said they'd go home* (omit comma) *and go to dinner later.* Compound verbs are not separated by commas the way clauses are.
4. Though they're pronounced the same, *Mackinac Island* is spelled with a *c* at the end, and *Mackinaw City* is spelled with a *w*. Let's not confuse the tourists more than they already are.

Checking my copy twice, I printed the list on paper taken from the middle of a ream. Using a tissue in order to leave no fingerprints, I put the magazine and the letter into a mailer. I made an address label and applied it, touching only the edges. Slipping downstairs as quietly as possible to avoid waking anyone, especially Buddy the dog, I weighed the envelope on Faye's postage scale and applied more than enough stamps to assure delivery. Back upstairs, I put it under the jogging pants I'd laid out to wear on my morning walk.

It isn't that I'm ashamed of what I do. It's just that people make so much fun of what are called "Grammar Nazis" that I prefer to remediate discreetly.

After consulting the Weather Channel the next morning, I put long johns under my sweat-pants and Tacoma University sweatshirt and pulled on a hat Faye bought me that looks a little like a periscope. In the worst weather, it allows me to cover everything but my eyes. Today's temperature didn't demand that. The air was a crisp ten degrees, but the biting Lake Huron wind was absent, so it wasn't unbearable for a Michigan native. Once I'd gone a few blocks, I pushed the hood back, relying on the ear-band under it to keep me comfortable.

I vary my morning walks, going in a different direction each day for four days then mixing it up for the next four. Heading west it's only four blocks to the lake, but from there I turned south, toward a little strip mall where I knew there was a mailbox. After mailing my packet from the night before, I fast-walked to a park where a paved oval track is kept plowed for walkers. A few fast turns around the track got my heart rate up and my lungs pumping. No one else was there, which I prefer. It isn't that I mind sharing the space, but meeting other walkers leads to suggestions like, "We should partner and encourage each other." In exercise, as in most things, I'm used to depending on myself.

That brought Rory to mind: Rory and the possibilities a romantic relationship. I've been on my own for almost ten years, and after the last time I'd vowed to remain that way. Of three long-term relationships I'd had, two had ended with demands I couldn't meet. Early in my career, a man I thought I loved had asked me to move to China with him. It turned out I didn't love him enough to live the gypsy life of an international shipping agent, and I'd returned to Tacoma after only a year.

Some years later, a lawyer I worked with proposed marriage, but he'd expected me to give up my career to raise the large brood of children he envisioned for us. I said goodbye, knowing he wanted a woman I'd never be content to be. Looking back on those relationships, I could hardly recall what either man looked like. But then, I barely recognized that long-ago Barbara Evans, either.

My last and best relationship had been with Hollis, who made no demands and loved me exactly as I was. When ALS took him, our time together was cut short, and what might have been my happily-ever-after became instead the waking-and-sleeping nightmare society gives the innocuous term "care-giving." Watching him die had been so painful that I'd decided I was better off alone. Like Simon and Garfunkel sang, "An island never cries."

What did my past say about a future I might have with Rory? He didn't seem the demanding type who'd insist I give up my home or the agency, but what other problems might arise? Would he hate that I eat out most nights? Would he find it weird that I share my house with my sister and her husband? Would he discover my secret Correction Events and make fun of me or demand I stop so as not to embarrass the police chief?

There's a lot more to maintaining a relationship than people want to admit.

Jogging lightly to raise my metabolism, I came back to Main, which on road maps is Michigan Highway 9. It was still dark, since sunrise in January comes around 7:30, but as a northbound car passed, I saw the driver's face in the glow of a street lamp. A hard-looking man in his thirties, he had eyebrows the size of newborn kittens. He watched the road intently and didn't even glance at me. Once the car had gone by, though, a head rose in the back seat, and a face peered out the rear window.

It was Winston Darrow. It was a split-second impression, but the guy looked terrified.

Staring after the car, I deduced that our client was in more trouble today than he'd been in yesterday, though that had been bad enough.

I continued home, wondering about what I'd seen. The authorities might have sent Darrow from the Bonner County lockup to somewhere else, but it didn't feel right. There were no official markings on the car, the driver hadn't been in uniform, and Darrow looked scared. Who had him in custody?

"The FBI," Glass told me when I contacted him an hour later. He hadn't answered the phone until precisely 8:00 a.m., and I pictured him alone in his office, putting in billable hours. "He was supposed to come to my office when he was released this morning, but he texted to say a federal officer showed up wanting to interview him." His tone turned irritated. "I guess the feds come first, but it isn't like I've got nothing else to do."

As I ended the call, Faye came into the office. I'd heard her moving around earlier, but it's best to leave her alone until she's had coffee and at least one cigarette, which she takes on the back porch, shivering in an old flannel shirt that once belonged to our dad. The dog stumped along behind her, gave me a disinterested glance, and curled up under her desk.

As I caught her up on what I'd seen, the phone rang again. It was Glass. "The FBI never sent anyone!"

"What?" Pulling a notepad toward me, I took up a pen. "Tell me everything you can."

There was a pause, and I sensed Glass trying to gather his thoughts. "After I hung up from talking with you, I called the sheriff's office. He didn't know a thing about any FBI agent. I tried to call Winston, but his phone went right to voicemail."

"Darrow is somewhere with an unknown man who claimed to be a Federal agent but isn't." I spoke for Faye's benefit, and she looked up in surprise.

"That's right."

"What did Sheriff Idalski say?"

Glass paused. "That Darrow has lied to us all from the beginning. He stopped just short of saying Win made the whole thing up."

"Why would he do that?"

"To avoid being charged with his wife's murder."

"So the sheriff's treating this as flight from prosecution rather than kidnapping."

"I'm afraid so." Glass paused. "What are you going to do?" Though he'd been unsure about us yesterday, he seemed willing now to let us decide the next step.

"First I'm going to call the sheriff and tell him what I saw. I'll keep you informed."

My call to Bonner County was productive in some ways but not in others. On the good side, the sheriff's tone was collegial. "Chief Neuencamp told me you were looking into things, Ms. Evans," he said when I identified myself. "Says he's worked with you and you're okay." Rightly or wrongly, crime fiction conditions police officers to think private detectives will work behind their backs. I was grateful to Rory for paving our way.

The sheriff was pleased to learn the direction Darrow had been headed, though he didn't comment on my impression that he'd been afraid. "We'll find him," he told me, "and then we'll figure this out." Thanking me for the timely information, he promised to keep in touch.

True to his word, Idalski called back twenty minutes later. "We found the car you described a few miles north of Allport. There were tracks alongside. Someone picked two guys up out there."

"So at least two people were in on the abduction."

"Abduction?" I heard disbelief in his voice. "Ms. Evans, can you tell me why somebody would kidnap Darrow?"

I told him then about Basca's visit, ending with, "My sister says he said "we" a few times, which indicates he isn't in Allport alone. If Darrow knows what Basca looks like, someone else would have played the fake FBI man."

"There's no evidence Darrow didn't go voluntarily."

"I saw his face, Sheriff. He was scared."

"It was dark, though, right? When Darrow texted Glass, he seemed okay."

"But if he wanted to disappear, why text Glass at all? Why not just go?"

Idalski paused as if weighing his words. "I know you're supposed to prove the guy didn't kill his wife, but you have to at least consider that he's called in some friends to get him out of Michigan."

"And the fake FBI agent?"

I imagined the shrug that came with his reply. "Darrow could have made that up. He's no innocent bystander, Ms. Evans." I pictured him counting points on his fingers. "He was using a false name. He didn't report his wife's death. He tried to get her money out of the bank before anybody found out about it."

I had to give him that. Liars lie, and I had no proof Darrow wasn't lying now.

"But why did Basca try to get us to act as go-between?"

His tone changed a little. "Maybe they thought you ladies would cloud the issue." Use of the term *ladies* hinted at the sheriff's prejudices. He considered us gullible, probably because we lack certain body parts.

Setting aside my irritation, I tried again. "Sheriff, isn't the simplest explanation most likely? Basca wants what Darrow stole, so he grabbed him in order to get it back."

"Won't know till we find them." His tone turned brisk as he wrapped up the call. "We've got men on every road out of the area. Once we locate Darrow, we'll find out what's going on."

For the next half hour, Faye and I looked at Darrow's abduction from every angle we could devise. "What if this isn't connected to Stacy's murder at all?" Faye asked at one point. "Suppose that back in New Mexico, Win conned a guy he shouldn't have, our Mr. Basca. He comes to Michigan, thinking he's out of Basca's reach. After Win kills Stacy in a quarrel, the publicity surrounding the murder alerts Basca to where Win is. He comes up here and asks us to help him convince Win to return his stuff. We refuse. Afraid if Win goes to prison for murder he'll never get his stuff back, Basca sends a guy to grab him the minute he's released on bail."

I spun my chair from side to side as I played devil's advocate. "If Win stole something valuable, why has he been living on his wife's money for the last two years?"

"Good point." We stared at the walls, but no answers appeared there. Finally Faye said, "I've got paperwork to do on that child custody case. I'd better get at it."

As she took up the file, a ring sounded. I put a hand on my pocket, but it was Faye's cell. It took her a while to locate it, but she checked the I.D. "It's Retta."

"Hey," she said, "I was just about to call you—Really? Wait a sec. I'll put you on speaker so Barb can hear, too." That took even longer than finding the phone had, but eventually she said, "Okay, Retta, go ahead."

"I got a strange call from Winston. He needs my help."

"Where is he?" Faye asked.

"He didn't say, but he made me promise not to call the cops. He said 'Don't call the cops' several times, but he never said, 'Don't call your sisters.' I think he wanted me to call you."

"Could be." Quickly Faye caught her up on the morning's events. After Retta made noises of surprise and distress, Faye asked her, "What does he want from you?"

"I'm supposed to go out to his house, find this lockbox, and bring it to him."

"A lockbox?"

"He says it's a matter of life and death. There's a book inside it that somebody wants, and they're threatening to kill him if they don't get it."

Faye sighed. "Retta, the sheriff thinks Win's trying to make it look like someone else killed his wife."

"The guy is a sociopath, Retta," I said, raising my voice. "People like him use whoever is available. They have no real feelings for anyone. He appeared to really like you when you were out together, but now you're just—"

"He's not lying," Retta interrupted impatiently. "I heard a man say something in the background, and then he did something to Winston. He was saying that I had to hurry, and all of a sudden he screamed. I think the guy hurt him on purpose." She paused. "What kind of book would it be?"

My mind cleared suddenly, like my vision does when I put on my glasses. "It's something Stacy Darrow stole from Max Basca. She knew Basca was looking for her, which is why she never went anywhere, but somehow he found her."

Faye caught on quickly, but she frowned, asking, "Then why didn't they get the book before they killed her?"

Nobody had a ready answer, but after a few seconds Retta said, "It doesn't matter right now. They said they'll trade Winston for it."

I shook my head at her ingenuous statement. "They killed Stacy. Darrow won't live long once they have the book. I'll call the sheriff and have him intercept them."

"No! Winston said if there are cops, he'll be killed."

I gritted my teeth. "Retta, you can't—"

She went right on as if I hadn't spoken. "Besides, our local guys are good with teenage drinkers and shoplifters, but I wouldn't bet on them handling kidnappers."

"So what do you propose we do?" I asked in frustration. "Let them kill you, too?"

Knowing Retta, I guessed she'd decided her course, logical or not. "I cannot desert a friend who needs me!"

It's always like this with her. I could argue with the best of my lawyerly skills and experience. She'd agree and then go on with her plans as if I'd never said a word.

I tried once more. "You can't go blithely off to meet a couple of killers."

"I'm not dumb, Barbara. I didn't just agree to everything they said."

Suppressing my sarcastic tone, or at least trying to, I asked, "What *did* you agree to?"

"Well, they wanted to meet out in the middle of nowhere, but I said it had to be where there were people."

"That's good." Faye's tone was hopeful.

"Unless they don't care how many people they kill to get this book," I replied. Faye's face pinched with dread. "Where is this exchange supposed to happen, Retta?"

"A diner called the Lunch & Munch. It's about a mile this side of Lawton, a couple of miles from Winston's house. They said I have exactly one hour to get there." Her next comment explained the background noise we'd been hearing. "I'm already on the way."

I should have known.

Rising, I went to a Michigan map on the wall. Faye joined me and put her finger on the spot where the diner was. Having lived somewhere else for decades, I wasn't familiar with some of the outlying places, but I saw that instead of turning off to Darrow's house, we'd continue toward Lawton. Allowing for snowy country roads, the drive would take us forty minutes.

Bonner County's sheriff could get there faster, but would these unknown men carry out their threat and kill Darrow? I thought of calling Rory, but he'd mentioned he'd be in Mt. Pleasant all morning for a conference.

The best thing was for Faye and me to go to the diner. If Darrow was scamming Retta, we could call the sheriff's men from there. If he was telling the truth, we'd have to try to figure out a way to help. At the very least we'd see that Retta got out of there unharmed.

Retta interpreted our silence as argument and went into boss mode. "Do NOT call the police, Barbara Ann. Once Winston's safe, we'll be able to give descriptions of the men who kidnapped him."

I stared at the map, feeling obligated to do what I could to protect our client, the people at the diner, and our bull-headed sister. Since she had to stop to get the lockbox, we should be able to reach the restaurant before she did.

Faye looked to me, raising her brows in a question. With a sigh I said to Retta, "When you get to that diner, there'll be two ladies having lunch. Just ignore them, but when the chance comes along, get Darrow out of there as fast as you can."

CHAPTER TWELVE

The diner was one of those cramped places with a long, beat-up counter, a low ceiling yellowed with age and cooking grease, an open kitchen, and a dozen scarred tables ringed by pressed-wood chairs. Everyone in the place looked up as we entered, and the waitress called casually from behind the counter, "Yous can sit wherever you like." Barb glanced at the woman darkly and flinched at her terrible grammar.

While it was possible Basca would show up, Barb thought it unlikely. "Men like him let lesser mortals do the blatantly criminal stuff," she'd said as we drove, "The guy who grabbed Darrow will make the exchange."

We chose a table in the back, and I took the chair facing the door. If Basca did show, I'd see him coming and hurry to the ladies' room before he spotted me. Our greatest asset was surprise, I figured. No one would expect two middle-aged women to abandon their lunchtime chat to stand up and shout, "Stop in the name of the law!"

We'd ordered by the time the bell over the door rang and a cold blast of air hit my ankles. Barb didn't turn, but I nodded to let her know it was Winston and the guy whose thick brows she'd described to me. Win had a split lip, one eye was swollen shut, and he cradled one hand in the other. He looked terrible.

When he saw us, Win's face lit. I frowned a warning, and he suppressed his reaction. His companion led the way to a booth near the front, indicating with a gesture that Win should sit facing the door. He took the seat opposite Win, closer to the exit.

The door opened again, letting in a second icy draft. Another man entered, larger and somehow uncivilized-looking, like an animal granted a day in human form. With a glaring glance that sent patrons and staff alike looking at their hands, he sat down next to Win, forcing him toward the wall and pinning him in the booth.

When the waitress brought our lunches, a hot beef sandwich for me and a salad for Barb, she tipped her head toward the three men and asked, "There a Big Time Wrestling event goin' on somewhere?"

"If there is, we missed it," I told her.

Lifting her brows expressively, she moved to Win's table and asked, "Would yous like to see menus?"

The guy with the big brows said tersely, "Just coffee."

Gesturing at Winston's face, the woman said teasingly, "I hope the other guy looks worse than you, hon."

Win said nothing. "He'll have coffee," the first man said. The big guy ordered a Pepsi and agreed ungraciously to take Coke instead.

While the waitress fetched their drinks, the three men sat in stony silence, each glancing out the window from time to time. Win turned several times to look at me, and I wished he'd stop. I shouldn't be that interesting.

After a few minutes the bell rang again, the cold blew in, and Retta entered. She looked perfectly put together, as usual, and I couldn't help but wonder how she did it. Her married-now-single boyfriend calls with a strange, dangerous request, and she arrives looking like she had all day to get ready.

"Is it her?" Barb asked.

"Yeah. She's got the box."

Retta had a Chico's shopping bag that she held a little behind her, as if to keep it from being snatched away.

"Get the car," Barb said in a low voice. "Bring it to the east side of the building, where they can't see you."

"What are you going to do?"

"Get us all out of here together," she said, adding, "If we're lucky."

CHAPTER THIRTEEN

Barb

After Faye left the diner, I listened closely to what went on behind me. Retta approached the table where Darrow sat and said something in a low tone. A rumbly bass voice responded, ordering her to set the box on the table. I couldn't make out her reply, but from the tone I surmised she refused to give up the box until they demonstrated willingness to let Darrow go.

Faking a cough, I turned away from the table to get a glimpse of the scene. Retta stepped back, holding the bag behind her as if that would stop the brute who was rising from the bench seat with a menacing expression. He loomed over Retta's petite form like a skyscraper over a chapel. My sister raised her chin and stood her ground.

Retta was wise to refuse to hand the box over without assurance of good faith, but I doubted she'd get her way. All the guy had to do was reach out with one ape-arm and take the bag from her. No one in the place looked likely, or able for that matter, to stand up to him. It was up to me to throw a surprise into the mix.

Rising, I tossed cash on the table for the bill then turned, pretending to notice Darrow for the first time. In my best too-loud, old-lady voice I called out, "Winston?"

Darrow looked at me hopefully. His captors looked at me unhappily.

"Honey, it's been ages since I've seen you!" I hurried toward him, arms raised. "Come here and give me a hug!"

Everyone in the restaurant, customers and staff alike, turned their attention to us. There were grins all around as I stopped, put my fists on my hips in apparent irritation, and urged, "Don't get all macho on me, Winston Darrow. I need a big old cousin hug right now!"

I'd gambled Darrow's captors wouldn't know how to deal with a doting relative, and I was right. Though he glared, the big man moved out of the way and let Darrow step into my embrace. As I hugged him I whispered, "Faye's outside. Get in the car and don't stop."

Getting the idea, Retta set the box down on the table with a thump. "Here are the Girl Scout cookies you ordered," she said, her voice a shade higher than normal. "You enjoy, now!"

Darrow was already moving toward the door, and Retta and I followed. The two men hesitated, unsure what to do with a half dozen smiling observers looking on. As we exited the building, Faye pulled up beside us, and we piled in. Though she's usually a cautious driver, she hit the accelerator before we got the doors closed. Wheels slipping on the snowy surface, we took off like the old bats the kidnappers were no doubt calling us at that moment.

CHAPTER FOURTEEN

Retta

It was reassuring to enter the diner and see Faye and Barbara acting the part of ladies having a casual lunch. All the way over, I'd told myself that meeting the kidnappers in a public place would be safe, but Winston's desperate voice on the phone had made that hard to believe.

When Barbara Ann made her move, I followed her lead. The bad guys froze as we turned away, unsure what to do. I'd handed over the book, but they were losing their victim. While they puzzled out whether to make a scene, we jumped into the car and left. It was priceless.

As we drove away, questions rose in my mind. What if they chased us? Could we escape with "Fifty-five Faye" driving? What was this all about, and how did it relate to the murder of Winston's wife?

The first question was answered right away. Looking back, I saw the two men exit the diner, stumbling in their haste. They climbed into a whitish sedan, and as we turned the first corner they were backing out of their spot in a big hurry. "They're coming after us," I warned.

"Why?" Faye asked. "You gave them the box, right?"

"Just drive!" Winston ordered. "They'll catch us!"

"Maybe not," Barbara said, pointing. The lights of a police car showed at an intersection ahead.

"I said no police, Barbara. Did you call them anyway?"

"They're out looking for Win," she replied.

The car hit a chunk of frozen mud, and we all grabbed for a handhold. As Faye clutched the steering wheel with both hands to avoid skidding into a ditch, she said, "This is good. They can take Win into custody—"

"No!" Winston's shout echoed through the car, scaring us all. Putting a hand to his forehead, he began again in a pleading tone. "Not the Bonner County cops!"

We looked ahead to where the cruiser sat sideways in the road, positioned to monitor passers-by. Winston's voice broke as he begged, "I'll explain later, but don't let them have me!"

We didn't have long to make a decision and typically, everyone waited for Barbara to do it. "Okay," she said reluctantly. "You two make like a couple."

Winston and I obeyed without question, as people tend to do when she uses that tone. In a partially unzipped gym bag on the floor, I spotted a black knit hat. Grabbing it, I scooted to Winston's side of the car and used it to cover his hair and forehead. "Glasses!" I said to Barbara, and she took off her black-framed specs and handed them over. After I put them on Winston, I wriggled in close. He flinched when I bumped his little finger, which stuck out at a forty-five degree angle. It wasn't bad, though. In thirty seconds I'd made him as unlike his mug shot as I could manage.

When we reached the patrol car, Faye stopped and rolled down the window. A fresh-faced deputy approached, thumbs in his belt. "Hi, folks."

"What's the trouble, Officer?"

"Nothing you need to worry about." Glancing into the back seat he asked, "What happened to your face, sir?"

Before Winston could answer I said in an outraged tone, "We hit a deer last night over near Alanson. The airbags didn't deploy, and his poor face hit the steering wheel." Patting Win's arm I added, "I'm going to call those lawyers downstate that promise to get you money. It's a crime what the auto companies get away with!"

The guy's interest waned and he stepped back. "You folks can go on your way. Have a good day now."

He looked back the way we'd come, and his eyes lit with interest. Peeking out the back window, I saw that the driver of the white car had come over a rise, seen the sheriff's car in the road, and made a U-turn. Sprinting to his cruiser, the deputy started the engine. Soon the cherry lights came on and the siren wailed. Without another glance at us, he was gone.

"That'll keep them from following us home." I handed Barbara Ann her glasses and returned the hat to her little bag of emergency supplies. I noticed a paintbrush in there and what good that would do if her car quit. You can trust Barbara Ann to be prepared for anything, though.

As Faye drove on, Barbara turned to Winston with a questioning expression. He was tense beside me, his face ash-colored and his mouth clamped shut to slow the quiver that had taken over his bottom lip.

"What's going on here, Mr. Darrow?" Barbara demanded. "Who are those men?"

"They were going to kill me!"

Barbara looked doubtful, and Faye's split-second glance in the rear-view mirror indicated something similar. He turned to me, seeking a friendly face.

"Why, Winston?" I kept my voice sympathetic. He needed understanding, not anger.

"I don't know, honest!"

A look passed between Faye and Barbara Ann. "Tell us what happened since we saw you last."

"The guy who grabbed me. George, met me outside the sheriff's office. He said he was with the FBI and he needed to talk to me about Stacy's death. It was a big lie."

"George is the guy with the eyebrows?" Faye asked.

"Yeah. He had a badge and all, but instead of interviewing me like he said, he drove out to where Carlos, that's the big guy, was waiting in the white car." He shivered against my shoulder. "George is bad enough, but Carlos likes hurting people. Really likes it."

Barbara wasn't buying it. "The sheriff thinks you arranged all this as a way to escape arrest."

Winston held up his damaged hand. "Would I let someone do this? Wouldn't I just take off before the cops knew I was gone?"

"Okay. Tell us about this book."

Winston's voice shook as he answered. "They didn't believe me when I said I didn't know anything about it."

"You don't recall stealing a book from Max Basca?"

"I didn't! I never knew anybody named Max!" His voice rose again, and his breathing became rapid and shallow. "I would have told them if I could! They—they hit me. They said they were going to kill me. Even after Retta said she'd bring the lockbox, they laughed about how they'd take it away from her, and she wouldn't be able to stop them."

"Calm down," Barbara said. Her eyes met mine, acknowledging that Winston was close to breaking down completely. "Now that they have what they want, they'll leave you alone."

"But they don't!" His voice turned to a wail. "When they started hurting me, I made up a story about a book in a lockbox at the house."

Anger swelled in my chest, rising up my neck and burning my cheeks. "You mean I risked my neck to bring you something that isn't what they want?"

Tears leaked from the edges of Winston's eyes and he wiped his nose on his sleeve. "I didn't know what else to do! They were going to take me to the house so I could get the book. But once they knew I really don't know where it is, I was scared of what they'd do."

"So you made up a story." Barbara's tone said she'd expected no less of him.

"Right. I told them the cops were watching the house. I said my girlfriend could go there, make up some excuse to go inside, and get the box for them." Here a trace of the old Winston appeared. "I thought you ladies might think of a way to help me get away from them, and you did."

"And now they're after all of us," Faye said grimly.

His tone turned whiny again. "I was scared!"

Barbara sighed. "Sheriff Idalski can protect you until this gets sorted out."

"No!" Winston's whiny tone disappeared. "One of the local cops is helping those guys."

"Listen, Darrow—"

He raised his crooked finger under Barbara Ann's nose. "How do you think they found out where I was and when I'd be released? George has somebody on the inside!" He lost a little steam as he went on, "He bragged he could have had me killed anytime he wanted."

"We can talk to—"

He interrupted Barbara's attempt at logical argument. "I'm paying you to help me, not to hand me over to crooked cops." He fumbled for the door handle. "Just let me out. I'll get away without your so-called help."

Braking suddenly, Faye cranked the steering wheel to the left. The car's back end slewed a little as she turned down a skinny road that apparently had no name. When we were no longer visible from the main road, she stopped and turned to face Winston. "We're investigators, Win, not bodyguards."

He calmed a little, but not much. "Then investigate. Find out who at the sheriff's department is helping George and Carlos. Until you do, I won't go back there."

"We could go to Millden County," Barb suggested.

"And then what?" Winston shouted. "The Millden sheriff will turn me over to Bonner County!"

"He's right, Barbara," I put in. "Professional courtesy. Why would they believe Winston without proof?"

Winston tried to cross his arms, bumped his damaged finger, and winced. "If I had proof, I'd give it to them."

"If you take the book to the police, they're more likely to believe your story," Faye suggested.

He waved his hands in frustration. "I keep telling you, I don't *have* the stupid book. I don't know what they're talking about!"

Despite further questioning, Winston held firm to the claim he had no idea which of Stacy's books might have brought about recent events. In the end the four of us began sounding like talking heads on a 24-hour news channel, chewing a few scraps of information in endless, useless speculation as to what was happening and why.

When Barbara asked for the tenth time where the book might be, Winston put his good hand to his forehead and massaged. "I—don't–know. Get it? Maybe if I had time to think, I'd remember something."

Gesturing at his bruised face I said, "At least the police will have to believe someone hurt you."

The panicky note in his voice returned. "So they'll add theft to the crimes I supposedly committed. They already thought I killed Stacy. Now they think I faked a kidnapping to get out of Michigan. They'll just assume I stole this guy's book, too."

He was right. I turned to my sisters. "Can we at least discuss the options before we decide what to do?"

They weren't thrilled with the idea, but neither of them rejected it. After a moment Faye asked, "Retta, do those guys know who you are?"

I looked to Winston, who gulped before answering, "I never told them your last name, and in my phone you're listed as Ray's Automotive."

It was hard to be reminded that he'd lied to me and to his wife. I'd trusted too easily what this man told me, fooled by his charming ways and handsome face. *Never again!* I vowed.

Acting without Barbara's input for once, Faye put the car into gear, made a U-turn in the road, and announced, "We can't just sit in the open like this. We'll talk further at Retta's house."

CHAPTER FIFTEEN

Faye

Retta's classy brick home is located a few miles out of town, isolated from its neighbors by trees and protected by an alarm system due to her deceased husband's familiarity with statistics on home invasions. Entering Allport would have committed us to turning Winston over to some legal official, and while I was pretty sure we had to do that soon, I suspected it would be better if he came to the realization on his own.

When we pulled into the drive Retta got out, unlocked the side door of the garage, and went in to press the button that made the big door open with a low rattle. Pulling the car inside, I shut off the engine, and Retta closed the door behind us. Inside the house, Styx was already scratching an excited welcome on the back door.

"Somebody wants to go out," Retta sang as she opened the door—or tried to. Styx is a little dense and never gets the idea that the door can't swing inward with him in the way. Once Retta convinced him to back up a little we went inside. Knowing what was coming, I prepared myself. Styx, a brown Newfoundland hovering at a hundred forty pounds, is huge, with the temperament that earns Newfs the nickname, "gentle giants." He has his own method of greeting friend and stranger alike. Standing up on his back legs, he puts his huge paws on the person's chest and waits to be hugged. Some find it endearing. Barb does not.

Styx began with Retta, who took his massive head in her hands and scratched his ears. "You're such a good baby." Assured she still loved him, Styx moved to greet me and then Win, giving us each the chance to stagger under his affectionate weight. After we'd gamely taken our turns, Styx turned to Barb, who gave him a sharp "No!"

With a look that said it was her loss, Styx scooted past her. In a few seconds we heard the doggie door at the back of the garage swish open and closed as Styx entered the fenced back yard.

Retta refilled the dog's water bowl and food dish then turned her attention to setting the alarm system. "I don't use this very often," she muttered. "Hope I remember how it works, or we'll get a call in about thirty seconds." Apparently she did everything right, because her phone remained silent.

Styx returned about the time Retta finished her chores, and she tussled with him a little before he trotted off to his bed, a saggy couch in the den that was all his. I heard the click of his claws on the parquet floor, the squeak of springs as his weight settled, and his sigh of contentment at being able to relax with a relieved bladder.

"I'll make us some coffee." Retta moved into the kitchen, where half of her remained visible over the breakfast bar. Barb and I took off our coats and hung them on hooks near the door. Turning to take Winston's, I saw that he'd collapsed onto

Retta's meant-for-people sofa in the living room. Arms folded across his chest and chin sunk into his collar, he looked like he might barf on Retta's cream-colored upholstery. He still cradled his right hand with the other, and the dislocated finger looked swollen and painful.

Going to Retta's bathroom, I found medical tape and some OTC pain pills and returned to where he sat. Leaning down, I examined the finger. "I can put that back in place and tape it to the next one to stabilize it," I told him. He looked up at me, horrified, but I added, "I raised three boys. This isn't my first time as emergency nurse."

"Will it hurt?"

He wouldn't have responded well to a truthful answer, so I simply handed him three pills. While he was swallowing them, I wrenched the finger back where it belonged with a decisive movement. He yelped, but it was over quickly. Win looked away as I taped the damaged finger to the next one. When I finished, he laid the hand on his stomach, blinking rapidly.

Barb was in no mood for his vapors. "What was in the lockbox Retta gave those guys?"

His answer came in a monotone. "The deed to the house, an insurance policy, and some other stuff." He touched his swollen eye gingerly with his good hand.

"And you're absolutely certain you don't know what they want?" Doubt was apparent in her expression.

"I didn't steal any book!" he protested.

"Was your wife the one who did it?"

Win didn't look surprised, so I guessed the idea had occurred to him. "It's possible." He bit at his bottom lip, wincing as his teeth hit the spot where it was split. "When we met, Stacy told me she'd always had money, but after a few months with her, I realized that wasn't true. She was thrilled with being able to buy whatever she wanted. She ordered stuff online all the time, and she was like a kid at Christmas when it showed up at the door."

"You never asked where her money came from?"

Win's eye-roll said we didn't get it. "I had secrets, didn't I? I let her have hers too."

The phrase *marriage of convenience* came to mind. It had been convenient for Stacy to have a husband who didn't ask questions, just as it had been convenient for Winston to have a wife with lots of money.

"Whether you know about this book or not," I said, "those men think you do."

"I tried to tell them I didn't." His nose reddened. "I could be a corpse in a ditch right now."

Barbara shifted her feet, signaling a decision. "Rory needs to know about this."

"Rory?" Win asked. "Who's that?"

"The chief of police in Allport. He's a friend."

"I don't think so!" Win said. "I know these locals all talk to each other. George's guy will find out, and they'll kill me!"

"We could call the state police." Retta came out of the kitchen with a tray of mugs. Setting a coaster near Win's elbow, she put one mug on it. "Two sugars with cream." After he'd taken a drink she said gently, "Winston, you know you have to get this cleared up."

Barb seemed to like Retta's idea. "They're only a couple of hours away. They'd probably send someone to get him if we tell them he isn't safe in a local facility."

Win's mouth opened a couple of times, and I could almost see him strategizing. He guessed he couldn't argue Barb out of her decision. When he finally spoke, he used a pleading tone. "Can it wait until tomorrow?" He scrubbed his face with his good hand. "Please? I might figure this out if I can think things through without a bunch of cops standing over me, already convinced I'm guilty."

There was a long silence while Barb thought it over. "I'll ask Rory what we should do," she finally said. "Maybe he could be the one to call the state police. They're more likely to believe a fellow officer than two female detectives and the suspect's girlfriend."

"What if he wants to arrest me himself?" Win asked.

"Then that will be the smart thing to do," she answered. "Rory can be trusted to do the right thing." Rising, she brushed her pants in case she'd picked up a dog hair. "If he does think we have to call in the state police, I'll be there to handle any questions he can't answer."

Win went quiet, and he seemed to shrink before my eyes. He'd given up in the face of Barb's determination, and he could no longer care about the details of what was going to happen to him.

Retta did. As Barb went to the back door and took her coat from the hook, she hurried out and caught her arm, speaking low. As Win stared at the wall, apparently unaware of their exchange, I joined them.

"Barbara, Rory is a cop. If you tell him we've got Winston, he'll make us bring him in."

"That might be best, Retta. The guy's a fugitive, even if he didn't plan to be. I wouldn't mind giving him a few hours to recover, but that might not be possible."

"They'll say he's lying to escape a murder charge."

Barb's jaw tensed. "Rory won't. He listens to me."

"Because you and he are a thing?" Retta made a sniff of dismissal. "Don't make a cop choose between you and his duty, Barbara. The result might not make you happy."

I didn't take a side. Though it felt disloyal to doubt Chief Neuencamp, I didn't know him well, and Retta seemed sure of herself. The set of Barb's chin told me she was fed up with Retta's assumption that only she can analyze a situation correctly.

"To protect the agency's reputation, we cannot conceal a fugitive. Besides, the sheriff's men are out there right now, searching for Darrow. We can't let them go on wasting time and resources."

Retta had no answer for that. I was torn between knowing Barb was right and feeling Win might collapse completely if we pushed him any farther today.

Was it okay to break the law to assure our client's safety, or should we surrender Win and hope they believed us when we said he was in danger?

"All right. We'll do it your way, Barbara." Retta reached out and patted Barb's scarf into position. "If Rory says Win has to surrender, have him call the state police and explain the need for caution. As soon as you're done, come right back here. We need to get my car back from that diner."

Barb said nothing, which is how she handles it when Baby Sister starts giving orders. As Retta turned away to press the button to open the garage door, Barb looked up from putting on her gloves and met my eye. "Your job is to make sure everyone here stays put."

She meant that if Retta proposed some wild scheme to hide Win at the local Holiday Inn, I was to stop her. I found myself hoping the threat of Barb's disapproval was enough to prevent that, since Retta's tough to stop when she gets an idea in her head.

Once Barb was gone, I sipped at coffee I didn't really want. We were all a little lethargic as the adrenalin in our systems leaked away, and Win seemed even less aware than he had a few minutes earlier. When Retta asked simple questions like "Are you hungry?" and "Do you want to take off your coat?" he answered as if he were half-asleep. Post Traumatic Stress, I concluded. I felt it a little myself, and I hadn't been through what he had in the last few hours. Despite legal considerations and Barb's reservations, Win really did need time to rest before he faced re-arrest and hard questioning from the police.

"Why don't you lie down for a while, Winston," Retta suggested. She pulled off his shoes and, taking a quilt from a rack in the corner, tucked it around his feet. Her care for his comfort struck me, and I realized that Retta has no one who needs her these days. Was dating guys like Winston a search for someone she could care *about*, or someone she could care *for*?

He went to sleep almost immediately, emitting a soft snore, which left Retta and me sitting silently on either side of the room. It seemed rude to talk while he was obviously exhausted. Rising, she inclined her head toward the den, and we moved there. Styx napped on his couch, but his rest wasn't disturbed in the least by our intrusion.

Retta's den is a comfortable room where the furniture is a little worn, the TV is large and modern, and family pictures are everywhere. I noticed that some of the framed ones had newer ones stuck into the corners, waiting for her to have time to matte and arrange them. Retta sat in Don's old recliner, a red-and-yellow plaid she'd hated when he'd first brought it home. After he died, that chair became her favorite place to be.

It was soon obvious she hadn't given up the argument. "Barbara Ann is putting Winston in danger because she doesn't want to mess up her relationship with Rory."

"Retta, you know that isn't true. We can't hide a fugitive and then expect the police to work with us in the future. Rory's our best bet for navigating through this."

She didn't agree but changed the subject. "Do you think the book is a rare edition?"

"Basca didn't seem the type for that." I sipped my coffee, found it cold, and set it aside. "Once Win tells what he knows, the state troopers will sort it out from there."

She sighed. "Winston the conman got conned. Stacy didn't want a husband. She wanted a man to hide behind."

"That's why she didn't care if Win had money."

"She just wanted a guy who wouldn't question what she did, like moving here and never leaving the house."

"Stacy thought she got away with taking something from Max." Picturing Basca, I shivered a little. Only a tiny instance of his disapproval had made my skin crawl. "It took two years, but he found her."

"But why did they kill her before they got the book?"

I frowned. "I don't know."

Glancing toward where he slept, Retta said, "Winston's right. They'd have killed him too." Her tone turned earnest. "I know he's a mess, Faye, but he doesn't deserve this."

"Neither do we," I said in warning. "I doubt those guys will hesitate to kill us if we get in their way again."

CHAPTER SIXTEEN

Barb

"The chief's back from the conference, but he's at the county commissioners' meeting," Janet told me when I got to Rory's office. "If it's an emergency I can call him."

Unwilling to admit we were harboring a fugitive and needed advice, I said, "I'll come back in half an hour."

It was my intention to wait in the lobby of the city building, since it was warm, out of the wind, and removed from employees prone to idle chatter. After only a few minutes, however, I was irritated and agitated.

Who was in charge of the bulletin board? Without trying I spotted three spelling errors, not to mention such sloppiness as "Call 4 assistance" and "Thanx for Participating." The postings were encased in glass, so I couldn't correct them. When I caught myself plotting how I might pick the lock, I decided it was best to wait outside.

It was much less comfortable on the sidewalk. Snow had begun falling, big, wet flakes that melted into my hair and on the lenses of my glasses. Cold invaded my face, ankles, neck, and wrists, anywhere cloth didn't cover. I considered coming back later. I could take Retta to retrieve her vehicle from the diner, but that would take almost two hours, and Rory would be gone when we returned. Not only would I have to listen to her argue against my plan, but I'd have to show up at his house after working hours. Checking my watch, I decided to give him ten more minutes. Retta would have to be patient about getting her car back.

Pacing to keep warm, I wondered what Rory's reaction would be. Would he believe me, or would he suspect our client was conning us? Despite Darrow's pleas, I knew we had to inform the authorities that we'd located him. I told myself I'd chosen Rory because that made the most sense.

My eyes watered as frigid gusts of wind tore at my coat buttons and drove snowflakes at my face like tiny straight pins. Digging out a tissue, I wiped each eye, then my glasses, and finally my nose.

There wasn't much traffic, but the cars that passed were coated from the door handles down with brownish gunk, snow mixed with sand, salt, and other chemical substances used to keep the roads safe for driving.

The atmosphere was so dim that a man sitting in his car only a few feet away was only a dark shape, larger than most but otherwise anonymous. I thought for a second it was the big man from the diner, but this man's head was shaped differently and his hair was short, not the tangled mess I'd seen earlier.

As I waited, checking my watch and holding my coat closed at the neck, a man crossed the street, coming toward me. The Millden County Building sat across from the city offices, and he'd come from there. The small form seemed familiar, but most of his face was buried in his jacket. He was singing softly, and the voice was familiar too. Squinting, I recognized the thinning, sandy hair and eyes a little too close together. "Gabe?"

He looked up, recognized me, and glanced immediately over my shoulder to see if I was alone. I suppressed a grin. Gabe, a small-time criminal we'd met on a previous case, was a little in awe of me but terrified of Faye. "Um, hey, Miz Evans."

"How are things?"

He kicked at the sidewalk slush with a dirty tennis shoe. "Okay, I guess. I got out a month ago."

In large part due to our efforts, Gabe Wills had received only ninety days for his part in several crimes against Faye and me. While he'd certainly been guilty, ten minutes in Gabe's presence would convince most people that his lack of morals stems more from ignorance than an inherently evil nature.

Nodding at the building behind us I asked, "Visiting your probation officer?"

"Yeah. She's pretty cool," he said. "It was nice of you ladies to speak up at my hearing, too. I know Miz Burner was pretty mad at me, but she still told the judge I wasn't responsible for my actions. That helped a lot."

"Has your caseworker helped you find a job?"

He nodded. "I work on the snowmobile trail, but that's only while winter lasts." He gestured toward the pickup I recognized as his. "Gonna have to sell that, I guess."

A thought struck me. "Are you busy right now? I have a job that's worth fifty bucks."

Gabe's eyes lit up. "Fifty? Sure. I'll do it."

"Hey," I cautioned. "Ask if it's legal before agreeing."

Tucking his hands in his pockets, he gave me a big grin. "You wouldn't do nothing illegal, Miz Evans!"

I hoped that would still be true tomorrow. "Can you drive Faye to Lawton to pick up a car?"

His shoulders twitched. "I don't think she'd ride with me, since I kinda kidnapped her that other time."

"You don't have to become best friends. Just drive her to the Lunch & Munch Diner."

His snarled brows revealed reluctance, so I added, "I'll pay to fill your gas tank, too."

Gabe sighed deeply at the irresistible incentive. "I guess I can do it."

I handed him thirty dollars for gas and gave directions to Retta's house. "I'll call, so she's watching for you."

As he left, shaking his head, I took out my phone. Faye was not going to be any happier about it than Gabe was.

CHAPTER SEVENTEEN

Faye

While I wasn't thrilled with Barb's plan for getting me to the diner, I knew she wanted to see Rory as soon as possible. I considered sending Retta with Gabe to get her own car, but Win was comfortable with her, and I was the least likely to be recognized if the kidnappers happened to be watching the place.

Despite all that, a ride with Gabe wasn't high on my list of fun things to do. Because I was irritated, I almost missed a comment Barb made. "Darrow must be making me paranoid."

"Why do you say that?"

"Well, there's this big guy who was sitting in his car but he just got out. Now he's leaning against the building like he's waiting for someone. He's got a decent haircut, a nice car, and he's wearing a suit, but I feel like he's watching me."

"Maybe he's just admiring an attractive woman, Barb."

"This isn't Retta you're talking to." The sound changed, like she'd put her hand over the phone. "Make sure you aren't followed, and keep your phone where you can get at it."

"You sound like Retta," I said teasingly. "Does paranoia make a person bossy?"

After making a rude noise, she hung up.

Gabe didn't keep me waiting long, and I guessed the money was a big incentive for him. His truck wasn't what I'd call neat as a pin. In fact, I probably could have found a pin somewhere, since it appeared there was one of everything stuffed behind the seat. It made me wonder if he lived in the vehicle at least some of the time. Along with the smell of sweaty man was the odor of tobacco, though, which for me is a plus. "Do you mind if I smoke in your truck, Gabe?"

"Heck, no," he answered, reaching toward the dashboard. "I could use one myself."

We both lit up, and my heart warmed toward him just a little. I've been trying to quit, and I've cut down a lot, but when things get tense, nothing but a cigarette will do. I sat back, ready to enjoy my vice in silence.

To my dismay, my host felt obligated to chat. "How ya been, Miz Burner?"

Suppressing a sigh I replied, "Okay, Gabe. And you?"

"Good, good." After a pause he said, "Pretty damp out today, ain't it?"

I allowed that it was.

There was a longish silence as he tried to come up with a topic of conversation other than my health and the weather. Thinking of Henry Higgins' advice to Eliza Doolittle, I smiled.

Gabe cleared his throat. "You ladies on a case?"

"Yes." Rolling down my window a little, I expelled a lungful of smoke outside.

"That's great. I bet you'll catch the guy, just like you did that other time." He paused, embarrassed to have brought up the instance where he had been, if not a bad guy, at least a bad guy accessory. "I got a job now, and I'm turning my life around."

"Really."

"Yeah." Gabe's cigarette rested forgotten between two fingers, filling the cab with a haze. "I got a girlfriend, Mindy. She volunteers at the jail, helping guys get their GED and stuff, and we kinda hit it off. She's real nice, but she don't take no sh—don't let me get away with nothing. She told me about Jesus, and I let him into my heart so I won't sin no more."

"That's good, Gabe."

"It's kinda hard sometimes, because Jesus don't help with money and stuff like that." He glanced skyward briefly as if searching for understanding. "I mean he *can*, if he *wants* to, but you can't just say a prayer and win the lottery. You gotta work for it, so He knows you mean it."

"I suppose that's true."

"So I got a job grooming trails. I'm looking for full-time work so Mindy and me can move out of her mom's house and get our own place."

I guessed Mindy's mom prayed for something similar every night.

"I owe it all to you."

I was too flabbergasted to speak, but he went on, "And Jesus too, of course. If you hadna come along, I woulda kept hanging out with guys like Zack and ended up going to prison, not just to jail. So you and Mrs. Evans saved me."

"That's good to know, Gabe."

"And Jesus."

"Of course."

CHAPTER EIGHTEEN

Barb

Because I was checking my phone to see if Gabe had arrived at Retta's, I didn't see Rory's approach. "What are you out here in the cold for?" he chided when I admitted I was waiting for him. Mentioning the mistake-riddled bulletin board seemed wrong. He touched my arm briefly. "I'll tell Janet it's okay for you to wait in my office anytime. Don't be shy about doing it."

Once we were inside, I recounted the day's events, ending with why we'd taken Darrow to Retta's. "He's a basket case right now," I concluded. "He says he needs time, but I know that isn't possible."

Rory scratched his chin. "Does Wade know you have Darrow?"

When I shook my head, he picked up the phone and punched a button. "Sheriff Idalski, please. It's Chief Neuencamp."

As we waited, Rory didn't meet my eyes. My heart thumped in my chest as my emotions flickered between anger and dread. Retta had been correct: Rory was a cop first, and our friendship fell somewhere farther down his list of important things. With no discussion whatsoever, he was going to turn my client in.

"Wade? Rory Neuencamp." He glanced at me. "I have good and bad news. The good part is that Barbara Evans and her sisters have Winston Darrow in custody." Another glance at me. I stared back impassively as he went on. "The bad part is that someone at your office might be helping the opposing team."

He explained the situation, stressing the treatment Darrow had received from his abductors. "He says someone in your department is keeping them informed."

The sheriff's voice rose as he asked questions, and I bit my lower lip as they discussed what should be done. Idalski spoke for a long time, and though I couldn't hear the words, his stress came through. Finally Rory looked directly at me, and he said, "I know you'll get to the bottom of this, Wade, but until you do, I have a suggestion. Only a few people know where Darrow is right now. How about if we leave it that way?"

The sheriff asked a question, and Rory replied, "I'm saying I'll take responsibility for him while you figure things out." He paused. "How about if I put him in the custody of a deputy for tonight and hand him over to the state boys in the morning? That'll give you time to get your problem under control before they descend on you."

Rory was giving Idalski a chance to clean up his own house before other law enforcement agencies got involved. No doubt the sheriff would appreciate that.

"I will," Rory was saying. "If I learn anything new, I'll contact you first."

I imagined Idalski's dilemma. He'd be reluctant to let a possible murderer remain on the loose. He'd be embarrassed at the prospect of betrayal of one of his own. He seemed to trust

Rory, though. I doubted I'd have gotten the same response if I'd called to suggest he had a crooked cop in his department.

"Good. You can tell your people Darrow's in custody," Rory told Idalski in closing. "That'll turn the heat down."

When he set the phone down, Rory's grin revealed satisfaction and something more. "What?" I asked.

"I'm going to need a new deputy to handle this, one nobody knows about."

I pressed a hand to my chest. "Me?"

"Yup." Reaching into his desk, he took out a badge and tossed it to me with a playful grin. I caught it deftly, and thirty seconds later I was a sworn deputy of the county, as Rory himself was. It's common practice, assuring that a city policeman's jurisdiction doesn't end at the city limits. My term would last only as long as the present situation did, but it would allow me to keep Darrow away from the men who wanted him dead.

Pleased as I was to have arranged our client's safety, I also anticipated having time to pick his shallow little brain. Once Darrow was in custody, Glass would no doubt advise him to say nothing. This way we might learn more about the wife Darrow apparently hadn't known well.

My face warmed with embarrassment. While Rory had neatly solved several large problems, I'd jumped to the conclusion he didn't trust me. He'd proved the opposite.

He didn't seem to begrudge me my suspicions. "Now let's discuss where your prisoner might spend the night."

"Retta's house is out of town," I said, "and we made sure nobody followed us there."

"That's okay temporarily," he replied, "but not long-term. If these guys have a source at the sheriff's office, they'll soon find out her name."

That was an unsettling thought. "So what do we do?"

He checked the time. "Can Faye handle the office tomorrow?"

"Of course."

"All right. I know a spot where both he and Retta will be safe." He explained what he had in mind, and though the location he suggested didn't appear on my Bucket List of places I wanted to visit, it was about as safe as Darrow could get. And right now, safe was better than sorry.

CHAPTER NINETEEN

Retrieving Retta's car took longer than expected. As Gabe and I traveled west, the dark sky dropped wet, dense snow on us. The roads were treacherous. Half-frozen ruts made by previous drivers pulled Gabe's worn tires first one way then the other. He handled it well, keeping his attention on the road and both hands on the wheel as the slush hummed wetly beneath us.

When we reached the diner, a plow truck rattled back and forth in an attempt to clear the parking lot. The body was half rust, and its gears ground with each change, but in Michigan anybody with the engine power and a snow blade can make extra money removing snow in winter.

We got out and went to Retta's Acadia, which was coated with an inch of heavy snow. As I started the engine, Gabe cleared the windows, headlights, and taillights. The plow-truck driver waited politely for us, and I glanced at him apologetically. He was on the phone, probably setting up his next job. That made me feel less guilty about holding him up.

Through the diner's window, I noticed a man watching us as a waitress poured coffee for him. When he picked up the cup, it almost disappeared in his sizeable paw. After a sip he returned to looking out at Gabe and me. Barb's description of the guy who'd been watching her came to mind: big man, short hair, nice suit.

"Gabe, did you tell anyone we were coming here?"

He paused with the snow brush in mid-air. "Some guy at the gas station asked how the roads were. I mentioned we were coming this way. He said he was, too. I told him he'd be fine as long as he took it slow."

A third ape had joined the Hulk and Monster Brows. Where were these guys coming from?

I surveyed the parking lot. Besides Retta's SUV, Gabe's truck, and the plow vehicle, there was a sedan with a dozen faded stuffed animals lined up in the back window, a rusty conversion van, and a gray, late-model Audi. "Gabe, park in front of that car and just sit for a while."

"What for?"

"Just do it, okay?" I gave him the rest of the money Barb had promised. "If the driver tries to leave, pretend your truck quit and you can't get it started."

Peering at the diner window, he said, "That's the guy from the gas station. What if he asks where you went?"

"Tell him I hired you to drive me over, but you have no idea where I'm going now."

Getting into Retta's car, I quickly acquainted myself with the dashboard (Why isn't there a law that says they all have to be set up the same way?) and shifted into drive. The wheels spun briefly then caught, and I was on my way. Gabe did as ordered, backing his truck into a position where it blocked the gray car in. I watched in the rear-view mirror as we left the parking lot, anxious to see if the guy left the diner. He didn't. Big sigh of relief.

Not far down the road I came up behind a snowplow. I followed impatiently, not daring to pass but eager to get as far from the diner as possible. The huge blade on the plow's front threw wet snow to the side in a slushy rooster tail, at one point sending a mailbox spinning into the ditch. The owner would be irritated, but the other choice, a clogged road, was worse.

The plow eventually turned down a side road, but when I reached the main highway, there was plenty of traffic to slow me down. Everyone drove cautiously, and we edged along at the pace of a funeral procession. I checked the rear view mirror. None of the cars behind me was gray.

After a mile or so, a dark car three back from me started nosing into the other lane then disappearing again, anxious to pass a small red car but wary of crossing the slushy middle of the road. If I could have given him the benefit of years of winter driving experience, I'd have counseled staying in his own lane. Passing in winter is often iffy; passing in half-frozen slush is downright dumb.

Finally the driver made his move. I heard the beep of a horn as the red car's driver braked to let the dark car by. When the impatient driver pulled back into his lane, the slush caught his tires, sending the car sideways. The vehicle slewed wildly for several very long seconds, clipping the front of the red car lightly before hurtling into the snowy ditch, back end first. Though the car stayed upright, its airbags deployed, filling the window and obscuring the driver's face.

I braked, as did the car behind me, but there wasn't much either of us could do. Two cars farther back pulled over to help, turning on their flashers. With a final glance at the half-buried sedan I continued onward, glad the idiot driver hadn't hurt anyone. I was relieved he hadn't been passing me when he lost control, because I couldn't imagine telling Retta that I'd dinged up her beloved vehicle.

CHAPTER TWENTY

Retta

Winston was still sound asleep when I heard the garage door rumble open and looked out to see Faye pulling in. She closed the door behind her, but I heard the honk of a horn and, looking out front, saw Barbara's Escape pull into the driveway. I opened the garage door again, and she parked next to my car.

Already telling each other their news, my sisters entered and shed their winter wear. When I shushed them, pointing to Winston, Barbara rolled her eyes at Faye the way she does when she thinks I don't see it. I started for the kitchen, but the sound of yet another vehicle sent me back to the window. Rory Neuencamp had parked his truck at one side of the drive. I had a moment of irritation. Not only did Barbara insist on consulting her boyfriend, she'd brought him along, too.

Pasting a smile on my face, I went to the front door to let him in. Pulling off his gloves, he said, "Hello, Retta."

There'd been a time when Rory first arrived that I thought he and I might hit it off, but I soon figured out he wasn't my type. Reserved, even a little cold. Like Barbara. It was no wonder they enjoyed each other's company.

"Come in, Chief."

He politely toed off his shoes and left them by the door. "Barb told me what's going on. I think I can help."

I led the way to the kitchen, where Barbara had pulled the spare chair up to the table and Faye was setting out plates for cake. When we were all seated with cake and tea or coffee, Barbara Ann said, "Rory deputized me." She added a half-teaspoon of sugar to her cup. "Darrow is ours until tomorrow, when the state police will take custody."

"We'll stay here?" I asked.

"Rory thinks we should snowmobile to his cabin."

"Me?" Faye's voice was a squeak.

"No sleds in your future," Barbara said with a tiny smile. "Your job is manning the office."

"Good," she replied. "If I remember right, the last snow vehicle I rode was pulled by a wooly mammoth."

I turned to Rory. "Where's this cabin of yours?"

"On the Paling River. It needs work, but I tightened up the seams and put in a generator, so it's habitable."

"It's a hunting camp?"

He chuckled. "So far I haven't found time to hunt. It's just a place to get away."

"Nobody knows about it?"

"Nobody who'll guess you'd be there." Leaning back in his chair, he glanced at Winston, who'd begun to stir. "Barb says he needs time in a safe place." He turned his mug back and forth on the tabletop, making a grinding sound. "There's more here than a marital quarrel."

It was nice that Rory accepted what we'd told him—well, what Barbara Ann had. "Thank you, Rory. We don't know who these men are, how many there are, or what their intentions are, except that they aren't honorable.

"Barb says you have snowmobiles?"

"Two of them."

"And enough gear to outfit all of us," Barbara put in.

"Great," Rory said. "Show me where the machines are kept, and I'll check them out."

I took keys from a hook by the back door. "Pole barn's out back. Fuel's in the red can."

After he left I said, "You're going along, Barbara? You aren't exactly Ms. Outdoors."

She shrugged. "Rory promised the sheriff we'd keep Darrow in custody. That means he doesn't leave my sight."

"Okay." Going to a double-wide closet in the hallway, I began pulling out snowsuits, boots, helmets, and accessories. As I worked I heard an engine start, and soon a machine roared up to my back door and then idled down to a low growl. A few seconds later another engine started, roared, and came toward the house, where it, too, idled down.

By the time Rory rejoined us, I had four piles of clothing. "Nice machines," he commented.

"My daughter and family were home for Christmas," I said. "I had them tuned up so we could ride together."

"You're an experienced rider. Who else?" Rory asked.

"Not so much," Barbara said. She probably tried snowmobiling once—in the Kennedy era.

Winston stumbled into the room, rubbing his head like a sleepy six-year-old, and frowned at the gear as if he'd come upon alien relics. I introduced Rory then asked, "Ever ride a snowmobile, Winston?"

He looked blank, and Rory and Barbara exchanged knowing glances. "You take him," Barbara said. "I'll ride with the chief."

I handed her a navy blue, one-piece snowsuit. "This is Tony's from high school. Rory and Winston need the bigger ones, so it's the closest I've got to your size."

Barbara took the suit and held it against her body. It looked long, but her hips would take up some of the slack. "It'll be fine." Her nose wrinkled at the slightly gassy smell the fabric tends to retain. She was probably reluctant to complain with Rory there, but her mouth turned down in silent disapproval as she started getting ready.

"We're going to ride snowmobiles to somewhere out in the woods?" Winston's voice revealed disbelief.

"All you have to do is ride along," Rory assured him.

"Can't we borrow somebody's pickup?"

"That's the point," Faye said patiently. "You'll be safe out there, because it's only accessible by snowmobile."

He frowned. "But it's getting dark. And it's cold, too."

"You'll enjoy it," I said, hoping to perk him up. "It's pretty out on the trails."

"Pretty noisy!" Barb muttered, but I don't think anyone heard except me.

Taking the two-piece suit I offered, Rory tossed his coat aside, stepped into the bibbed pants, and topped them with the short, matching jacket. The nylon fabric whistled as he dressed. "Riding double will be tough in this wet snow, and it's at least ten miles from here. The trip's going to take a while."

Winston looked on helplessly until Faye picked up the snow pants I'd set out for him and held them out. He just stared, so I took them from her and pressed them onto his chest. "Put them on." When he'd done it, I held the jacket for him then fastened the zipper. Leading him to a bench near the door, Faye helped him put on the snowmobile boots, tying them for him as if he were a backward kindergartner.

"We won't be able to use our phone out there," Rory said, "too many trees. I've gotten texts, though, so we can communicate that way."

"Good. Text to let me know you made it." The waver in Faye's voice revealed she wasn't thrilled about being separated from the rest of us.

"We will." I swept a stray hair off her shoulder.

"And when I figure out what's happening tomorrow," Rory said, "who should I call?"

"Faye," Barbara replied. "She can relay the message."

"Okay." Rory turned to me. "Do you have a couple of sleeping bags, Retta?"

"Sure," I answered. "I'll get them."

As I burrowed in a different closet, I heard Rory closing the zippers that ran down his pant legs and snapping the bottoms around his boots. His movements were confident and efficient, and I couldn't help comparing him to Winston, who looked on vacantly as Faye helped him with his gloves. I reminded myself that Winston had been through all kinds of trauma today and Rory had not, but Winston still suffered in the comparison.

Returning I asked, "Faye, can you put these in a couple of trash bags to keep them dry?" She went to the kitchen, and I turned to help Barbara with the zippers and snaps on her suit. She let me, though her expression said she'd rather I didn't.

"There." I checked everyone over. "Are we ready?"

To my own suit I added a tight-fitting nylon hood to protect my neck and most of my face from the cold. Pushing the bottom edge under the suit's collar, I adjusted the face hole so it covered my chin and forehead. After snapping the suit snugly at my neck, I handed helmets to Win, Barb, and Rory and then put on my own and tightened the chin-strap. Last I pulled on my mitts, which have clever, fold-back tops. I can uncover my fingers when I need full dexterity, but otherwise they stay warm.

"Styx!" I called. "Come here, baby!" He followed me into the garage, where I set his food and water dishes at the back wall. The doggie door would allow him into the back yard when he had to potty, and he'd sleep on a pile of old blankets in one corner. Before I closed the visor of my helmet, I turned to Faye. "Can you come out and feed Styx in the morning?"

"Sure. Just don't be gone too long."

I gave her an awkward hug, since my outfit made it impossible to get close. "We'll be fine, Faye." In her ear I said, "Barbara will hate it, but it'll do her good to try something different."

Barb, Winston, and Rory joined us, and we trooped out of the garage. The light had died quickly, and the single headlight of each snow machine showed bluish in the dark of the yard. Faye stood on the sidewalk, lighting a cigarette as she watched us go. She tried to smile, but her success was iffy at best.

CHAPTER TWENTY-ONE

Barb

Rory set a brisk but not taxing pace, handling the snowmobile with confident ease. Retta stayed back a little for safety's sake. Riders were sometimes hurt when one driver stopped for a deer or a downed tree branch and the one behind him couldn't do the same.

After following the highway for a mile, we turned due north, taking a trail maintained by groomer drivers like Gabe. Using various types of vehicles, they flatten and smooth the trails periodically during sledding season.

Aside from the noise, it wasn't an unpleasant experience. Over Rory's shoulder I saw that our speed was forty miles an hour, a bit fast for my taste but not particularly worrisome on a groomed trail. The first segment passed through lightly inhabited areas, mostly farms protected by barbed wire and warning signs. After that we entered heavily wooded land where the trail was the only thing that didn't belong to Mother Nature.

Retta was correct about it being beautiful. Our headlamps revealed ghostly tree-trunks and blue-white snowdrifts, often dotted with the tracks of rabbits and other small creatures. At one point Rory gestured at a deer that bounded into the woods ahead, desperate to avoid the oncoming monsters.

The ride got scary when we left the trail. Without the packed surface, the machine bogged down. The engine whined with strain and Retta backed off even farther. Grasping the handlebars firmly, Rory gunned the motor. The machine bucked and fought its way forward.

"Lean right!" he ordered as we came to a clump of trees. He did the same, turning the skis in that direction. I obeyed, though it felt like the wrong thing to do. I thought for sure we'd tip over, but the track dug in and we made the turn. Again he cranked up the gas, and we surged forward. "If we slow too much we'll get stuck," he shouted. I hung on, wishing the trip were over, but Rory was in control, and somehow the machine chewed its way through the deep snow, bouncing off buried rocks and pushing small trees out of our way.

It was probably only a mile farther to the cabin, but it seemed to take forever. When the trees opened before us, I realized we'd turned onto a road. A two-track, I guessed, usable in good weather but buried now under snow.

The headlight's reach was limited, and I was peering around Rory's substantial shoulders, so I couldn't see much of what was ahead. When the road curved sharply, Rory stopped beside a clump of trees. "I think this is it," he muttered, "but everything looks different at night." I could tell we were at the edge of a steep decline, but it was impossible to see what lay below us.

Retta pulled her sled up beside us and shut it down, and darkness descended like a heavy blanket. Along with it a dense, repressive silence settled. A cloud of exhaust fumes enveloped us, making me cough.

Rummaging in her sled's storage compartment, Retta called, "Here, Rory," and handed him something. I heard his suit fabric rustle, a click, and a light came on directly over his eyes. It was a headlamp, held in place on his helmet by a wide elastic band. Retta had one, too, and soon her light complemented his, one above my line of sight, the other below it.

Rory waded a few feet to the right and directed the light over the sharp drop-off. About fifty yards away and fifteen feet below us was the cabin, tiny, forlorn, and half-buried in white. Overhangs all the way around it kept the snow back from the walls, but beyond them it had filled the valley halfway to the height of the roof. From above we could see only part of the front wall with its large square window and plank door.

Darrow peered over Retta's shoulder. "*That's* where we're spending the night?"

"You could be in the Millden jail," I reminded him.

"I could be dead." He added glumly, "I just hope I live through this."

Rory led the way to the cabin, wading through waist-deep snow. I followed, dragging my feet to clear the spaces between Rory's prints. Darrow was next, and I heard him grunting behind me. Retta came last, angling her headlamp downward to light our feet. Stumbling and panting, we made toward the building. Somewhere behind it I heard water: the Paling River, narrowed and possibly covered by ice in places. Dangerous.

When we reached the cabin door, we were all out of breath. Darrow groaned in wordless complaint. Focusing his head lamp on a padlock threaded through a hasp-type fastener, Rory inserted a key and opened it. Setting it on the windowsill, he turned the knob, shouldered the door open, and led the way inside, spilling snow onto the floor.

"Come in," he said. "You're probably freezing."

Though the temperature had dropped to a few degrees above zero, I was surprisingly comfortable. Veteran snowmobilers advise, *Dress for it and you won't get cold,* and in my case they were correct. It wasn't true for Darrow, though. His teeth chattered like castanets.

The cabin was musty, dusty, and almost empty. Rory turned in a circle, showing us a single room with only a wooden table, two chairs, and a sink with a broken hand pump on one side. "No water," he said, "but I stopped on the way to Retta's and picked up some things." Pulling the light off his helmet, he handed it to me. "Barb and I will get the groceries."

As I followed Rory out I heard Darrow ask Retta, "Is he kidding with this place?" Hoping Rory hadn't heard, I closed the door and put the light on my own helmet.

Clambering back up to the road, we got the sleeping bags and a small duffel bag from the sleds' saddle bags. Back inside, I shook out the bags while Rory opened the duffel and removed an eight-pack of bottled water, four deli sandwiches, and a box of candy bars. "Not gourmet provisions," he said apologetically, "but it'll keep you alive until I get back."

Winston glanced around doubtfully, but Rory rubbed his hands briskly. "I'll get the generator going. Barb, come with me so you can see how it works."

He led the way around the side of the cabin, where the overhang had kept the way almost clear. Halfway down was a small metal shed, its low door fastened with a padlock. Opening the lock, Rory ducked inside. I remained where I was, there being no room for a second person.

The generator, about the size of a small steamer trunk, was painted red. As I focused the light, Rory pulled a cord and the machine chugged to life, emitting a low, continuous growl.

"See how I did that?" he asked.

"You turned that and pressed that."

"Right. There's gas in that jug." He showed me where it would go when the time came. "Good for ten hours." Backing out of the shed, he stood upright. "Are you going to be okay?"

"Yes," I said firmly, though I'd begun to wonder what I was doing out here in the woods in the middle of the night.

Stepping close, Rory put his arms around me, and I raised my face for his kiss. The world recedes a little when someone you care about kisses you, and I felt my fears ebb. If Rory thought I could do this, I could.

When we separated he said gruffly, "Someday there won't be a murder investigation between us."

"That'll be good," I replied.

"Yeah." He touched my cheek. "Guess we'd better go in and turn on the lights."

When we entered Darrow asked, "You guys get lost?" I bit back a nasty reply, recognizing that it was spooky in there with just Retta's headlamp. I focused my light on Rory, who reached up and pulled the chain on a fixture much like those in any home. The room glowed to visibility, and we squinted at each other as if assuring ourselves we weren't alone.

"Let there be light," Darrow sneered sarcastically.

"Just one so far." Rory sounded apologetic. "I have plans, but I haven't done much yet."

Retta's nylon snow-suit whistled as she stepped forward and set her headlamp on the table. "You couldn't have known you'd have company out here in January."

"At least I brought in wood, so we don't have to dig in a snow bank to get a fire going." Kneeling at the blackened stone fireplace, he began crumpling paper from a cardboard box at one side and tossing it in. He added kindling, stacking each piece at an angle to the one before it, and set two small logs on top. Taking a grill lighter from the mantel, he set the paper on fire. Flames licked at the kindling pieces, which in turn lit and went to work heating the logs to their burning point. As the fire took off we all moved toward it, watching the hypnotic dance of the flames while we waited to feel the warmth.

When it was clear the fire was viable, Rory sighed. "I should get back to town." Pulling on his jacket again, he started for the door. "By the way, the outhouse is on the far side of the generator shed." He grinned, catching my eye. "You'll hate it, but there are no other options."

Rory's gaze stayed on me, and I knew he wanted to tell me to be careful. I was fighting the same urge. In this primitive setting, I was safe, though uncomfortable. He would return to a soft bed and central heating, but what if he had to face Basca and his men?

As the whine of the single snowmobile faded, I stood in the center of the room, uncertain what to do. "We might as well make the place as clean as we can," Retta said briskly.

I agreed, not so much for aesthetics as to keep moving. The fire was only beginning to warm the cabin, but with its light and the lamp above, the need for housekeeping was obvious. Finding an old hand towel, I used it to wipe the cobwebs from the corners, the mouse droppings from the table, and the dust from the chairs. Retta swept the floor, using a broom so old it might have served at Castle Dracula. Darrow just watched until she handed him a towel and ordered him to help. With a pained expression he swiped at a few spots, his nose wrinkled with disgust.

When the place was as clean as we could make it with no water and few tools, we ate some of the food Rory had brought. The bread on my sandwich was slightly stale, but the water was nice and cold—not that we needed chilling. When we finished, we moved the table and chairs against one wall and laid the sleeping bags out near the hearth.

"Who'll keep the fire going?" Darrow asked.

Retta had taken off her snowsuit and boots, and she slid into her bag, wriggling into the most comfortable position she could manage. Darrow and I followed suit, avoiding each other's eyes. "One of us will wake up when it starts to cool down in here," she said confidently.

She was correct. An hour, maybe an hour and a half after we settled down to sleep, I felt the room's warmth start to fade. Shivering, I rolled out of the sleeping bag and tossed a couple of logs on, wrestling them into place with a metal rod that served as a poker.

Later I heard Retta do the same thing. She groaned a little as she stood up, and I grimaced in sympathy. No one over forty is meant to sleep on a bare wood floor. I never heard Darrow get up and feed the fire, but then, I hadn't expected to.

CHAPTER TWENTY-TWO

When I went out to Retta's the next morning, my husband insisted on riding along. In the fifteen years since the accident that almost killed him, Dale has struggled physically and mentally. He understands his disabilities but finds it hard to no longer serve what he considers a useful purpose. It doesn't matter to me. He's still the guy I fell in love with at sixteen. We didn't even mind much when I got pregnant at seventeen. By then we'd already decided to spend our lives together.

For years Dale provided for me and our three boys, and the jobs I worked were only for extra money. Things changed after he was hurt, and while his conscious mind recognizes that, Dale's subconscious keeps trying to prove he can still contribute. His coping mechanisms are harmless, consisting mostly of helping me in ways that aren't all that helpful. Mostly he gets in my way, but recognizing his need, I go along.

Dale had sensed my nervousness when I returned the night before without Barb, so I'd shared some of the details of the Darrow case with him. When I said I had to see to Styx in the morning, he said, "I'll go out there with you. I'm not Chief

Neuencamp, but I can call for help if there's somebody around Retta's house that shouldn't be there."

I knew my sisters were okay, having gotten a terse text from Barb. Still, the chief had figured Basca and his men would eventually find Retta's place. Having a man in the car might serve as a deterrent if they were watching the place, so Dale's presence was welcome.

Still, it always takes a while to get going when my husband is involved. While I put on my coat, I heard the weather channel girl start talking, despite the fact that Dale had tuned in fifteen minutes earlier and a half hour before that. He often checks my iPad, too, in case there's a difference in the forecasts.

Long ago, I made up my mind to give Dale leeway in the areas of life where he has some control. While he checked one more time, I waited in the kitchen, filing my nails. Once he was sure that the weather was no worse than most January days in Michigan, we left.

"Whose truck is that?" Dale asked when we pulled in to find a vehicle parked at the edge of the paved space.

"The chief's," I replied. "He should be back by now."

Getting out, I went and looked into the truck. The glove box door was open, and items lay scattered over the seat. I'd seen the chief put the truck keys into the pocket of his snowsuit the night before, but now they lay under the brake pedal as if they'd been tossed there in disgust.

Someone had been waiting when Chief Neuencamp returned last night. They'd taken his keys and searched his truck, no doubt looking for the mysterious book.

Dread shivered down my back. He wouldn't have given up his keys willingly.

"Dale!" I called. "I think the chief's here somewhere, and he might be hurt." *Or worse.*

He got out of the car, moving as fast as he was able, and I handed him Retta's spare keys. "Check the garage and the house while I look out back. Be careful!"

Opening the door, Dale disappeared into the garage. Soon Styx came bounding out to greet me, and I figured Dale had sent him to be my protector. First he put his paws on my shoulders so I could hug his big, shaggy body, but after that he turned away, nose in the air. "Go on, boy," I urged. "Find the chief."

Styx started around the house. The sidewalk to the pole barn hadn't been shoveled in a while, but feet and snowmobiles had packed the snow down, so the going wasn't too bad. Skirting the burlap-wrapped shrubbery, I trailed Styx to where Retta's sleds were kept.

When he reached the door at the side of the structure, Styx clawed at it, whining. I tried the knob. Locked. Peering through the foot-square window, I saw a snowmobile inside. Rory had indeed come back, but he hadn't left, at least, not in his truck. Impatient with me for not opening the door, Styx gave a yip of distress and clawed at it again.

Dale appeared in the garage doorway. "The alarm is still on, so nobody went inside."

I rattled the handle of the pole barn's door. "See if the key for this is hanging in the garage."

While I waited, I waded through ice-crusted snow to the window on the other side. From that angle I could see Chief

Neuencamp lying motionless on the dirt floor. His helmet had rolled into a corner, and his gloves lay at his side, one atop the other.

"Got it!" Dale called, and I trudged across the yard to get the key from him.

"The chief's in there," I said. "Call for an ambulance."

My fingers trembled so much it was hard to fit the key in the lock. Steadying one hand with the other, I ordered myself to calm down. Neuencamp needed help, and it was up to me. Opening the door, I hurried to where he lay.

The chief's muscles were slack, but he was breathing. Putting my fingers on his carotid artery, I felt a pulse that, while I was no expert, seemed okay. Years ago I had first aid training, but there'd been no lesson on helping victims of a violent attack. Taking off my coat, I covered him with it. Keeping body heat in had to be good.

Not sure what else to do, I lit a cigarette to calm my nerves, stepping away from the chief every few seconds to take a brief, comforting puff. In between I patted his shoulder and told him help was on the way. He moaned once or twice, which I took to be a good sign, but he didn't seem aware of me, which was really, really scary.

The EMTs arrived, and I held Styx back, explaining to him it wasn't a time for hugs. He behaved well, standing meekly off to one side as a young woman checked Rory's vital signs before her partner fitted him with an immobilizing collar and they lifted him onto a cot. Dale and I watched, feeling helpless, though the EMTs said we'd done well.

Barb had found someone she cared about, and he might be dying. It felt like I should have done more, though I didn't know what it would have been.

As the ambulance sped off, Dale asked, "Are you going to call your sister?"

Barb was already stressed. Could it help to add more stress? "I'll wait until we get a prognosis," I replied, adding silently, "*If she wants to be with him, I'll go out to that cabin and babysit Winston myself.*"

CHAPTER TWENTY-THREE

Barb

I never claimed to be a camper, and no one who knows me would predict I'd be a happy one. In fact, when our parents sent Faye and me to camp the summer I was twelve, I called after one day to demand they come and rescue me. Faye stayed, learning how to ride a horse Western Style, shoot arrows from a bow, and make ugly ceramic ashtrays. She'd gone back three more summers, but I'd refused, claiming my time was better spent at the library.

After Rory left for Allport, the adventure leaked out of the experience, turning it into an uncomfortable inconvenience. Around three a.m., when it was necessary to go out in the cold to visit the outhouse, I began to wonder why I'd stayed. I could have gone back to Allport with Rory, leaving Retta to babysit her smarmy boyfriend. I'd have slept in my own bed and visited my own bathroom to quell the urge that hits sometime around two a.m., no matter where I am.

Once I'd braved the disgusting, crooked, splintery, but frozen and therefore less odiferous outhouse, it was hard to get back to sleep. I quieted my mind by planning some Correction Events. I needed to fix the corkboard at the Chamber of

Commerce, where someone had misspelled *February* in the usual, infuriating way. I'd also had my eye on a sign at my hairdresser's that said EVERYONE NEEDS TO KEEP TRACK OF THERE OWN BELONGINGS. I could cover the initial *t* and the final *e*, making the sign read HER OWN BELONGINGS, acceptable for a mostly female clientele. What I hadn't figured out was how I'd get to the errant signs while no one was looking.

I added the city's bulletin board to my fix-it list. I could offer to help Retta with one of her many projects and get the key under the guise of posting the event. I'd have to be careful not to arouse her suspicions, though, since I wasn't in the habit of supporting her civic do-gooding. Pondering how to get those things done took my mind off my uncomfortable situation, and I dozed off again.

A couple hours later, when I woke up achy from sleeping on a chilly hardwood floor, I promised myself I'd be a trouper. I'd keep the drawbacks of primitive living to myself. Therefore, when I mentioned how creepy the outhouse was, it was a warning, not a complaint.

"Of course it's creepy, Barbara!" Retta put on her coat and boots in preparation for her own visit. "Who expects an outhouse to be anything but?" She clomped to the door and left, closing it with a vigorous scrape.

"An outhouse!" Win shuddered. "Germs and bacteria."

Despite my own repugnance, I felt a responsibility to defend Rory's territory in his absence. "If you'd lived in the Tudor era, you and everyone you knew would have used one. One castle I saw has an outhouse built into the upper wall, and another one had a two-holer. I did wonder about people who went in there together, but—"

"I'm in no mood for a history lesson." Darrow turned his back, letting me ponder ancient outhouses on my own.

When Retta returned he asked, "How bad is it?"

"You'll survive," she replied tersely.

He pointed at me. "She said creepy. Does that mean things are creeping around in there?"

Retta rolled her eyes. "It's January, Winston. There aren't any bugs."

"Bugs aren't the only things that creep," he grumbled. "Maybe I'll just wait."

With a sigh, Retta unzipped the duffel bag. "That's totally your choice."

Breakfast was a candy bar and a bottle of water. Since there were only two chairs, one of us had to stand to eat, and Retta and I let Darrow play the gentleman's role, each taking a chair without bothering to ask if he minded. When his chocolate was gone, he raised his nose a little and asked, "Are there any more sandwiches?" No one answered him. He looked longingly at the remaining candy bars, but Retta shook her head.

"Until we know how long we have to be out here, we need to be careful with the food."

"Hey, I'm a growing boy!" He tried to cover his argument with a jovial tone. "Besides, I thought women were always watching their figures."

"Maybe the women you consort with," I said bluntly. He went quiet, eyeing the remains of Retta's candy bar with longing. Either she didn't notice or she didn't care.

The cabin was drafty, its corners cold. I'd set my chair directly in front of the fireplace, but it wasn't a perfect place to break my fast. There was nowhere to set my cup of water except on the floor, and I had to rotate the chair ninety degrees every few minutes to keep from frying like bacon in a pan. Despite my resolve, I heard myself mutter, "My rear's burning and my face is freezing!"

"Then don't sit so close!" Retta snapped. Without waiting for me to act, she rose and pulled my chair, with me in it, backward, making a scraping sound that raised the level of my irritation exponentially. "You and Winston should have a griping contest," she said in a voice that sounded like our mother at her angriest. "You're both really good at it."

Darrow's bottom lip protruded at her criticism. I also resented being repositioned against my will, and I opened my mouth to say so.

Retta changed the subject. "You should have told Rory to let us know when he got home." She checked her watch. "Text his personal cell. I'm sure you have the number."

Reluctant to obey her imperious command, I checked my own watch. Seven a.m. Rory was either getting ready for work or on his way. "Give him another hour," I said. "By then he'll have talked to the state police, and we'll know who's coming to get us.

CHAPTER TWENTY-FOUR

My stressful morning continued. I could get no word on Chief Neuencamp from the hospital, since I wasn't family. In desperation I called Tom Stevens, the deputy chief. We'd known each other since high school, so I figured he'd give me something.

"He's awake and coherent," Tom said. "They're being cautious, checking him out six ways from sundown." He chuckled. "He isn't happy about it. Chief ain't a guy who likes to wait around for other people." He sounded just a touch critical. Tom isn't known as a man of action, which was probably why Rory was brought in when the chief's job came open.

"Is anyone with him?" I couldn't imagine waking from a traumatic event with no friendly face beside me.

"His daughter's somewhere down south," Tom said, adding as an afterthought, "The girls sent him flowers from all of us."

"I'm sure he'll appreciate that."

"They said he asked about you first thing."

"Me?"

"Well, all of you, you know. Retta and Barb and that guy you arrested."

"Winston Darrow."

"Yeah. He wanted to know if anybody heard anything."

"I'll contact him. Thanks, Tom." Before he could start asking questions, I ended the call.

A snuffy little sigh sounded at my feet, and I reached down to scratch Buddy's ears. He'd followed me around all morning, settling under my desk when I sat down to work. When it looked like that was going to be his spot of choice, I went and got an afghan one of Dale's aunts made for us. A hideous mix of browns and purples, it was nevertheless soft and warm, so I spread it under the desk for the dog to lie on. He followed me to the bedroom and back, apparently curious to see what I intended, but when I sat down again he turned around a few times on the blanket and settled in for a nap.

Buddy was both a joy and a concern. There was evidence he'd had training at some point. He scratched at the back door when he needed to go outside. He was used to a collar and didn't mind a leash as long as I was at the other end. He wasn't fussy about food, only about who offered it. He didn't like visitors, and I'd have to work on that. It's hard to interview clients while your dog growls at them. On the other hand, not all strangers are good guys, so Buddy's suspicious nature might turn out to be helpful at times.

That reminded me of Chief Neuencamp. If his condition was good, he'd be anxious to know that Barb and the others were okay. If he wasn't doing well, I'd have to let Barb know. When I called and asked for him, a woman informed me he'd been taken to the lab for tests. "Can you give him a message?" I asked. "Please tell him things are all right at the agency."

She agreed to pass the message on. The chief would know what I knew—almost nothing. Nothing is good in some cases.

The next problem was how to answer Barb's texts. I didn't want to lie, but I also didn't want to tell her the whole truth. Not yet.

CHAPTER TWENTY-FIVE

Barb

By ten o'clock, I'd texted Rory once and Faye twice and received no answer from either of them. The cabin became a prison as we tried to guess what that meant. I paced, Retta checked her phone constantly, and Darrow stared out the single drafty window, where there was nothing to see but snow. He drew designs in the frost at its edges, scratching at it with his fingernail. The noise got irritating after a while, especially since he asked every few minutes, "Do you think something bad happened?" I wanted to scream at him to stop.

To pass the time, I led Darrow again through the events of the last few days. If it triggered a memory he hadn't yet shared with us, great. If not, at least it would stop the ice-scraping.

It was clear to me that the men who'd kidnapped Darrow had also killed his wife. Because his story remained the same after repeated questioning, I believed he hadn't known about the book. Stacy had stolen it, probably before they met. Though Max Basca believed otherwise, she'd never trusted Darrow enough to tell him what she'd done.

Turning to him I asked for at least the eighth time, "There's no book around your place that's different?"

Because I was facing Darrow, I saw the tiny light in his eyes at my wording. "You've thought of something."

"No, I—"

Before I could finish, Retta was toe to toe with him, her finger under his nose. "Winston Darrow, we've had enough of your lies. We risked our lives to help you, so don't you dare hold out on us!" Her message was punctuated with pokes to his chest, and he leaned against the wall to try to escape them. Her face close to his, she asked pointedly, "Did Stacy mention a book that was special to her?"

"She didn't, honest. But I might have seen something."

"When? Where?"

He raised his hands as if in surrender. "I didn't lie. I never saw any odd book in the house. But when Ms. Evans said, 'around your place,' that reminded me of something."

"Tell us," Retta demanded.

Darrow's eyes focused on nothing as he remembered. "One day I went out to the barn to ask what Stacy wanted for supper. It was summertime and the ground was soft, so I didn't make noise coming down the path. The stable door was open a little, and she was standing in the middle of the room. She had a book—not a story-type book, but one you'd write stuff in."

"A ledger?"

"More like a journal. She put it into one of those zipper-type plastic folders then put that in a canvas bag."

"To keep it clean and dry," Retta murmured.

"I wanted to see where she was going to put it," Darrow went on, "but the stupid horses smelled me and got all spooky. Stacy turned to look, and I backed around the corner of the building. She came to the doorway and called my name, but I didn't answer. When she went back inside I heard noises, like stuff sliding across the floor. I went back to the house the long way, through the trees. She never knew I was there."

"What did you think it was?"

Darrow shrugged. "Her diary, maybe."

"Did you ever try to find it?" Retta asked.

"I went out there a few times when she was out riding, but like I said, those horses hate me. Whichever one was left there always made a fuss."

"Stacy never mentioned keeping a diary?"

He shook his head. "I never saw her writing anything."

An idea buzzed in my mind. "You said she did the banking."

Nodding, Darrow said, "Once a month she figured out what we needed for household expenses. Then she went to the bank and put money in our joint account to cover it."

"What's your bank?" I asked.

"Um, BB&T in Allport."

"She went there once a month."

"On the first Monday, like clockwork."

"Did she take anything with her?"

"Just her purse." He sniffed. "If you call that suitcase she carried a purse."

"It was big?"

"Well, no bigger than some others I've seen." His eyes flickered to Retta, whose purses are large enough for a long weekend getaway. They usually have more buckles than a suit of armor, and I'm supposed to call them handbags, not purses. She gives me a look if I forget.

Terminology aside, I was pleased. After multiple retellings of his story, Darrow had revealed a worthwhile tidbit. Turning, I looked at Retta speculatively.

"What?"

"Can you pull off a little deception?"

She snapped her fingers. "Any day of the year. What do you have in mind?"

I began pacing. "Here's what I think happened. Stacy—or whatever her real name is—stole a large amount of money from Max Basca, a man she shouldn't have crossed. Possibly to keep him from coming after her, she also took a book filled with information that can hurt him."

Retta caught on. "Right, but for some reason, the protection it was meant to provide didn't work out. She had to run."

"They were looking for a thirty-ish single woman, so she figured she'd be safer as a wife. Winston here happens along, thrilled to be offered a meal ticket."

Darrow turned from the window to glare at me. "I told you, it wasn't like that."

"Who made the first move?" I demanded.

"Well, she did."

"And who suggested marriage?"

His head drooped. "She said she knew from the moment we met." What sounded romantic then sounded suspicious now, and for once he had no more to say.

I looked back at Retta. "Instead of having it all, the way she'd imagined it, Stacy was afraid, every single day. She moved to a remote spot in Michigan. She became less and less comfortable in public." To Darrow I said, "Did Stacy begin acting differently recently? Even less willing to leave the house, maybe?"

He thought about it. "Yeah. Last time she went to the bank, she came back looking upset, but she said she was fine. She spent the rest of the day on her computer."

"Booking a plane ticket." Retta's airbrushed nail emphasized her point on the tabletop.

My mind was still working on the details. "You said she often ordered things on line?"

His answer came with a snort. "All the time! Why?"

"That's how people who try to disappear are found. They keep something they shouldn't: membership in a group, a subscription, even an RSS feed."

He got it. "Stacy wasn't really Stacy? She was a fake?"

"Changing identities seems to be in fashion, *Walter*."

Retta stepped in. "What do you want me to do, Barbara?"

I took a moment to think it through. "Go back to Allport. When you get there, tell Faye all this. She needs to find out who Stacy Darrow really was. While she works on that, visit the bank and learn what you can about whatever Stacy had going."

"How am I supposed to do that?"

"You'll think of something." Going to the corner where we'd piled our snowmobile clothing, I started tossing items to her. "When you get to the main road, call Rory and ask him to meet you at your house. I don't think those guys will be around, but we should play it safe."

She stopped with her snow-pants halfway up. "They might be at my house?"

"You're the girlfriend, remember?"

Her eyes got big. "And if they are there?"

"They'll take off when a cop car pulls in." I gestured for her to resume dressing, and she obeyed. "Pack what you need for a couple nights at our place. Go to the bank and find out what you can about Stacy's personal visits the first of every month."

Retta was already plotting. "Rory will probably help."

"He might. Once you learn what you can, go back to the office and stay until this is over. Rory's called the state police by now, so they'll come for me and Darrow soon."

CHAPTER TWENTY-SIX

Retta

The trip back to Allport didn't take as long as the trip out had. I had a trail to follow, and the sled went faster with only my weight to carry. Once I got to the groomed trail, the way was familiar, so I pressed the throttle and headed for home.

When I parked the machine behind the house, I came around the garage to find Tom Stevens waiting in his patrol car.

"Good morning, Tom," I called as I approached. "Is Rory busy?" His somber expression told me something was wrong. "What is it?"

"Someone attacked him out here last night. Faye found him this morning when she came to see to your dog."

Barbara had been right to be afraid. "Is he all right?"

Tom shifted his feet. "Still doing tests, I guess."

I glanced around my yard. "They were waiting here?"

"Someone whacked him then searched his truck." He put his thumbs in his belt, which called attention to his oversized gut. "What were they after, Retta?"

"That's what we're trying to figure out."

"You girls have Darrow stashed out in the woods, don't you? You should bring him in where we can protect him."

"There's some question about how to protect Winston right now, Tom. Rory tried to, and look what happened to him. Besides, he deputized Barbara, so it's legal."

Tom made a clicking sound with his tongue, but he didn't argue. "I checked your house out. There are footprints all around, like somebody peeked in. You might not want to—"

"I'm staying with my sisters," I interrupted, shutting off the advice Tom was prone to press on others. "If you'll wait a few minutes, I'll pack some things and follow you back to town."

He seemed about to object, so I added, "I made a red velvet cake you might want to try." That was enough to assure I even had time for a shower, if I was quick.

As I dressed, I thought about what must have happened. Winston's enemies had found out about me, as Rory had predicted. They'd come here, looked in my windows, and noted the presence of alarms and a very large dog. Rory had come along at precisely the wrong moment, unaware of the danger. But why had they attacked him?

It came to me in a flash. Basca and his men had thought Rory was Winston. The snowmobile suit and helmet would have made him anonymous. Once they realized their mistake, they'd searched Rory's truck, looking for some indication of where we'd gone. They probably hadn't cared much whether Rory was alive or dead once they knew he wasn't their man.

The incident made me decide to take Styx to town with me. The threat to me hadn't seemed real before, but now it did. If the men who'd hurt Rory returned, I didn't want my dog in their way. Loading food, his favorite bowl, and Styx into my SUV, I followed Tom to town. When I turned off Main Street, he beeped the horn twice and drove on. At the office, Faye suggested Styx could spend the day with Dale in his workshop.

"We'll bring him in the house tonight, but right now it'll be easier if he stays outside. Buddy's a little territorial." Her tone was apologetic. "He's decided I'm okay, but so far, nothing else that moves can come near him. He already hates the vacuum cleaner and the mail lady, and Dale hasn't had any luck making friends, either."

"He'll like Styx," I told her. "They'll be friends before you know it."

Faye was unconvinced. "Maybe in time." She thought about it. "We could take them somewhere neutral, like the park, and introduce them there."

That was just plain silly. Styx is the friendliest dog in the world. Buddy would feel safe here on his home turf, and Styx would be polite, being a visitor. I decided not to push it, though. I'm not nearly as bossy as Barbara Ann says I am.

"How's your dog's leg?" I asked.

"Buddy's break is healing nicely," she said, emphasizing the name a little, which I guessed meant we were stuck with it. Glancing toward the kitchen she added, "He hasn't let it stop him from exploring." She ran her tongue over her teeth. "I hope when Barb gets back he'll accept that she belongs here."

My instincts had been right. Strays are unpredictable, and Faye had saddled herself with a nasty one. It wouldn't bother me to put up with the dog for a day or two, and Styx would be fine in Dale's workshop. But what if this new dog took a dislike to Barbara Ann? What would happen to their partnership then? For the good of everyone, I decided that when I got back from the bank I'd start some firm but gentle re-training on Buddy.

Faye hadn't heard anything new about Rory's condition, but hospitals are notoriously cautious about head injuries. I told her what we'd wrung out of Winston at the cabin, ending with Barbara's idea that I should see what I could find out at Stacy's bank. I thought Faye might object, since she is a partner in the agency and I'm not, but she'd never pull it off and she knew it. The woman has no talent for deception.

Instead she said, "Now that I know Stacy changed her name, I'll take another shot at finding her." She turned to her computer, but a thought struck her. "The state police! If Rory never made it home, they don't know what's going on." She picked up the phone. "We'd better call them."

I checked the time: 11:40. "Wait." I put a hand on Faye's shoulder. "Right now we have no proof of anything. Once I talk to the bank people and you do some on-line research, we might be able to hand them the whole case on a platter."

Faye seemed doubtful. "But we're supposed to turn Win over to them."

"And we will," I assured her. "But right now we know he's safe." Picturing myself explaining the details of the case to Barbara Ann and that snooty trooper who refused my request for information, I finished, "One hour, two at the most, and we could have all the answers."

"Barb won't like it," Faye said, and I tried to hide my irritation. It was always about what Barbara would think!

"I'll call them, but I want to get to the bank before the manager goes to lunch." When she still looked uncertain, I said, "They know me at the state police post, remember?" I took up my coat. "See if you can find the real Stacy Darrow. When I get back we'll be in a much stronger position to prove Winston is innocent." I set my purse strap on my shoulder and pulled my gloves out of a side pocket. "It will be so much nicer for him if he isn't considered a wife-murderer."

Faye had one more objection. "Should you go to the bank alone? What if someone's watching us?"

"I'll be careful." I checked my hair in the small mirror of my compact then clicked it closed.

"All right, but we have to call as soon as you get back, whether we've got more to tell them or not. Barb shouldn't be stuck out there any longer than she has to be."

Grinning, I gave her a little slap on the arm. "You never told me what a wimp Barbara Ann is. She went on for an hour about having to use an outhouse." Loyal to a fault, Faye didn't answer, but she couldn't hide a tiny smile. "How will you get the bank people to share information about a customer?"

With my best innocent expression I replied, "You'd be amazed what girls will tell other girls when they think they're just chatting."

Businessman's Bank & Trust is a local entity known for friendly tellers and silly rules. Loans depend on the whims of a board of old men (I think they added a token woman when the millennium changed). Acting on principles only they understand, BB&T might refuse a home loan to a respectable young couple while a guy with a string of past bankruptcies can borrow and default at will for decades. Rumor has it their decisions reflect the condition of their collective digestive systems.

The bank is a 1950's style stone building with a flat roof, wide doors, and a metallic smell. When I entered, two tellers looked up brightly. The third was on the phone. I stopped to glance around, since I'd been there only a few times. There were two offices opposite the tellers' windows. On the door of one it said MRS. DIANA SELLERS in block letters. The other said MR. PULARSKI in slightly larger letters. Easy choice. "I'd like to see Mr. Pularski, please."

It didn't matter if he was the top dog (which I guessed he was) or second banana. Men are so easy to manipulate.

I had to wait a few minutes, which was fine, since I needed time to get my story straight. Ignoring the muted sounds of busy-ness around me, I prepared myself for my little charade. Barbara had sent me, and she was deputized, which meant it was almost like I'd been deputized, too. I represented the Smart Detective Agency (which will have a new name as soon as I get a chance to talk to my sisters about it). I guessed a guy working at a small-town bank had never met a real P.I. before.

"Ma'am?" The teller tilted her head toward the door, where a man in his forties ushered an elderly couple out. When they were gone, I approached with my hand out. "Mr. Pularski? I'm Barbara Evans of the Smart Detective Agency. Could I have five minutes of your time?"

Though I don't work in the business world, I know how things go. You treat people a certain way, confident but not overbearing. You limit what you ask them for. Five minutes is something even a busy person can spare. You use the person's name. You look him in the eye. And if he's male and you're a reasonably attractive woman, you add a smile that says you find him interesting.

I was seated in a padded chair and urged to call Mr. Pularski Ralph. He was very much a gentleman, as many men who spend most of their workday with women are.

"So you're a shamus, eh, Mrs. Evans?" Barbara hates the "Isn't she cute" attitude some men adopt when faced with a female detective. Irritation flickered in my mind, too, but I've learned to use such things to get what I want.

"Please, call me Barbara," I urged. "We're on the Darrow case. I'm sure you've heard of it."

"Guy killed his wife, right?"

I leaned in conspiratorially. "That's what the general public thinks."

"Really?" I had his attention now, and not just because of the low-cut, silky blouse I'd chosen. Since I was pretending to be Barbara, I'd considered dressing down but decided instead to use *my* femininity to *her* advantage. I hoped word of her vanilla wardrobe and Puritan plainness hadn't gotten around to local bankers and tellers.

"The police can't talk about it yet because it's a complicated situation, but Chief Neuencamp wanted me to contact you with some questions."

He wasn't stupid. "Why didn't the chief come?"

"You didn't hear? He was attacked, almost certainly by the real killer."

"That's terrible!" Now I really had his interest.

"He'll be all right, but the investigation needs to continue. I'll brief him later." I gestured toward the phone on his desk. "Call his office if you like. They'll tell you I'm legally deputized."

Shoving some folders out of his way, Pularski took up his phone, pausing to glance at me as if I might try to stop him. When I only smiled in my most charming manner, he made the call. "Can you tell me if Barbara Evans is working with the chief on the murder over in Lawton?" ... "I see. Thank you."

When he hung up, Pularski checked me out again. "Even if you are working with the chief, I can't share customer records without authorization."

I waved a hand. "I'd never ask you to, Ralph. Your bank has a stellar reputation, and I understand you work hard to maintain it. What I'd like is to speak to the tellers about their impressions of Mrs. Darrow. If you'll ask them to cooperate, it would be a great help."

Resting his chin on his knuckles, he tried briefly to think of an objection to that. "Okay," he finally said. "I'll stick around, though, so they don't pass on anything they shouldn't."

"Not a problem." I gave him a look. "I really appreciate this, Ralph." As we left the office, his hand was at my back, and accidentally, I'm sure, it slid down a little, feeling the curve of my rear. That's when a girl is thankful for Zumba.

The first teller I chose to speak to was Marian, a forty-something woman with a pleasant face and arms that needed toning. Once Ralph explained the reason for my questions, he stood back and watched, like a father listening to the conversation between his daughter and her first young man.

I started by thanking Marian for her time, saying I knew she was very busy. I asked her a little about herself: how long she'd worked at the bank, what days she worked, what times of day were the busiest. Once we got past that I asked, "Did you know Stacy Darrow on sight?"

"Yes. She came in every month, so we all knew her."

"Was she friendly?"

"No." She corrected herself. "I mean, she wasn't unfriendly, she was just...distant, you know? She brought in her—" She glanced at Pularski. "She did what she came to do and left."

"What did Mrs. Darrow look like?"

"Excuse me?" The victim's picture had been splashed all over the local news for days now. When I waited expectantly, Marian laid a hand on her chest. "Well, she was pretty, long black hair, dark eyes, tall. She didn't try to attract attention, but you couldn't help but notice her."

"What did she wear?"

"Um, dark clothes, mostly. Leggings with tank tops under baby-doll dresses, big sweaters with UGG boots, stuff like that."

"Did she ever wear sunglasses or hats?" Pularski moved behind me, and I sensed his growing boredom.

"No. I don't recall her ever doing that."

"Thank you. I appreciate your time." With a smile for her and a glance at Pularski, I moved to the next teller, a winter who wore colors all wrong for her complexion. When I began the same way, asking the same questions, I heard him sigh. I proceeded slowly, asking about the teller and her work before turning to Stacy's looks. When I got to the question about her clothes, the phone on Pularski's desk buzzed and blinked. He looked toward it, hesitated, and turned back to me.

"Did she wear jewelry?" I asked. "I heard she liked long, dangly earrings."

Pularski cleared his throat. "Ms. Evans, I have a call."

Touching his arm I said, "I'm almost done here. Again, I appreciate your help, Ralph."

His answering grin was weak, and he walked away. At first eager to help with a murder case, he'd ended up irritated by my petty questions.

It was exactly what I'd hoped for.

The third teller, Teresa, was my best chance for information, based on what I'd observed. She was chewing gum, and I was surprised Pularski hadn't banned chomping away like a camel during work hours. She'd been on the phone when I came in, and she was still talking. Though she tried to pretend it was a business call, the look fake-serious on her face told me otherwise. As I approached, she glanced up and changed her tone. "Thank you for contacting BB&T, and please don't hesitate to call if you need help again."

She turned to me with an innocent look. The gum disappeared into some secret place in her mouth, but I could still smell the spearmint. Her eyes glittered with interest. This woman loved gossip. Just the kind of person I needed.

After I'd introduced myself, I started with the same questions. The other two women listened at first but soon returned to their work. I wandered a few steps away, ostensibly to look at a poster but actually moving Teresa out of range of her co-workers' hearing.

My source was primed. Her boss had okayed my questions. Her co-workers had already answered them. This time, I would learn more than what kind of boots Stacy Darrow wore.

"I've got the basics figured out," I told her, "like what Mrs. Darrow's big purse was for."

The gum cracked once before she remembered and returned it to its hiding place. "I used to wonder what would happen to her if some of the low-lifes around here knew how much cash she carried around in that thing."

I waggled my head gravely. "Not very wise."

She nodded enthusiastically. "That comes with a cash business, though." I wanted to ask, but I didn't have to. Teresa went right on. "Can you imagine? Car washes all over northern Michigan? She must have spent half her time on the road." Leaning toward me she said, "I told her once she should bring her deposits in more often so it wasn't thousands of dollars at a time, but she kind of blew me off." She shrugged. "Her decision, even if it was dumb."

Realizing she'd criticized a customer, and a dead one at that, Teresa backtracked a little. "I guess she knew what she wanted. It just seemed funny to me. Not real businesslike."

Outside, I called Faye and told her what I'd learned.

"No way," Faye scoffed. "She wasn't operating a business unless it was Internet-based, and they didn't find evidence of that on her computer."

"Winston says she never went anywhere, so there was no business. She lied to them."

"To explain why she brought in cash every month and deposited it in her account."

"Owning a string of car washes would make used cash in small bills look legitimate."

"And she deposited it a little at a time, to avoid suspicion."

"That's my guess."

"So she brought cash, probably stolen, from New Mexico. How'd she get it here without Winston knowing?"

I tapped my phone with a fingernail. "She could have put it in boxes, like it was furniture or something."

"Books!" Faye almost shouted.

"Books?"

"Readers are the ultimate hoarders."

"Oh my gosh. Stacy packed cash in with her books!"

I shivered as a draft of cold air surged through an alley and hit my face like a slap. "Text Barbara and have her ask Winston exactly what Stacy brought along when they moved here."

"Okay." Faye hesitated, and I heard her fidget in her chair. "We're assuming the money belongs to Basca, right? Where do you think he got it?"

"Drugs would be my guess."

"We need to get the state police here ASAP."

"I'm on my way. You find out who Stacy really was."

As I turned my body to block the wind, I noticed a man across the street, a stranger who was big enough to start on the Lion's offensive line. When our eyes met, he turned toward a store window and pretended to look inside. A few seconds later he walked away in the opposite direction.

I was almost certain he'd been watching me. Did he know I'd gone into the bank to check Stacy's finances? If he was one of Basca's men, he probably knew more about where her money came from than I did.

CHAPTER TWENTY-SEVEN

Barb

After Retta left, Darrow grew agitated. Staring out the window, he scratched at the frosty pane again, muttering phrases like, "No way out" and "Sitting ducks."

Having little talent for babying spineless whiners, I ignored him, busying myself with feeding the fire, checking the generator, inventorying the food we had left, and pacing. Though the order varied, that was pretty much it.

Around noon, his eyes got the wild look I'd seen when we rescued him at the diner. "We're dead meat, I tell you!"

"They can't find us out here, Mr. Darrow."

"What if they do? Retta and your cop took the snowmobiles. Are we gonna run across the snow like rabbits?"

"They'll be back for us when this is sorted out."

"How do you know that? They might both be dead!"

His scenario was irritating, being both hysterical and possible. We were isolated, unaware of what was going on. It was beyond nerve-wracking. Still, I had to prevent him from losing it completely. "They're fine. They're going to get us back home."

His mind jumped to another track. "When the cops come, you'll tell them I didn't kill Stacy, right?"

I nodded. "I believe you, so does Chief Neuencamp."

"The sheriff doesn't." His mind jumped again. "Do you think he knows who's helping George and the others?"

"Since we haven't heard from them yet, I'd guess not."

He smacked the windowsill with a fist. "Call your cop friend. Find out what's going on!"

Though I didn't like his tone, and though he seemed to think I could make the cell phone work by magic, I sympathized with Darrow's frustration. Retta had been gone for four hours, Rory for twelve. Why wasn't somebody telling us something?

They were. When I picked up my phone, an icon indicated I had a text. I'd missed the signal due to Darrow's ranting.

I navigated to the message from Faye. DID STCY RCVE SHPMTS FROM NMX AFTR MOVE?

I grimaced. Did my sister realize I was stuck in a rustic cabin with an annoying client and an *outhouse*, for crying out loud?

Assuming the question had a point, I read the message to Darrow, who shrugged. "She brought her clothes in the car, and we bought furniture once we got here."

"She brought only clothing, nothing else?"

He thought about it. "Some other stuff came later by UPS." He huffed in disgust. "Boxes and boxes of books." Poking his chest he added, "Guess who did all the lifting when they came."

"Did you help her unpack them?"

"No. She said she wanted to categorize them herself."

I began to understand the question Faye had asked. Stacy had shipped something north, probably whatever she'd stolen from Max Basca. Darrow had been served as unwitting accessory to the crime she'd committed.

A text wouldn't do. I had to call the office and actually speak to Faye, but there wasn't even one full bar in the upper corner of my phone's screen.

I moved around the cabin, holding the phone before me. Nothing. Setting it down, I slithered into my snowsuit and pushed my feet into the boots, tying them loosely.

"Where are you going?" Winston asked.

"Out to find a signal."

"Cool. Are you going to get us out of here?"

"I'll let you know."

Outside, I went up the path we'd made to the ridge and tried the phone. Still no signal. Guessing the trees blocked the signal, I looked for a spot that was more open but higher than the cabin. I'd heard stories of people in remote areas standing on whatever was available, including tree stumps, to get a few bars on their phones. The cabin roof was high and open, but I didn't see a way to get onto it. There were no stumps around, nor any trees that looked climbable. I looked again, slowing myself down and considering each possibility.

Of course. The outhouse.

Going to the woodpile, I took two substantial logs and carried them to the back of the small plank building, where the slanted roof was lowest. Setting them about a foot apart, I pressed the bottom ends into the snow and braced the tops against the wall. They made clumsy steps, but Correction Events have made me creative about getting to hard-to-reach places. Stepping onto one then the other lifted me to a point where my chest was at roof level. Brushing away the snow, I found a knothole and hooked two fingers into it. With that assistance I pulled myself up and caught a second handhold where two boards had shrunk, leaving a crack. It pinched a little, but I swung one leg up and pushed with the other, lifting my lower body up. With an extra push and a grunt of effort, I found traction and sprawled onto the roof.

The building was rickety, so I didn't stand but instead spread my weight along the line where the roof met the wall. Digging my phone out, I held it before me. Two bars! I pressed the button that would connect me with Faye.

"Barb!" I heard a few seconds later. "Are you okay?"

"Not comfortable, but we'll survive. What's going on?"

"A lot." The phone made a rustling sound and the volume faded a little. "Someone attacked Rory when he got back to Retta's last night. He's in the hospital."

I felt like someone had punched me in the gut. "Is he—Is he all right?"

"He was unconscious when I found him, but the EMT said that was a good thing. His body shut down to protect his brain." She cleared her throat. "Barb, I'm sorry."

Waves of fear splashed through my mind, drowning logical thought. I wanted to be at Rory's side. I wanted to know he was all right. I wanted the danger to be over, for him—for all of us.

Dragging my focus to the question she'd texted, I said, "Darrow says Stacy had boxes of books shipped north. I guess you think books were mixed with something else."

"Stacy's been feeding cash into her bank account with a cover story about running a string of car washes."

"No large deposits to call attention to herself. Clever."

"—Says Basca wants his money back, plus—" I missed the last words as the phone cut out.

"I'm losing you. So we'll be out here a while longer?"

"Yeah." Now her voice sounded scratchy. "Like to get— more food, but—Retta."

"Don't worry about that. Just get someone to arrest Basca and his boys."

"—will. Take care, Barb."

Stuffing the phone into my suit pocket, I clambered down from the outhouse, missing my step and landing on my back. It didn't hurt, but I got a healthy dose of snow down my neck.

As I made my way back to the cabin, I digested what I'd learned. If our pursuers had waylaid Rory, they hadn't found the book they were so desperate to get back. Rory's injury was an emotional blow and a practical one. We'd lost our inside man, the one who believed in us, which left my sisters the job of convincing the state cops that hiding a murder suspect in the woods had been a good idea.

And Rory was unconscious. Was there brain damage? Had anyone called his daughter? I didn't know her name or where she lived, but surely he'd written it down somewhere for emergencies. Was she on her way right now to sit by her dad's bedside, as I would if I were there? I hoped so.

Remembering how his last kiss had made me feel, how his hand slid up my neck and into my hair, how he'd looked into my eyes afterward, I wanted to be there with him.

And what? I asked myself. Elbow his daughter aside? *Announce* you're his girlfriend?

It was far too early for that. Better that I had other things to occupy my mind and my time. Pushing the cabin door open, I went inside to give Darrow the bad news.

Faye

After the static-laden call from Barb, I felt anxious and antsy. Usually the two of us discuss things, like our last case when we'd solved the problem of disappearing funds from a local charity's collection jars. Looking at the evidence we collected, we'd concluded the thief was the director's teenage daughter. I can't say which of us figured it out. Barb and I complement each other, and it was difficult to only be able to exchange a few sentences.

Hearing click-click-click-tap, I turned to see Buddy coming into the office. His cast made the odd click sound, but he didn't seem to feel pain when he put his weight on it. He explored the room, perhaps suspecting I had a second dog hidden on the premises. I watched in case he decided to mark his territory, but he didn't.

In an attempt to make friends, Dale had offered the dog a bit of his homemade jerky at lunchtime. Not only did Buddy ignore the gift, he'd also snarled when Dale got too close. Dale had definitely been miffed as he set out the items he thought I needed to make a peanut butter and jelly sandwich. When he turned away, I put the banana back and substituted grape jelly for strawberry, which is his favorite but not mine.

Retta had put her things in the den, which doubled as our guest room. To give her privacy, I moved my laptop next to my chair in the living room. She could watch my TV in the den, and I could play card games on the computer while Dale watched *Gun-smoke* and *Wagon Train* reruns in the living room.

Styx spent the morning with Uncle Dale in the workshop and settled in for a nap around 11:30. Knowing better than to separate him from Retta all night, I got another old blanket and laid it on the floor in the den. My plan was to sneak him through the front door once Buddy retired to our bedroom. As long as he didn't actually meet Styx nose to nose, I thought Buddy would be okay. He seemed to be an out-of-sight, out-of-mind kind of dog.

I did office chores, worrying a little about Barb as I worked. She'd insisted she was fine, but for someone who preferred being alone and staying busy, it had to be torture to be stuck with a whiny client and nothing to do but wait. I hoped Winston was behaving, for his own sake.

Retta came in rosy-cheeked. "Brrrr! Where's Styx?"

"With Dale in the workshop."

"Has he met your dog yet?"

I frowned. "Buddy's new here. He needs more time."

She waved a hand. "Your dog needs to meet your people, Faye, and he might as well meet Styx, too." Before I could argue she was heading for the door. "I'll get him before I take my coat off. Bring your dog out here, and we'll introduce them."

Though I sensed impending disaster, I went. I'm not one to argue, and Retta's hard to stop when she gets an idea in her head. Buddy was napping on our bed, apparently convinced it was more comfortable than his. I should have scolded him, but he looked cute curled up between the pillows, nose resting on his paws.

"Hey, kiddo," I said softly. "How are you feeling?"

His tail thumped, and I'd swear he smiled at me.

"Would you like to come out and meet some company?" I kept talking and petting him as I slipped the leash onto his collar, telling him how much he was going to like having another canine to play with. Buddy didn't respond one way or another. He followed me calmly down the hallway until we got to the office and he saw Styx.

Retta had at least had the sense to put a leash on Styx, but with him it's all about affection. He danced with excitement at the prospect of someone new to greet.

Buddy's reaction was the opposite. Lowering his front half, he barked loudly, growling in between to stress his point.

I pulled him away and picked him up. Styx looked at us in confusion. He's used to patient people who give him affection, not angry dogs who don't.

Over the din, Retta said, "I was afraid of this." Glaring at Buddy she ordered, "Doggie! Be nice!"

A person's dog is like any other member of the family. While you might gripe about him, get mad at him, and even scold him, no one else should.

"There's a strange dog in his house, Retta. It's a natural reaction." Holding my face close to Buddy's ear, I said, "Calm down, kiddo. It's okay." As I patted his head, barks faded to growls, complaining but not as aggressive as before.

"At least he responds to your commands," Retta said. "There's hope for him."

My face got warm and I pressed my lips together to hold back the "I told you so" that threatened. Unwilling to discuss my dog's faults, I carried Buddy back to the bedroom, set him on his bed with a pat, and shut him inside. When I returned to the office, I glanced at the blanket under my desk. It was Buddy's place, and we'd been content with each other's company until Retta came along with her big ideas about a doggie date.

Retta was unhappy with the results of her experiment, but she tried not to show it. She took a seat by my desk, and Styx plopped down beside her, beautiful but clueless. He really is sweet, but in a brains contest, I knew Buddy would win.

With the dog problem on hold, Retta explained her trip to the bank in more detail. "It's a little more information," she concluded. "We just have to keep putting things together until something makes sense."

Dale came in with a cup of coffee for each of us. "Break time," he said cheerfully, setting down a tray with two mugs, some packets of sweetener, and a plate of cookies.

"Thanks, hon. You're the best."

When he left, Retta's brow quirked. "Fig Newtons?"

"Yes." I tried to keep my voice neutral.

"You hate figs."

I sighed. "He wants to help."

"By bringing you cookies you hate?"

I chuckled. "He loves them. To him it's the best gift."

"And you don't say anything."

"Retta, if everything you were able to contribute was suddenly taken away—"

"I've noticed he's always at your elbow when you're cooking. How do you stand it?"

I grinned. "It drives me nuts sometimes." Feeling disloyal to Dale for saying it aloud, I turned to our case. "I didn't find Stacy's real identity. It's good you got some answers at the bank."

Retta bit her lip. "There was one weird thing. When I left the building, a guy on the street seemed to be watching me."

"One of the men who kidnapped Win?"

She shook her head. "This guy was big like Carlos, but he wore a suit and tie and had a decent haircut."

I got a bad feeling. "Barb saw a man in a suit hanging around the city office, and your description sounds like a guy who was at the diner when Gabe and I got your car."

Retta stood and began pacing, reminding me of Barb in problem-solving mode. Styx looked up expectantly but relaxed again when she didn't head for the door.

She tapped her upper lip with a finger. "Three sightings can't be coincidence."

I nodded. "We've seen Basca and the two who brought Win to the diner, so they sent a different guy to spy on us."

"Four guys to find one book. It must be important."

"They came to get it from Stacy, but something went wrong. They killed her before they got the book."

Retta bit at her lip. "They thought Winston could tell them, but he got arrested for the crime they committed."

"That brought them to us. They needed someone to contact him in jail and make a deal for the book."

"Wasn't it risky, involving you?"

"Not if you think everyone's willing to cheat for money. If it worked, they'd have been gone from here in a few hours. When I refused Basca's offer, he simply walked away. Even if I'd called the police, I didn't have much to tell them."

Retta took a few steps, thinking it over. "So when you refused to be bribed, they went to the hands-on method."

"Right. Basca sends a guy to waylay Win with a story about being a government agent. They planned to get the book from him, kill him, and hide his body in the woods somewhere. The police would think he ran off rather than face trial for murder."

"But we got Winston back, and they still don't have the book. Now they're pulling out all the stops."

"Which means we need to be careful."

"Really careful," Retta agreed. "They killed Stacy Darrow, smacked Winston around, and left Rory to freeze to death. I doubt they'd hesitate to murder one of us."

I realized that Retta and I were figuring things out together like Barb and I usually did. I felt a little disloyal, but Retta wasn't bad at tossing ideas back and forth to reach the truth. Would Barb even consider—

"Ohmigod." She was looking past me, toward the front door, where a vaguely familiar figure rounded the snow bank and started up our walk.

"Is that the guy?"

She looked at me, eyes wide. "It's him!"

I glanced around the room, looking for something I could use as a weapon. There was nothing, and I promised myself I'd get a baseball bat at the very next opportunity and put it under my desk. We tensed as the big man entered the office, closed the door behind him to shut out the cold, and turned to us. He seemed even bigger up close. I doubted the two of us stood a chance against him.

Should I call for help? Even if Dale had been able, he'd gone back to his workshop. I glanced at the phone. If this man meant to hurt us, help would never arrive in time.

Desperately I looked again for a weapon. The only solid object on my desk was a stapler. I considered launching it at his head, but what good would that do unless I scored a direct hit?

Suddenly Buddy came rocketing out from the hallway, scrabbling a little as his casted leg slid on the slippery floor. He raced past Styx, who'd been napping. He turned, curious to see what the unfriendly dog intended. Buddy stopped a few feet back from the intruder and lowered his head, barking furiously. Not to be left out of the fun, Styx got up and started barking, too.

Dancing a little and snarling a lot, Buddy skittered in a semi-circle around the intruder, letting him know in no uncertain terms that he was to stay where he was.

With an excited "Woof!" Styx bumped past Buddy to greet the newcomer. As Buddy made more noise than a dog his size should be able to, Styx set his huge paws on the man's shoulders, pinning him to the door.

"A little help here?" The guy seemed less worried than he should have been, maybe even a little amused.

Retta spoke sternly. "Are you armed?"

"As a matter of fact, yes."

I tried to recall how they handle such things on TV. "Hand it over," I ordered, "or we'll let the dogs have you."

Now I was sure I saw a glint of humor in his eyes. "I can't give you my weapon. It's against the rules."

Rules? With a Newfie on his chest and a mutt at his ankles, he kept the criminals' code of behavior in mind?

Retta asked, "What are you doing here?"

Raising his voice to drown out my noisy canine he replied, "I came to discuss your current case."

Discussion sounded better than the threats I'd expected. "Buddy, be quiet!" I ordered, and surprisingly, he obeyed, backing away until he was at my ankle. Satisfied that he'd subdued the interloper, he licked his chops and sat down.

Despite the odd situation, I noted that Buddy's protective behavior involved mostly making noise. That was good. No one wants a dog that bites—unless, of course, biting is justified.

Retta pulled Styx back, and the guy wiped a little drool off his jacket. "My neighbor has a Newf," he said. "They're great dogs."

To prove she wasn't affected by praise for her dog, Retta gave a snotty little sniff. "That's nice, but you might as well leave," she informed him. "We don't discuss our cases with un-involved parties."

Still friendly, still smiling, he said, "Oh, I'm involved."

He *was* part of Basca's gang! Just before I reached for the phone to dial 9-1-1, he added, "I'm with the DEA."

That stopped me, but Retta said, "That story's been tried. Tell old Max we aren't as easy to fool as Winston Darrow was."

"You know Max?" he asked.

"We know lots." That wasn't exactly true, but her tone was confident. "My sister is going to call the cops. One more and we'll set the dogs on you again."

Styx held himself back with effort, his rear end all a-quiver, and I hoped a stranger didn't realize he wanted a hug more than he wanted a piece of his arm. Buddy still growled softly every few seconds, though he stayed beside me, ready to defend his home and his human mommy.

"Look," the big guy said reasonably. "I can tell right now the big dog isn't going to hurt anybody, and as far as the other one goes, I'll take my chances. He looks pretty beat up." Raising his arms, he said, "Reach into my front coat pocket and you'll find what you need."

Retta moved gingerly toward him. Buddy growled again, and I bent and took hold of his collar. He strained his neck, snarling at the stranger. Apparently Retta had become part of his family, and he meant to protect her, too.

The man didn't move as she took a dark leather wallet from his pocket, opened it, and read aloud, "Special Agent Lars Johannsen, U. S. Drug Enforcement Agency."

When Retta gave the agent his badge back, Buddy growled again. "Be quiet!" she commanded, but it had no impact. Picking him up, I petted his head to let him know things were okay. "I'll shut him in the bedroom again."

As I left the room I heard Retta say, "Would you step into our office, Agent Johannsen? It's more private." I was shocked at her use of "our" to refer to the office I considered Barb's. Still, Barb wasn't there, and it couldn't hurt to present a professional attitude to a federal agent.

I left Buddy in the bedroom a second time, closing the door more firmly than I had before. "We're okay," I told him. "Take a nap." He didn't object.

As I returned, though, I wondered if we were okay. Badges can be faked. George had shown Win a badge before taking him prisoner. I'd be more careful than Retta, who seemed willing to believe what any man told her.

Before I joined her and the supposed agent, I went to my desk and picked up the stapler. There weren't any weapons in Barb's office, either, and I wanted some kind of edge over the as yet unproven Special Agent Johannsen.

Retta had played hostess, and our visitor was seated in one of the padded guest chairs. She sat in Barb's ergonomic chair behind the desk. As I came in I took a long look at our guest, trying to see past my distrust. Built like I pictured the ancient Vikings, he exhibited good posture and had reddish-blond hair with silver sidewalls clipped very short. His suit was neatly pressed, and he looked good in it. His face, while not handsome, was interesting, which some say is better. From Retta's funny little smile, I guessed she'd agree.

When I was seated in my usual place, Johannsen asked Retta, "Are you Ms. Evans?"

She had the grace to look embarrassed. "My sister is away on business. I'm Margaretta Stilson, and this is Faye Burner." Removing the leather wallet from the breast pocket of his suit, the man flipped it open and passed it to me. "There's a number you can call if you want to check me out," he offered.

I almost reached for the phone, but Retta said, "That's okay, Special Agent. We don't doubt your word."

Handing his badge back, I set the stapler on the corner of the desk as unobtrusively as possible. Folding my hands in my lap, I smiled as if I'd never planned to bonk Johannsen on the head first chance I got.

He slid the wallet back into his jacket. "I understand this agency is investigating Stacy Darrow's murder."

Retta cleared her throat, and I guessed she was adjusting, as I was. We'd been prepared to lie, but now we would tell the truth and hope to get help from the United States government. "That's true."

"The sheriff in Bonner County tells me Darrow is in custody, but not in his custody."

Retta's gaze flickered to me for a half-second. "I believe that's also true."

"We'd like to speak to Mr. Darrow."

I noticed the pronoun and wondered if there were other agents in the area or if he used the "royal we" to hint at the power of the agency.

Retta gave him a run-down of the situation, explaining how with Rory's support, we'd hidden Winston to protect him. I was afraid he'd throw accusations of misconduct at us, but overall, he seemed to approve.

"I wish the locals had contacted us right away," he said. "We could have protected your client and maybe caught the guys who killed his wife."

"How could they know the DEA was interested in an apparently ordinary couple and a death that looked like domestic violence?" Retta asked.

"True," Johannsen admitted. "We had no idea where Mari was until yesterday."

"Mari? Is that Stacy Darrow's real name?"

He nodded. "Almost three years ago in New Mexico, Maria Constanza Verdugo, known as Mari, agreed to testify against her boyfriend, Maximilian Santiago. She was his bookkeeper as well as his lady, so she knew a lot about his business."

"Which is drugs, since the DEA is involved."

He nodded. "Max controls a large chunk of drug traffic in New Mexico. We wanted him badly, and the agent in charge thought he'd convinced Mari to help put him away."

"Why would she turn against her boyfriend?"

"A few black eyes, to start with." Johannsen unconsciously brushed a hand over his own eyes. "Each time Max got upset, he got more violent. Mari began to be afraid she wouldn't live through his next temper tantrum."

"Poor thing." I didn't realize I'd spoken aloud until they both turned to look at me. A DEA agent and a cop's widow might be used to stories like this, but it made me sad. Maria/Mari/Stacy had probably never known real love.

Johannsen went on, "As part of the deal, Mari was going to bring us Santiago's record book. That and her testimony would have sent him to jail for life."

"It didn't happen?" Retta folded her hands on the desk.

It occurred to me I should be taking notes, but I didn't want to ask, being totally out of my depth. The DEA? Drug runners? I concentrated on remembering so I could tell Barb everything.

"It did not. We'd arranged for her to go into the witness protection program." Shifting in his chair, he went on, "Unfortunately, Mari had her own scheme. After she milked everything she could get from her handler about how to disappear, she used the information to drop completely off the grid."

"On her own? That took guts."

"She took the book and a great deal of Max's money."

Retta glanced at me, pleased that our guesses were proven correct. "This woman cheated a drug lord and scammed the DEA? Was she really dumb or really brave?"

Johannsen ran a hand over his hair. "She fooled us all."

"The least she could have done was mail the book to you." Retta seemed ready to side with the authorities on this one, but I saw Mari/Stacy's side. That book was supposed to be her protection. She'd wanted it nearby to ease her fears that Max would find and kill her.

Retta asked, "Can you tell us what's in the book?"

Johannsen shrugged, indicating that secrecy didn't matter. "Santiago's contacts: Who he bribes, who supplies him, and who he supplies."

"So the book can still hurt Basca."

"We know the man you call Santiago as Max Basca," I put in. Briefly I recounted Max's visit and described him.

"That's the guy."

"Why do you think Mari broke her deal with you?"

He smiled thinly. "I can give a few million reasons."

I whistled. "That's how much she took?"

"It's an estimate. It was drug money, most of it in small bills." His nostrils flared. "Mari insisted on waiting until the end of the month. The agent was so eager to keep her happy that he missed all the signs."

"That she planned to take the money and run."

"Mari never intended to go into Witness Protection."
Johannsen's tone was bitter. "She was just waiting for
Santiago's haul to be as fat as possible."

Retta's right brow rose. "I bet your superiors weren't happy
with you."

His face flushed. "You guessed right. I was the agent who
should have known better."

"I believed Winston when he said he was divorced." Retta
waved a hand, dismissing human frailty. "It's not a sign of
weakness to think the best of people."

Her comment seemed to please Johannsen. "How much did
Darrow know about his wife's past?"

"Not a lot." Briefly Retta recounted Win's path from
factory worker to gigolo.

"No wonder I didn't find much information on him," he said
when she finished. "Two crooks who found each other, neither
aware of the other's dishonesty."

"Which one of them led you here?" I asked.

"Neither. I've been keeping an eye on Santiago and his
boys. One of them, George, flew up here ten days ago. Later,
Santiago and two others followed. I wanted to see what they
were up to, but while my request for travel was working its way
through the chain of command, we learned that Mari's
fingerprints matched a woman who'd been murdered up here."

"Bet that speeded up your permission to come north."

He chuckled. "Big time. When I checked in at the Detroit
office, they told me the victim's husband had been abducted by a
fake FBI agent. I rented a car and drove up." He gestured at the

snowy scene outside the window. "Can't say I enjoyed the drive. How do you people do it?"

"Practice." Retta set her elbows on the desk and leaned her chin on folded hands. "Agent Johannsen, can you clear some things up for us?"

He chuckled. "If it gets me to Darrow, I'll try."

I thought it was nice of him not to use his authority to demand we do as he said, but Retta promised nothing. "Stacy ducked out on the DEA because she wanted Santiago's money."

"Yes."

"But she lived pretty conservatively. Why was that?"

Johannsen's expression turned glum. "When I first approached Mari, I implied we had more on Santiago than we actually did. She thought she was just a part of our case, but she was pretty much it. Once we lost her and the book, we couldn't touch him."

"When he remained free, she knew he'd come for her."

He nodded. "All she could do was stay low and hope we got him some other way."

"I suppose she thought her disappearing act ruined her chances of getting any more help from the DEA."

His sigh said a lot. "Let's just say my boss wasn't happy with either of us. It had taken us almost a year to set things up, and we walked away with nothing."

"To escape Max, Mari became Stacy Kern then Stacy Darrow, a not-very-interesting wife from Michigan."

Johannsen gestured at the computer on the desk. "Bet you didn't find any photos of her."

"Barb found one from their wedding day," I replied, "but she's looking down."

"I taught her that," he said with a hint of satisfaction. "It's hard to avoid getting your picture taken these days, but if you look down, it messes with facial recognition software." He added, "Mari learned her lessons well."

"We figure Basca traced her through Internet activity," I said. "Maybe some mystery readers' group."

"We warn them about that." Johannsen took a deep breath, and his massive chest got even bigger. "Some people can't give up their favorite things, though. The sheer size of the Internet makes them think they can fly under the radar." After a pause he asked, "How did she explain the money?" When Retta told him what she'd learned at the bank, he raised his brows in appreciation. "Car washes? That's a good one."

Next Retta told him about the boxes Win had described. "A couple million in small bills is a little cumbersome," he commented. "Darrow was a good choice. Most guys would have been way more curious."

"He's an aging professional boyfriend," I said. "He took the meal ticket she offered and never questioned it."

Retta seemed uncomfortable with the subject of Win's women. "You contacted the local police when you arrived?"

"I started with Sheriff Idalski, who told me about an odd incident at a local diner."

"Where I saw you a few hours later."

"Yes. Idalski said Darrow came in with two men and left with three women. The descriptions I got from the help confirmed my suspicions that the men were George and a big guy named Carlos. Idalski mentioned that some 'lady detectives' had been hired to help Darrow prove his innocence, so I guessed you took Darrow away from George. I decided to do some investigation on my own before I introduced myself."

"I thought you were one of them." Feeling my face warm I added, "Sorry I had Gabe block your car in."

He waved a hand, dismissing my interference. "You didn't know. I think that plow guy called someone, though. Probably he told George you'd come back for the car."

Remembering the black SUV that had ended up in the ditch, I realized he was right. If not for the driver's inexperience with winter roads, they'd have followed me right to Retta's, and we'd all have been in trouble. The urge for a cigarette tingled in my blood, but I resisted. There was more to hear.

"Idalski says someone in his department has been helping George out, but he hasn't figured out who it is yet. He suggested I work with the police chief here, but when I stopped in yesterday, he was out. Today when I went back, they said he was unavailable." His eyes locked on Retta. "While I was there, I heard one end of a call from a bank manager, saying Mrs. Evans of the Smart Detective Agency was asking about Mrs. Darrow."

Retta blushed prettily. "A small lie, since Barbara Ann can't be in two places at once."

"And the police chief?"

"In the hospital."

Johannsen's sandy eyebrows twitched. "Did he run into George and Carlos?"

"Apparently. He's okay, but he can't help us now."

"So do I get to meet Mr. Darrow?"

"That depends." Retta gave him a coquettish smile. "Are you the outdoor type?"

He frowned. "For scuba diving in Baja, yes, but I bet you've got something else in mind."

"Ever driven a snowmobile?"

"Can't say that I have." He added gamely, "But I can learn. You've got him out in the woods somewhere?"

"Safest place for him." Retta was rearranging Barb's desktop as she spoke, and I made a mental note to put things back the way Barb likes them. "We'll take two machines and bring Winston and Barbara back. She's the deputy Sheriff Idalski mentioned."

"I see."

Checking her watch, Retta frowned. "It's too late to go today. You need to get outfitted, and I've only been out there once. I'll need daylight in order to find the place."

"Sounds reasonable."

"Go to the Sled Store on Carroll Street and get outfitted. Tell them I sent you, and they won't sell you anything extra." Retta's glance was coy, and I rolled my eyes at the idea she could flirt in such serious circumstances. For all the notice either of them took of me, I might as well have been that stapler.

On the back of one of our business cards, Retta wrote the name of the store she'd mentioned as well as her home address. Handing it to him she asked, "Do you have a card so I can contact you if something changes?"

Taking out his badge wallet again, Johannsen withdrew a business card for each of us. "Thanks," Retta said, rising. "Be at my house at eight tomorrow morning. We'll start with a lesson on how to make a snowmobile go."

"I hope you'll show me how to stop, too." The agent was teasing her! My eyes rolled again as Retta agreed with a giggle that stopping was also a necessity.

Johannsen rose to go. "Thanks, Margaretta, and—" Realizing he'd forgotten my name, he merely waved.

"My friends call me Retta," she called as he exited.

Once he was gone I asked, "Would you know a fake DEA badge from a real one, Retta? Because I wouldn't."

"No," she admitted.

I stood, leaning over her in an earnest need to make her listen. "This is life or death stuff. You can't go riding off with that man without knowing he's the real deal."

With a look that said I was over-reacting she said, "Why do you think I asked for his card?"

"Anybody can make a business card!"

"That's why we're going to check it out." Consulting the card, she turned on Barb's computer and navigated to the DEA website. In a few minutes she'd ascertained that the main number on the card was indeed the Albuquerque, New Mexico, office. Punching in the numbers, she asked, "May I speak to Agent Johannsen, please?" After a moment she said, "That's all right. I'll try his cell. Oh, wait! Maybe you can answer my question. I'd like to get him new swim fins for his birthday. Any idea what size shoe he wears?" At the response, she laughed. "Yes, I thought so, too. The biggest size they have should be good."

Replacing the phone, she told me, "They have an Agent Johannsen, but he's away for a few days. He has very large feet, as you might have noticed."

"Okay," I said. "He's for real, and you're going to take him out to the cabin."

"It solves our problems." She counted three points on her fingers. "We need two machines to bring Barbara and Winston back. Johannsen doesn't think Winston killed his wife, and he can help us prove it. And DEA agents carry weapons at all times. It'll make me feel better to have a man along who's armed, trained, and authorized to kill if necessary."

CHAPTER TWENTY-NINE

Barb

By five o'clock, the shadows of snow-laden pine trees dimmed the window at the front of the cabin, darkening the grubby, wavy glass. I kept the generator filled with gas, afraid if it stopped I wouldn't get it started again. To give him something to do, I'd ordered Darrow to feed the fire. Though he complained about having to wade out to the stack at the side of the cabin to bring in more wood, he seemed a little less anxious when he was busy. From his demeanor each time he pulled on his boots to go outside, it appeared that keeping a fire going was the hardest job anyone has done in the history of the world. For someone who'd spent his life catering to women, he certainly seemed unwilling to continue the practice with me. I was apparently not his type—and I thanked my lucky stars.

Our food was almost gone. Rory had expected our stay to be short, but that changed when Darrow's enemies—our enemies now—put Rory in the hospital. My mind kept returning to him, wondering how he was doing. Each time, I pushed the thoughts away. I couldn't change anything. I couldn't even get an update, since my phone's battery was dying fast.

Dinner was a Hershey bar each and as much water as we cared to drink. When we'd finished (Darrow licked his wrapper), I took up a battered deck of cards and a cribbage board I'd spotted atop a rafter. "Do you play?" I riffled the deck like a professional, but its age ruined the effect.

"I haven't for years," he replied, "but my dad taught me when I was a kid."

It wasn't my best idea. Darrow couldn't concentrate, and I ended up keeping score for both of us. Time after time he tossed points into my crib, and I ended up skunking him. I started a new game, which ended the same way. When I won a third time, I stubbornly dealt again. At least while we played he had to pretend to consider his hand, add cards to the count, and deal every other round.

Around eight o'clock, when he passed me a king and a five and kept no points whatsoever for himself, I gave up. Darrow retreated to the window, now a black square, while I slumped in my chair, staring into the fire.

I'd left my phone on the table, so this time I heard the tone and hurried to see the message. TOMORROW A.M.

"Retta's coming in the morning," I told Darrow. He opened his mouth as if to ask for more information but didn't, accepting that was all I knew.

"Then I'll eat that last candy bar," he said. "Unless you want some."

As a matter of principle, I took half. While we nibbled I asked, "Now that you know more about Stacy, do things make sense that didn't before?"

He spent a few seconds chewing. "Sometimes she said things about her childhood that didn't fit with growing up in the east. Like she said she took a fall as a kid when her pony shied at an armadillo. I said, 'Armadillo?' and she laughed. 'I meant *porcupine.* I get those two mixed up.' Who confuses an armadillo with a porcupine?"

"Did she ever talk about former relationships? Husbands or lovers?"

Darrow's lips pressed into a tight line. "When I got upset, even at a baseball game on TV, she'd get this scared look, you know?" He laid a hand on his chest in dramatic fashion. "I never hurt her, but somewhere in her past, somebody did."

CHAPTER THIRTY

Faye

I woke Retta early the next morning so she'd have time to fuel the machines and get ready for the ride out to the cabin with Agent Johannsen. I suggested she take Styx and leave him inside the house. "He'll bark if someone comes around, and his size is intimidating if you don't know what a cream puff he is."

Balancing on one leg to put on a boot, she glanced out the kitchen window. Styx was playing in the snow while Dale swept tiny V-shaped drifts off the porch with a broom. The dog rolled in the freshly-fallen snow in the yard, digging his nose into it, flipping it into the air, and then biting at it as it fell back to earth. It was a game only a dog could love.

"But what if those men come back?"

I thought of Buddy, locked in a cage in my bedroom. "If they'd wanted to break in, they'd have done it already."

When we stepped onto the porch, Styx came running as if we'd been apart for decades. "He is a teddy bear," Retta said, ruffling the dog's fur, "but if someone tried to hurt me, I bet he'd have them for brunch. It's too bad you had to lock your little guy up."

Buddy's imprisonment in the dog carrier was due to his animosity toward Styx and the fact that he'd figured out how to open the bedroom door. The house was old, and the latch didn't catch securely. Buddy, begin smart, had figured out that he could simply bump at it until it jiggled open. Twice the night before and twice that morning, I'd refereed between him and Styx until Dale had taken Styx outside to give me a break. In order to let Retta have her breakfast in peace, I'd put Buddy in the carrier, promising him that our company would only be around for a little while longer.

"You can't ride on the sled, Sweetie," Retta was saying to Styx when I returned my focus to her. "Momma's going to have a passenger on the way back. Is that okay?"

Styx seemed agreeable, but he always agreed with anything Retta said. As she drove off, Styx made good-bye nose prints on the passenger side window.

I worried about Retta a little, but that's because I worry about everything. *Between the dog and the DEA agent,* I told myself, *she's as safe as any of us right now.*

A while after she left, the office door opened and Rory Neuencamp came in, his torso tilted forward like a man on his way to somewhere. He slammed the door, looking over my shoulder into Barb's empty office.

"Chief!"

He looked rougher than I'd ever seen him: unshaven, with his hair mashed down in the back where a pillow had squashed it. There was a bald patch above his right ear with at least four neat, black stitches across it. He wore no coat, and the collar of his tan shirt had a rusty brown stain.

"What's going on at the cabin, Faye? Tom doesn't know anything."

"Are you supposed to be out of the hospital?"

"I stayed twenty-four hours, as ordered, and they did every test they could think of."

"And I bet they told you to go home and rest."

His shoulders rose and fell. "I don't remember hearing that part." He glanced past me, and I turned to see Buddy limping into the office. I'd released him as soon as Retta and Styx were gone, but he'd pouted a little, his shiny black eyes accusing me of colluding with the enemy.

The chief knelt to a crouch. "Who's this, and what happened to him?"

"That's Buddy. He was hit by a car." As he reached out I cautioned, "Be careful. He's a one-person dog."

The chief put out a hand for him to sniff, but Buddy responded with a growl. "I see what you mean." He surprised me with a smile. "You're his one person?"

"He's begun to tolerate my husband, but just barely."

"I had a dog like that once." There was no disapproval in his tone. "Some people don't get it, but it's kind of comforting to know there's one being on earth who loves you and nobody else." Standing again, he said to Buddy, "You're okay, mutt."

That's when I began thinking of Chief Neuencamp as Rory.

"So tell me," he said. "Where are Barb and Retta?"

Knowing it was hopeless to repeat the doctors' advice, I filled him in on what he'd missed. When I finished he asked, "How far am I behind Retta and the agent?"

Glancing at the clock I replied, "Thirty minutes."

"Any chance you'd give me a ride out to her house? My truck's out there."

If I said no he'd just get someone else to take him. If I said yes, I could be in on whatever he had in mind. "I'll get us each a coat. You're about my husband's size."

"Thanks. Nobody could find the one I was wearing, and I didn't wait around."

Once we were in the Escape, Rory took out his phone and made a call. "It's Chief Neuencamp. Is Wade there?" … "Will you ask him to call me? Thanks."

We were just out of town when the sheriff returned the call. "Wade? What's going on?" Rory waved a hand impatiently. "I'm fine. The news people made it sound a lot worse than it was. So what have you got for me?"

He listened, asked a couple of questions, and thanked the sheriff. Putting the phone in the pocket of Dale's coat, he said, "They found out who's been helping the wrong side. Apparently the janitor at the county building spends too much time at the casino, so he accepted some extra cash when George approached him. He claims nobody was supposed to get hurt."

"Have they got any leads on Santiago and the others?"

"No one's seen them lately." He touched his wound gingerly and winced. "Nobody but me, I guess."

"Maybe they gave up and went back to New Mexico."

He frowned. "Even if they gave up on getting the money back, they need that book. I'd bet it represents a life sentence for all of them.

CHAPTER THIRTY-ONE

Retta

My sisters complain that I'm often late, but I was ready for the snowmobile trip by seven fifty-five. Faye had practically shoved me out the door, babbling about not keeping Lars Johannsen waiting. It's been my experience that making men wait a little keeps them interested, but since this was important, I did as ordered.

The morning was brutally cold, but the sky was clear, so the sun would soon take some of the chill away. The snow was crisp, and it crunched underfoot like Styrofoam packing. Already light reflected harshly, but my helmet had a tinted second visor I pulled into place behind the clear one. I'd dug out a pair of wraparound sunglasses in case the helmet Agent Johannsen brought didn't have something similar. Riding trails with all that light on white can do real eye damage.

When I heard a car pull in, the sleds were idling behind the house and Styx was secure inside. Johannsen parked behind Rory's truck as I came out to meet him. He'd called the hospital, he reported, and learned that Rory had been discharged. At least I could give Barbara Ann some good news when we reached the cabin.

Johannsen had been lucky in getting outfitted. They'd even found snowmobile boots big enough for him. He wore bibbed pants with thin but effective insulation and a jacket with more zippered pockets than a '90s rapper. "Not sure how my expense voucher will go over back home," he said drolly. "This isn't the usual Albuquerque DEA look I'm sporting today."

Leading the way to the back of the house, I showed him the basics of operating a snowmobile. I shut the machine down and had him start it again. Then he took it around the house a few times to get the feel of steering, turning, and stopping. He did well, and when he came roaring back the second time he wore a kid-like grin. "This is awesome!"

"Then let's get going. Keep me in sight but don't follow too close. If we meet other riders on the trail, stay to the right." I showed him the hand gestures I'd use to indicate changes in direction, which are about the same as the ones used before cars had turn signals and brake lights. He listened and nodded understanding. "I'm ready."

We took off, following the road until we reached the place where the snowmobile trail crossed it. Snow was banked high along the roadway, and I gunned the machine up one side, bumped down the other side, and stopped a few yards in to see if Johannsen could manage it. He did, raising a mittened thumb in a gesture of accomplishment when he joined me on the trail. Giving him a wave in return, I turned forward, heading west.

CHAPTER THIRTY-TWO

Faye

When Rory and I arrived at Retta's house, exhaust fumes still hung in the air. "We just missed them," he muttered.

Dialing Retta's number for the third time, I waited for several seconds then gave up. It was unlikely she'd hear her phone over the roar of the engine.

"You might as well go back to town," Rory said. "I'll stay here and wait for them."

"I'll let you into the house," I offered. "It's warmer."

When we approached, I heard anguished whines from inside. Styx made it difficult to open the door, as usual, and I had to coax him into backing away. His feet drummed on the floor, and he groaned and cried as if the world was ending.

"Calm down, Sweetie," I ordered, but he was more agitated than I'd ever seen him. As soon as there was enough space for him to get by, Styx bolted past, knocking me out of the way. Rory made a startled sound as the dog flew by him, bounded across the yard, made a hard left turn, and disappeared down the road. "Styx!" I called after him. "Styx, come back here!"

It was out of character for Retta's dog to leave the yard, even more out of character for him to ignore a command to return. It was clear he intended to follow Retta's trail.

I ran to the end of the drive, calling to the dog with no result. Rory joined me, looking concerned. "We passed a truck with a four-sled trailer up near the trailhead," he said. "I noticed because the driveway where it was parked hadn't been plowed. Those guys saw me come in on a sled. What if they followed the agent yesterday, saw him buy snowmobile gear, and figured out that Retta was going to take him to Darrow?"

"Where would they get snowmobiles?"

"From one of the locals who set up trail rides for fudgies. Some provide sleds, gear, guidance, and can even make simple repairs if a sled breaks down on the trail."

Recalling ads I'd seen in pamphlets on the wonders of northern Michigan, I agreed that tourists ("fudgies" to the locals) were wise to make such arrangements.

Styx had stopped and was looking back at us as if to ask why we weren't following his lead. Nodding in that direction, I said, "Retta's dog wants to take us to her."

Rory grimaced. "Maybe he can follow them on foot, but there's no way we can."

We paused, at a loss for what to do next. "I need a sled," Rory said. "Tom has one."

There were several things wrong with that idea. It would take time. He wasn't dressed for riding. He'd just been released from the hospital. None of those would convince Rory not to go. "Do what you need to," I said. "I'll get Styx and take him home with me."

Rory waited while I backed out of Retta's drive then followed me down the road. Styx still waited at the spot where the snowmobile trail crossed, his tail wagging anxiously. I stopped beside him, got out, and opened the hatch. Rory slowed as he passed, probably wondering if he should help me with the dog. "I can handle him," I said.

As I took hold of Styx' collar, I looked in the direction he was looking, down the trail. There were no snowmobiles, but I did see something slow, large, and as noisy as a train engine. The groomer.

"Rory!" I shouted. He'd just started pulling away, but he stopped and turned to look where I was pointing. "Gabe drives the groomer! He could take you to the cabin."

"Gabe?" It took him a tick to remember. "Oh, the guy with the bad decision-making skills."

"He claims he's gone straight." I wobbled a little as Styx struggled to get free and investigate the approaching stranger. "Stop him and explain the situation. I'll go back to Retta's and get you warm clothing, so you don't freeze to death."

He thought about it. "Hurry. When I get your buddy turned around, I'll be on my way."

"Come on, Styx," I ordered, but the dog broke away, heading up the trail toward the groomer.

"Let him come along," Rory said. "He might scare the bad guys away just by his size."

Styx danced atop the snow, twenty yards from me. There was no way I could catch him, so I turned my car around and headed back to Retta's.

The closet was pretty much stripped of winter wear after the initial trek to the cabin. Rory wore the boots she'd given him originally, so his feet would be warm enough. The rest of what would fit him came from the back of the closet, which amounted to the bottom of the proverbial barrel. I found a blaze-orange Carhartt coverall Don had worn for changing the oil in his vehicles and other messy jobs. It had a tear at the crotch, a missing snap on one cuff, and lots of stains. With it and the accessories I could find that were big enough for Rory, I hurried back to where I'd left him.

Rory stood at the trailhead. Gabe had turned his equipment around and was unhooking the trailing piece that flattened the snow. Better to leave it behind, since speed was a necessity. Taking the clothes from me, Rory held them to his chest as he climbed onto the track vehicle. He patted the seat beside him, and Styx climbed aboard as if he'd done it a thousand times.

"Call the sheriff and tell him what's going on," he ordered. "He should take Ponzer Road out to the turn-off for the state forest campground and then watch for a signpost that says WILD ACRE. From there they'll have to snowmobile in. They should be able to see where I left the trail and follow my tracks to the cabin."

"Are you sure you don't want me to take Styx?"

Patting the excited dog, Rory smiled. "I doubt either of us could make him go home with Retta out there." He gestured to Gabe, who waved once then put the vehicle into gear. I stepped out of the way, and they rumbled off, focused on their goal.

Stomping the cold from my feet, I watched the vehicle disappear from sight. It sank into a dip on the trail, and the last thing I saw was Rory's head, now encased in the red plaid hat with ear-flaps that had been the only one left in Retta's closet.

When I reached Sheriff Idalski, he didn't fuss about Rory's decision but promised to send help as soon as possible. "We'll have to do some organizing," he told me. "A guy who knows the country out there real well guides us in cases like this. Don't worry," he said in a confident tone. "Your sisters will be all right."

With Rory and Styx on the way, a DEA agent for backup, and the sheriff alerted, I prayed he was correct.

As I drove back to town, things Winston had told us echoed through my mind. We knew almost all of it now, and I felt another stab of pity for Stacy. It was her mess, but she must have been so scared, hiding out with her books and her horses—

The horses! We'd focused on the humans involved, but was anyone caring for the beasts? Shut up in a barn, the poor things couldn't feed themselves. Had anyone thought of them? Their situation bothered me, in spite of—maybe because of—my inability to help Barb and Retta. If I couldn't get my sisters home from the cabin in the woods, I could at least tend to a couple of neglected animals.

"There's been a lot of snow since Friday," Dale objected when I got home and told him my intention. "There's probably no path to the barn."

I knew what was bothering him. His physical therapist was on her way, so he couldn't go with me.

"I'm looking for my big boots," I replied, my voice muffled because my head was buried in the coat closet.

"Can't the humane society people do it?" he asked. "You've got a lot going right now with Retta and Barb out in the woods and all."

"It's the weekend," I reminded him. "I'll call them on Monday, but those horses shouldn't have to wait."

"Faye." Dale's tone made me turn. "You think I don't know what's going on, but I'm not deaf."

"I'll be careful," I promised. "If there's one sign someone's at Win's house, I'll drive on by."

He didn't like it. Just then Buddy limped past as if Dale didn't exist and rubbed against my leg, almost upsetting me as I pulled on my second boot.

"I'll take the dog," I said. "He's pretty protective."

"True," Dale agreed. "He'd as soon bite a guy as look at him." Buddy was still ignoring his friendly overtures.

Maybe I could get him his own dog, I thought. That was followed by, *Right—Barb will be thrilled to have two in the house.*

"Here." Dale handed me gloves, a hat, and a scarf. When he turned to speak to the dog, I replaced the scruffy yellow scarf with a purple one Barb had given me for Christmas.

"Go with your mom," Dale said to Buddy. "If there's anyone at that house, I expect you to chase him off." The dog made no sign he'd heard but followed me to the car and waited expectantly to be lifted onto the front seat. Once there, he made a little huff of contentment and settled down for a nap.

As I backed out the driveway, my phone sounded. Pulling over to the curb, I checked the caller ID: MEADOWS.

Great.

"Hello."

"Hi, Mrs. Burner, it's Delia. It's Harriet's day to take a bath, but she says she won't."

I suppressed a sigh. "Put her on." After some muted pleading and strong objection I heard, "What?"

"It's bath day, Harriet."

"I just had a bath."

That wasn't true, though it might have seemed so to her. Or she was simply feeling cantankerous. I kept my voice light. "That's okay. Hilda Fordham wants your spot, and I told them to let her have it."

Hilda was one of the few other women in the nursing home who still had "it," meaning, I guess, that she could still flirt with male residents and remember where her room was.

"She can't have my spot!" Harriet shouted. "Why in the world would you tell them that?"

I didn't have to say more. She was still ranting about my interference when Delia took the phone back. "Thanks," she said softly. "You always seem to be able to handle her."

"Decades of experience, dear."

"But now she's angry at—"

"I don't mind if she's mad at me as long as it makes your job easier."

It really was okay, because Harriet forgot old complaints quickly. Mostly because she so easily thought up new ones.

On the drive out to the Darrow place, we added something to the list of things Buddy didn't like: cigarette smoke. He snuffed, he sneezed, and he let me know in no uncertain terms that he didn't like that smell. With a sigh, I put out my cig. I didn't smoke in the house, since it was Barb's. I couldn't smoke in most public places. Now I couldn't even smoke in my own vehicle. Maybe it was time to give it up. The only person who might possibly be sorry to see me quit was Gabe Wills, and really, did I need more of Gabe in my life?

There was no car in the driveway at Darrow's house. Winston's car had been pulled from the ditch, leaving a gouge that was almost filled in by recent additional snowfall. I pulled into the drive and waited. Nothing moved. I got out, carrying Buddy to keep his cast dry, and peered into the garage windows. Both the Darrow vehicles were parked inside.

I went to the door, noting fresh footprints. Several people had come onto the deck, turned, and gone away. Reporters, no doubt, hoping for a scrap of information no one else had.

There was no sign that anyone was inside. To be sure, I rang the doorbell. No answer. I knocked sharply then tried the door. Locked, as I'd expected. Taking a last glance at the yard, the deck, and the empty road at the other side of the frozen lake, I followed the walk around the side of the house and headed for the barn.

Set back from the house and off to the south a little, the barn was a neat structure just large enough for a couple of animals, some tack, and grain and hay storage. Un-shoveled for days, the way was as difficult as Dale had predicted. Carrying Buddy threw my balance off, so I took small steps, testing the snow to be sure of my footing. I was huffing and puffing by the time I got close, and my boots were full of snow already melting to icy water. Plaintive nickers from the horses told me my mission was necessary, and I slogged on. Buddy growled at the sound, but I gave him a pat. "Quiet," I ordered. "It's their house, so you have to be nice."

Kicking the snow away from the door, I slid it open and stepped inside. The barn was dark, its windows shuttered against the weather. Feeling along the door frame, I found a switch and flipped it on. A single fluorescent light flickered, flickered again, and came on, showing me the interior in two tones: glaring white and dim gray.

The place smelled like barns everywhere, a mixture of hay, manure, and sweat. On my right was a large stall where a pretty little buckskin eyed me warily. I wasn't the person she expected, but I might be someone who could help. Farther down, a chestnut with a white blaze stepped to the front of her stall, nodding a greeting. She didn't appear to care who I was as long as I was there to feed her.

I set Buddy down and waited to see what he'd do. I attached a leash to his collar but let it lie slack, giving him room to explore a little. He made a cautious circle around my feet, barked twice, his way of announcing our presence, and set his rear down as if to say he was okay with the place. I looped his leash over a convenient nail on the center post, limiting him to a three-foot circle that kept him from reaching the horses.

Ahead of me, square hay bales three rows deep took up the whole back wall. The stack at the rear reached all the way up to the rafters. The middle row was almost as high, but in front there were single bales, left as steps so Stacy could reach those higher up. A square bale weighs over fifty pounds, so it's not something most women toss around easily. I pictured her pulling one off the stack and sending it tumbling to the floor, where she'd cut the ties and break it in half for the two beasts.

There was hay, but I thought horses needed more, so I kept looking. The wall to my left was taken up with shelving and cupboards for tack and supplies. Bits and bridles hung from pegboard hooks. Near me was a large bin with a hinged cover. It was almost full of grain and topped by a handy scoop. Moving back and forth, I filled the feed boxes with what I estimated was the right amount for a hungry horse.

Next I gave them water from a spigot fitted with a hose. Taking it to the chestnut's stall, I filled her trough. She started drinking right away, and the buckskin complained about having to wait her turn. When the first horse had enough water, I transferred the hose to the other trough, giving the buckskin her drink.

There was loose hay in a pile, so I tossed some of that into the stalls. They needed mucking out, but I wasn't dressed for that, nor was I sure enough of the horses' gratitude to climb into their bedrooms with them. The Humane Society people would be better suited for that.

When I tossed the grain scoop back into the bin, it made a hollow thump that didn't sound like grain. Though I dreaded finding a dead mouse or even a rat, I gingerly scraped through the oats with the scoop. An object buried in there was harder than a critter and much bigger. Brushing the grain away with a gloved hand, I uncovered a large plastic tub. I found the lid's lock-on mechanism, unhooked it, and pulled it off.

Money. The bin was half full of mixed denominations in used condition: a twenty missing a corner, fives that had been crumpled then flattened again, and hundreds bunched with rubber bands. I'd found the money Stacy stole from her former boyfriend, the source of the cash she'd deposited at BB&T each month until she died.

Being a horse lover myself, I should have suspected Stacy would keep her secrets not in the house she shared with Winston, but in the barn, where only she spent time.

That meant the book might be out here, too. If I found it and turned it over to the authorities, Santiago and his men would have no more reason to harass us. In fact, they'd have every reason to leave Michigan.

I began with the shelves and cupboards, where I found bridles, saddles, leather conditioner, black salve, ropes, reins, and blankets, but no books. Next I returned to the grain bin, thinking she might have buried it at the bottom. Pulling the tub of money out, I climbed into the bin and sifted through the grain along the bottom and sides. I got nothing except a coating of dust on my pant legs and sleeves and a fine, dry cloud that made me sneeze.

Crawling out of the bin with no dignity whatsoever, I began searching the room. The pile of loose hay yielded nothing. The rafters, the door frame, the corners—nothing. Moving along the back wall, I kicked the hay bales, listening for something that didn't sound like hay. About a third of the way down, I heard it: plastic hitting the barn's plank wall. Pulling two bales from the front stack out of the way, I exposed the second stack, its bales alternated like bricks to steady the pile. Carefully I pulled one bale halfway out. Behind it was a second tub. I kicked the next bale and heard the same thud of plastic hitting wood. There were more tubs back there.

Working up a sweat and a dust that dimmed the light to a pale glow, I maneuvered the hay bales away from the tubs. I let gravity do most of the work, pulling bottom bales out and stepping back to let the stacks fall helter-skelter. Once they were on the floor, I pushed a pathway through the mess to the tubs.

There were four of them. The first had money stacked all the way to the top. I dug around. No book. It was the same with the next tub. And the next.

By the time I reached the fourth one, I was winded. Setting the last lid aside, I sat down on a bale and stared. On the side was a label: 18 GALLONS. How much money did a tub that size hold? My unscientific answer was "A lot." Retta's DEA man was sure to be happy.

That reminded me that Barb and Retta might be home by now, or at least somewhere their phones worked. As I reached into my pocket to get mine out, Buddy, who'd watched my activity with casual interest, growled angrily.

"Just a minute," I said.

He growled again, straining against the leash, and I realized he wasn't looking at me.

A voice said, "You don't need to call anyone, Mrs. Burner. I'll handle things from here."

Max Basca stood in the doorway. He looked much the same as the day he'd come to our office, still underdressed for the weather. The difference was that he held a gun now, and it was pointed at me.

If you've never had the experience, let me tell you, it's like nothing else. A video ran through my head, some Internet tutorial that showed how a person could disarm an attacker with a handgun. You were supposed to lean to one side, push his gun hand in the opposite direction, and do this thing to his wrist so the gun fell to the ground.

There are several problems with that. First, if your opponent is experienced, he stands back so you can't reach his arm. Second, if you haven't practiced the moves over and over, they don't come naturally when a threat appears. And finally, if you're so scared you can't move, it's impossible to follow three simple steps, even if you do remember them. Instead of plotting my opponent's defeat, I found myself wishing I could have one more cigarette before he shot me. Even half would be okay.

Buddy's growl dropped to a deeper tone, and he took a leap at the newcomer. He had more courage in one of his fifteen pounds than I had in all of my...more than fifteen, but the leash stopped him. The growl cut off abruptly as his collar choked him to silence.

"Santiago," I croaked, my throat dry from dust and fear.

He smiled thinly. "You've been talking to Johannsen."

"He's going to arrest you."

He shook his head, but his hand remained steady. "He and I will not meet again, I think."

An image rose in my mind of Oversized Brows and the Neanderthal Man shooting my sisters, the agent, and Winston as they crouched in a corner of Rory's cabin. They'd probably ambush Rory and Gabe, too. My hope that a police chief and a DEA agent would make things turn out right suddenly seemed unlikely. These men were killers, and we were all in their way.

"It was good of you to find my money," Santiago said in a conversational tone. "I didn't think of the barn, though I should have. Mari was always loco for horses."

Blocking out another wave of pity for Stacy/Mari, I focused on my own peril. "I didn't see a car." Basca understood that thought fragment to mean I was surprised at his presence.

"George brought me out here. He'd heard Darrow tell your sister where the spare key was hidden, and I thought I might make Mr. Darrow's help unnecessary."

"But he and the others are on the way to the cabin."

He bowed at my correct guess. "I have no interest in learning to ride one of your snow machines." He sounded as if he couldn't comprehend such things.

He glanced out the door. "When I saw you come out here, I said to myself, 'She knows something.'"

"I didn't," I said. "I was concerned about the horses."

His left eyebrow rose. "Ah. A Good Samaritan."

Our discussion was underscored by Buddy's sounds of disapproval. Straining against the leash he growled, yipped, and grunted. Frowning in irritation, Santiago turned the gun toward him. As his hand tightened on the grip I said sharply, "Buddy! Lie down and be quiet!"

The dog obeyed, lapsing into aggrieved silence. I'd hurt his feelings, but Santiago returned his attention and the gun to me. I'd known from the moment Santiago entered the stable that I was going to die, but Buddy didn't have to. He deserved a better life than he'd had so far. He'd get used to Dale in time.

Buddy didn't get that death was an option. He growled once deep in his throat, signaling willingness to rip this guy's throat out if I said the word.

Santiago glanced at the tubs. "Is the book in there?"

I tried twice before my voice worked. "No."

"Too bad. Still, it must be here somewhere." He peered into corners of the room. Almost to himself he said, "She'd have kept it somewhere nearby."

I watched warily as he walked in a circle, bending to look at possible hiding places. Curiosity overcame fear and I asked, "Why kill Stacy before she gave up the book?"

Without looking at me he answered, "I was not present, and you know the cliché about how hard it is to get good help. Stacy gave up *a* book, and my man believed it was *the* book. Then she tried to run, and—Well, you know what happened." Again to himself he added, "Such a simple thing I asked of him."

Losing patience, Santiago kicked the remaining bales at the back wall. The resulting sounds indicated only wood behind them. Next he checked the cupboards I'd already looked in. Then all that was left were the horses' stalls.

His expression revealed the same worry I'd had. One doesn't just climb into a horse's territory and have a look around. Santiago's hand twitched on the gun butt, and I bit my lip. Like my dog, the horses were expendable if they stood in the way of what he wanted.

He stepped tentatively toward the chestnut, who moved her feet and nodded a warning. Glaring at her, he stepped back and raised the gun. Though she couldn't have understood the danger, the horse sensed it and tossed her head wildly, eyes white with agitation. His hand twitched again, and I begged, "Don't hurt her!"

He turned to me, his eyes hard, and pointed the gun at my chest. "Then go in there and search the stall."

Forcing my legs to obey, I stepped woodenly toward the buckskin. She moved nervously around her space, huffing a warning. *Great,* I thought. *I can be shot or stomped to death by an angry horse.*

Recalling my long-ago experiences with horses at summer camp, I spoke in a low voice to calm her before I moved closer. "Whoa, girl. It's okay."

"Get in there!" he repeated, louder this time. Behind him the chestnut reacted with a whinny of fear, bumping her chest against the gate to her stall. Santiago turned, momentarily distracted. Taking advantage, I slipped Buddy's leash off the nail I'd hooked it on. I was hoping he'd escape, but instead he launched himself at Santiago, spanning the space between them like a bird taking flight. His front paws caught Santiago's arm, and Buddy skittered wildly to steady himself. His hard claws raked the hand that held the gun, and the pistol discharged. The shot went wild, hitting the barn wall. Twisting his body, Buddy closed his jaws on Santiago's wrist. With a howl of pain, the man lost his grip, and the gun fell to the floor.

Clutching his hand, Santiago fell backward against the gate of the chestnut's stall. The topmost cross-board cracked loudly when his shoulder hit it, and he broke through, landing hard against the second board. He rolled onto his chest, trying to pull free, but his movement allowed the splintered board above to sag downward. Its jagged edges dug into his back and he hung there, pinned by the broken ends of the upper board to the unbroken one below him.

As Santiago fell, Buddy dropped to the floor in a heap. Rolling over quickly, he scrambled to his feet and ran at the man, biting at his ankles. Santiago kicked ineffectively at the dog while he smashed at the boards with his hands and elbows. His movements only drove the board's raw edges deeper into his fine leather jacket, slicing it—and his back too, I hoped.

That wasn't enough for Karma. The chestnut mare, seeing the chance to punish the interloper in her stall, stretched out her neck and nipped Santiago smartly on the exposed skin between his hairline and collar. Again he roared in pain, but by that time I was no longer paying much attention. I was on the floor, avoiding his flailing feet as I picked up the gun he'd dropped.

CHAPTER THIRTY-THREE

Barb

Just after nine a.m., we heard them. Sleds had passed for some time, making far away, high-pitched buzzes that rose and then fell. This time the sound grew steadily louder. Two sleds, I thought. Retta had brought help.

Looking out the window, I saw her unique pink-and-purple helmet appear at the top of the ridge. A second rider, this one taller in the saddle than most, stopped behind her.

"Wait for me here," I ordered Winston.

He retreated to the back of the cabin. "I hope that's our ride out of this icebox."

"You and me both."

Stepping outside, I climbed up to where Retta was taking off her helmet. The man with her removed his own helmet and looked down at the cabin with interest. I recognized the guy I'd seen waiting outside the police department.

"Barbara Ann, meet DEA Special Agent Lars Johannsen," Retta said.

As I opened my mouth to speak, more sleds roared up and stopped about thirty feet back. The new party consisted of three machines, two with single riders and one with two. The guy in the lead climbed off and raised the visor of his helmet. Though I'd never seen him before, he asked, "Are you Retta?"

"Yes."

"These guys hired me to bring them out here. I guess you're old friends."

There was a sharp report, and the speaker jerked spasmodically. His friendly grin turned to stunned incomprehension, and he crumpled to the ground.

"Get inside!"

I looked toward the sound. Retta's companion had grabbed her by the arms, and he pushed her down the slope toward the cabin. "Inside!" he repeated, and this time I got it. A glance past him revealed that the man with the gun was now aiming in my general direction.

Launching myself over the incline, I rolled to the bottom and stumbled toward the cabin. More shots were fired, but we were for the moment below the shooters' line of sight. When we reached the cabin and tumbled inside, the big man slammed the door closed and pushed the wooden bolt into place to secure it. Judging by dull thuds I heard on the other side, two bullets hit the door a second afterward. Since my face was level with the agent's shoulder, I noticed a hole in his coat sleeve where red oozed out. "You've been shot!"

Ignoring my comment, Johannsen pushed us all to the rear of the room. Turning the table over, he gestured for Darrow and me to get behind it. His gaze scoured the cabin, assessing its possibilities as a shelter from killers with guns. His expression said he didn't whole-heartedly approve, but he pointed at the stone fireplace. He and Retta took shelter in its corner.

As Darrow and I crouched behind the table in very close quarters, Retta slid the agent's jacket off and examined his wound. Surprisingly calm, she took off her scarf and bound the arm tightly. "It went through the fleshy part," she said. "If we stop the bleeding, you'll be okay until we get you to a hospital." When had Retta become an expert on gunshot wounds? For his part, Johannsen never stopped looking out the window.

"What happened up there?" Darrow asked.

"They killed that poor man!" Retta's tone revealed she wasn't feeling quite as cool as she was pretending.

"Who?" Darrow crouched between the two of us, his eyes wide. "Who did they kill?"

Retta bit her lip and Johannsen said, "A guide, I think. Once he got them here, he was no further use to them."

"Like us," Retta said. "We led them here, and now they'll kill us."

The agent checked Darrow out dispassionately. "As long as we've got him, we stay alive."

The silence that followed that remark was creepy. Actually, the silence outside the cabin was creepy, too. What were they doing? How would they try to get Darrow away from us?

"Who are you?" Darrow demanded.

"Agent Lars Johannsen," the tall guy said. "DEA."

"That's good," Darrow said. "You guys travel in packs, right?"

Johannsen licked his lips. "Sometimes. Not this time."

Darrow moaned, and I wanted to moan along with him.

Johannsen asked, "What's the fastest way to get help?"

"No such thing as fast out here," Retta answered. "I'll send texts to the Milldon and Bonner County sheriffs." As she thumbed the keyboard she added, "There's no road within a mile of here that's maintained in winter."

"So how will they get to us?"

"The same way we got here." Her eyes widened with surprise. "There's a message from Faye: RORY ON HIS WAY TO U.

"What does that mean?" Johannsen asked.

"Rory is Chief Neuencamp. What 'on his way' means, I can't say. As far as I know, he hasn't got a snowmobile, and mine are both already here."

"Hey, you inside!" It was George. "Send Darrow out. Once he tells us what we want to know, we'll leave!"

"Don't let them take me! Please don't!" Darrow pleaded. He touched the fading bruise on his cheek unconsciously as if fearing the pain to come.

"We won't give you up, Winston," Retta assured him.

"That's right," Johannsen agreed. "You're going to show me where your wife hid her secret stash."

"I keep telling people, I don't—"

"Later," I interrupted. No sense letting the agent know Darrow was useless to him until we were out of this mess.

The cabin window exploded, causing everyone to jump and some of us to scream—all of us, in fact, except the G-man. Cold air rushed in. The fire leapt and roared as it sucked in fresh oxygen. From then on, though, the warmth drained away as the fire's heat was neutralized by the cold that came through the gaping hole. I looked longingly at the corner where we'd piled our winter wear. Was it better to freeze slowly or die quickly of a gunshot wound?

Johannsen solved my dilemma, crawling across the room and tossing the items to us. Getting the clothes on was awkward, and Darrow kept kicking me as he pulled his own snow pants on, but we managed.

Retta watched from her crouched stance, and my fears were reflected in her eyes. "We have to get out of here."

We turned to Johannsen, who glanced around. "One door, one very open window, both in front. No other exit."

Retta surveyed the room, no doubt hoping he was wrong. I didn't. I'd spent the last day and a half here, and Johannsen was right. There was no way out.

Except there was. Without raising his head, Darrow pointed upward. "There's that octagon-shaped one up there. You can hardly see it except when you're sitting by the window."

We followed his gaze. On the back wall at the apex was an odd little window about eighteen inches across. Apparently designed to let in light, it had over the years been made less effective by large pines that had grown up behind the cabin.

"Nobody could get out that opening," Johannsen said.

"I can." Retta was right. At a hundred twenty pounds, she has hips like a ballerina.

"How would you get up there?" I asked.

"Agent Johannsen can lift me."

He looked at the window then at Retta. Turning to me he asked, "Ever fired a pistol?"

"Yes." I saw where this was headed. "I'll cover you."

Without further question he handed his sidearm over. "Stand by the window. If anything moves out there, take a shot.

Don't waste ammunition, but don't be shy, either. I'd rather not take one in the kidney while I'm boosting your sister up."

"Got it." I moved to the wall beside the window, kicking shards of broken glass aside. The clink they made was how my insides felt, brittle and shattered.

"Retta," Johannsen was saying, "when you're out, circle behind them, get to the trail, and lead the sheriff's men here."

"Check your phone when you get up on the flat," I added. "You might get a signal."

She nodded. Her face was pale, and for once she didn't amend the plan. "I will."

"Take off your coat," Johannsen said. "It's too bulky to get through the opening."

"Boots, too," she said. "I'll toss them out first." Taking off her boots, she tied the laces together and hung them around her neck. Johannsen set his back against the wall and made his hands into a basket. Turning to me, Retta smiled before putting her coat collar between her teeth. I smiled back, but mine was as weak as hers had been. She didn't want to do this, and I didn't want her to. Baby Sister was the only one who could.

Turning away, Retta put one foot in Johannsen's cupped hands, put her own hands on his shoulders and lifted herself up. Once she was stable, she set one foot on his shoulder then the other, straddling his head as she reached to open the window. It was stuck, and she had to hammer at it. I tried to concentrate on my job, watching the hillside above us, but when I glanced back again I saw blood on her knuckles.

The latch yielded, though. The window was hinged at the top, and a metal brace held it open. The next time I looked,

Retta's head and arms had disappeared through the opening. I imagined what she was thinking. She'd wriggle through and then what? Drop to the ground head first? The snow should cushion her fall, but what if there was something under it? She could be hurt, possibly killed.

When the shot rang out, I almost didn't realize what it was. Something whizzed by, thudding into the wall beside Johannsen, and Darrow swore in a tone of pure panic. Our attackers had tired of waiting and sent us a warning.

I'd forgotten the weapon in my hand, but Johannsen growled, "Return fire!" With a jerky motion I raised the gun and fired. Peering around the windowsill, I watched for a moment. Something moved, and I fired a second shot, actually aiming this time. I probably wouldn't hit anyone, but the idea was deterrence, not accuracy.

A hand touched my arm, and Johannsen spoke in my ear. "I'll take that now."

Handing him the gun, I backed away from the window. Looking up at the tiny opening overhead, I saw that Retta was gone. We had no way of knowing more than that.

CHAPTER THIRTY-FOUR

Retta

The hardest part was not screaming when I saw the drop.

Standing on Lars' shoulders raised me to where the window was just above my waist. Once I wrenched the rusty latch open, I pushed my coat and boots through and leaned out. There was no porch at the back, just a rich, white drift of untouched snow that curled softly toward the cabin wall at its tip. If all went well, I'd drop into a pillow of soft snow.

There were other scenarios. The snow might have a heavy crust, which would cut any unprotected skin like tiny knives when I broke through. There might be something under it I couldn't see, a piece of metal or a wooden frame. I wondered briefly if it was best to launch myself outward or drop straight down. Could I flip in the air and get my feet under me?

Lars stood patiently, waiting for me to make my move. Wriggling forward, I balanced my weight on the frame, releasing him. Without pausing to let my terrified side argue with my determined side, I pushed my body forward until my hips rested on the window frame. With a burst of effort I twisted myself around so that I sat in the opening, legs in and torso out. Clutching the frame with both hands, I looked down again.

The snow appeared deepest about three feet out. Setting my heels against the frame, I moved my hands to the inside of the window and grasped the trim. Once I had a firm grip, I pulled my rear up and brought one foot then the other to the outer edge of the sill. At that point it wasn't a matter of getting the courage to let go. I couldn't have held on for long anyway. I did remember to push off with my legs, which landed me near the spot I'd chosen.

The crust was cushioned by a few inches of new snow, so my landing wasn't bad. My rear hit first, but I rolled, taking some of the impact on my hips and thighs. I heard myself grunt and immediately felt the cold of a generous portion of snow up the back of my sweater. I lay there a few seconds, taking stock. Other than the fact that the snow was fast melting to ice water at my waistline, I seemed to be okay.

As I put my coat and boots back on, I formulated a plan. Behind me was the river, which was unsafe to cross since I wasn't familiar with its path, span, and currents. Out front were our enemies. I'd have to make a wide arc around them, but the snow was deep, so it wouldn't be easy. I could walk on the crust in some places, but in others I'd sink to my waist.

As I finished lacing up my second boot, one of the men out front shouted, "Hey in there! Are you going to send the guy out or are you all going to die?"

Nobody answered. I pictured Winston crouched behind the upended table, watching Barbara and Lars with fear in his heart. They wouldn't give him up, though. For one thing, it wouldn't save them. It was more likely George and his friends would set fire to the cabin and leave their charred corpses for the authorities to puzzle over.

I cut through the trees, crawling on all fours to better distribute my weight. Pushing through the heavily-laden pine branches shook snow onto my head and down my neck, and crawling was tiring. After a while I stood, hoping walking would be faster.

It was and it wasn't. Every three or four steps, I broke through. Each time, I fought my way back to the surface and went on. Breathing became difficult as my lungs fought to fuel my straining limbs. I went back to crawling, then walking, alternating the two. Before long, I was wet with sweat and every muscle in my body shook with fatigue. When I left the hollow where the cabin lay, not only was I fighting waist-deep snow, I also had to deal with the steep climb to the road.

At the end of the line of trees, I stopped to catch my breath and reconnoiter. I'd reached the snow-buried road, and I could see our attackers clearly. Getting past them meant crossing the road, and if one of them noticed me, I was dead.

I turned to see what lay in the opposite direction, but there were only trees. If I followed the road that way, it might come to an abrupt end or wind and turn until I completely lost my bearings. I couldn't help Barbara by wandering for hours through the frozen woods. The trail was my best chance. I had to hope those men were completely focused on Rory's cabin.

"It's only twenty feet," I whispered to myself, but it didn't help. For twenty feet, I'd be clearly visible in my bright pink snowsuit. I needed a distraction, thirty seconds or so when all of them were focused on something else.

Pulling out my phone, I texted Barbara. MAKE SOME NOISE. Sitting back under my tree, I waited.

And waited.

Barbara Ann is terrible at communication in the modern world. She often forgets to check her phone for messages. She still believes in email. She refuses to be part of Facebook or Twitter. As I sat there sweaty and scared, I worked myself up to real irritation with her. She'd probably shut her phone off to save the battery or put it somewhere she couldn't reach it or—

The sound of breaking glass echoed across the valley below me, and I looked toward the cabin. A stick—actually a broomstick held in a large hand that had to be Lars'—jabbed at the remaining shards of window glass, knocking them onto the snow. At the same time, I heard the sound of wood on wood and a voice shouting loudly, releasing frustration, anger, and primitive rage. Barbara Ann as I'd never heard her before, banging furniture and hollering like a Viking on the attack. It was enough to distract George and the others, to make them wonder what the cabin's occupants were up to. If I moved quickly and stayed low, they wouldn't see me cross the road.

Leaving the shelter of the pines, I ventured into the open and scrambled across, using hands and feet. I almost sobbed with relief when I reached the trees on the other side without any bullet holes.

My sister Barbara is pretty good at coming through when she's needed.

George and the others were no doubt trying to figure out what had just happened. Knowing there was at least one gun inside made them cautious, but how long would they wait to make a move? How long did I have?

Taking my phone out again, I checked the bars. None. I texted 911 anyway: RORY'S CABIN. HELP! and replaced the phone in my zippered front pocket. On the trail I might find a spot with better reception. Forcing my aching legs to move, I made my way through the trees, circling behind George and his buddies.

Then a better thought occurred to me. Five snowmobiles sat idle not fifty yards away. My own was too close to the men with guns, but the three they'd come on were farther back. On a sled I'd reach the sheriff much faster than I could on foot.

Could I sneak down there, start a machine and get away before they caught me? They'd chase me, but I was pretty sure I could outride a bunch of guys from New Mexico. The other option was trekking through a half-mile of snow to locate the trail, where I might walk for miles before meeting someone. Liking the sled-stealing option better, I ignored the inner voice warning that no matter how experienced I was as a rider, I was completely inexperienced at sneaking up on armed men, stealing their stuff, and getting away while they shot at me.

CHAPTER THIRTY-FIVE

Barb

It was maddening not knowing whether Retta had gotten away or not. When we heard nothing, I told myself that meant they hadn't caught her—hadn't killed her—yet.

"How long till she reaches the trail?" Darrow asked.

"No idea." In an attempt at encouragement I added, "If her text went through, she'll meet the sheriff's men there and lead them back here."

Johannsen was frowning at his phone, apparently becoming aware that a call was impossible. I saw no point in mentioning it might work from the roof of the outhouse.

"They won't get here in time," Darrow whined. "They'll find a pile of ash and a bunch of corpses."

"Don't—" I warned, but he was no longer in control.

"Those guys aren't going to wait out there in the cold for long." He jabbed a finger at the window, and his voice shook. "They'll come after us. We haven't got a chance!"

The agent looked at him. "Nobody has a chance once they give up." He said coldly. Though I noticed the grammatical error, I didn't correct him. *Nobody* is singular. *He* or *she* would give up, not *they*.

When my phone buzzed against my hip, I took it out, read the message, and smiled with relief. "It's Retta. She says we need to make some noise."

"Stand back." Johannsen grabbed the broom and went to the window. With energetic punches, he knocked the remaining glass from the frame, stomping on the pieces already on the floor to maximize the noise he made. Doing my part, I took up a chair and pounded it against the floor, adding something between a scream and a yodel that felt like catharsis.

When the glass was all gone and my throat was raw from yelling, we lapsed into silence.

"Was that long enough?" I asked.

Before Johannsen could answer, an engine growled to life somewhere near the road. A shout followed, then another. Someone barked an order about stopping. It sounded more like, "Stop her!" than just "Stop!"

Retta had stolen one of the snowmobiles! It was a genius move—if she got away with the stealing part.

Shots rang out, echoing through the trees so it was hard to tell how many there were. More shouts, and a second engine started and roared away. I took that to mean Retta hadn't been stopped—not yet, anyway. She was a good rider, and she had a slight head start. "Go, Retta!" I murmured, and across the room, Agent Johannsen nodded agreement40

CHAPTER THIRTY-SIX

Retta

With the three men focused on the noises coming from the cabin, I reached a snowmobile with no trouble. The problem would come when I started it. If I was lucky, the motor was still warm enough that it would start on the first pull. If it did that was good, but I still had to get the sled turned around before they shot me or dragged me off.

Taking a deep breath, I left cover and ran to the nearest machine. It was enough like my own that it took only a glance to see what I needed to do. Setting my feet firmly, I pulled the cord once. The engine roared to life, and three heads swiveled in my direction. After a brief pause of confusion, the three men pushed themselves to their feet. By that time I was on the machine, revving the engine and slamming it into gear. They started toward me, but I was riding a thousand pounds of metal. When I drove straight at them they dived for cover, as anyone would. One tripped and fell on his face in the snow. The other two jumped into a nearby clump of trees.

Once they were off their feet, I turned the machine in a tight half-circle and headed away. Shouts sounded behind me, though I couldn't make out words. A bullet flew over my head, almost stopping my heart. Crouching low, I gunned the engine and kept going. When a sled started up behind me, I let out a sob of fear. It was no longer a simple matter of fetching help. I had to outrun a killer as well.

Speeding down the narrow track, I glanced behind me every few seconds. Before long I caught a glimpse of my pursuer, crouched low over the handlebars. He seemed to get bigger each time I looked back. The guy wasn't afraid of speed, and I was his unwilling guide. He'd simply follow until he got close enough to shoot me in the back.

A dozen unhelpful questions rose in my mind. What does it feel like when a bullet enters your body? Would I die right away or bleed out in the snow? If I were wounded, would he finish me off with a smile as I lay there, unable to get away?

"Stop that!" I muttered aloud, trying to focus on my advantages. I was a hundred pounds lighter, so it would take him a while to catch up. When I reached the trail there might be other snowmobilers, which might force him to turn back. Then I remembered they'd shot their guide as soon as he served his purpose. How many more would they kill to get their way?

I pictured the trail ahead. Were there places I might turn off and lose him?

No. Off the trail, I'd leave a clear track for him to follow, and a snowmobile is not a silent mode of travel. There were no forks in the trail, either. It was a straight line into Allport, roughly following the path of the way.

The river! Years ago, my son Tony, always a bit of a daredevil, had scared us all by swerving off the trail and crossing the icy river on his sled. When we caught up with him, he'd laughed at our fears, saying, "You just keep your nerve and go hard. The sled will stay on top."

"Keep your nerve and go hard?" I'd repeated, not sure I understood.

"Right. When the sled hits the water you have the urge to slow down, but if you do, you won't make it."

The snowmobile trail crossed the river twice along this stretch, and both crossings had narrow plank bridges built over them. If I turned off the trail, headed through the woods, and crossed the river, two things could happen. The guy behind me might stay on the trail, and I'd lose him. If he followed me I could cross the water. He wasn't likely to know Tony's secret, so he'd have to give up. Either way, I'd get away.

There were a few things wrong with my plan. For one, leaving the trail meant I'd have to plow through deep, unpacked snow. My pursuer, following my track, would have the advantage. If by chance he'd watched extreme snowmobiling on TV, he might know how to make a sled skim the water surface. In that case my bold move would mean nothing. Worst of all, in order to even try a crossing I needed just the right spot, a narrow place where both banks were level with the water. There was no way to know how far I'd have to go to find it.

The bridge was coming up. What should I do: attempt the trick or try to outrun him?

Almost of its own volition, the snowmobile turned left, leaving the trail. The engine's drone dropped a few tones as the track engaged a more difficult surface to run on. The machine bucked under me as I fought to keep it heading forward, down a slight incline and between some trees. I stole a look backward.

The rider behind me followed my turn, his face grim. At least it would be harder for him to shoot at me now, since steering took more concentration.

All the tricks I'd learned in years of riding were required as I wove between stumps and hillocks and bumped scrawny tree trunks out of my way. The river flowed beside me, but the bank on the other side rose steeply, thick with trees.

It was slow going, and the machine behind me came closer. I accelerated slightly but I couldn't push it too much and take the chance that the rotating under the machine would dig itself a hole it couldn't climb out of.

A *ping!* at my right made me crouch lower, but I kept the throttle pushed forward. He was shooting again. While I doubted he'd be accurate in these circumstances, a lucky shot wasn't out of the question. The image of the gun pointed at my back made me feel like I might throw up.

There! I came over a rise to find that the river narrowed ahead as it passed through a rocky spot. The bank on both sides was almost level with the surface of the water. The opposite bank sloped upward at a gentle angle, fairly open. If I made it across, I wouldn't have to maneuver around any trees.

It was good that I had little time to think about it. Gunning the engine to full throttle, I turned sharply right, heading straight for the river. Though I tried to trust my son's experience, I couldn't help picturing myself sinking somewhere in the middle, the sled settling to the muddy bottom as frigid water washed over me, pulling my heavy boots and layers of clothing under the surface.

Focus on success! I ordered. *Imagine yourself riding away like Indiana Jones or Allen Quartermain while your pursuer shakes his fist on the opposite bank!*

I maintained speed as I approached the icy river, trying to forget that the water was traveling perpendicular to the direction I wanted to go. It was hard to tell where the land ended and the ice began, but when I heard cracking beneath the sled, I knew I was on ice. Water bubbled over the surface. I closed my eyes, bit my lip, and recalled my son's words: "Keep your nerve and go hard." He was right. I was floating—

And then I wasn't. I hit the bank with a jolt that shuddered up my spine and made my teeth click together. For a moment I feared the back of the sled would sink, but the spinning track caught against the rocks and pushed me forward onto dry land.

A few feet farther on I paused, chancing a look backward. If my pursuer followed successfully, I was lost. If he didn't, I was safe.

The guy was no coward, but he wasn't brave enough. A second before he hit the open water he let off the gas, and the sled didn't get the impetus needed to make the crossing. Halfway over, he sank like a stone in a bucket. The engine died as the carburetor filled with water, and for a moment there was only the purr of my machine.

Then the swearing began.

Rising from water almost up to his neck, that man called me every name he could think of. Abandoning the sunken machine, he started toward me, fighting the current, the mud, and his water-logged boots. Realizing my ordeal wasn't over quite yet, I turned to go.

That's when I realized I shouldn't have stopped. My sled had sunk into the snow, and the track spun uselessly. I looked back at the man, who was now only waist deep in river water. There were only thirty feet between us. Even on foot, he might catch me before I could get going again.

Fighting panic, I forced myself to think. I'd been stuck before, and I knew what I had to do. Setting one foot against a nearby tree trunk, I rocked the sled from one side to the other, freeing the track of snow. Then, sitting as far back as I could on the seat, I gave it gas. The sled strained for a moment, the engine whining. I was enveloped in a cloud of exhaust. But when I shifted my weight the machine jerked forward, chewing its way along until it was again atop the snow. I looked back once to see my pursuer staggering from the river, but he was too late. Turning right, I traced the bank, knowing I'd find the trail again and head for the road, this time with no one in pursuit.

CHAPTER THIRTY-SEVEN

Barb

Shots, at least three. Snowmobiles starting and roaring away, definitely two. What was happening?

When the engine noise faded it was quiet outside for some time, and I guessed the men were waiting, as we were, to learn the outcome of Retta's escape attempt. There was nothing.

We squinted out the window. Sun on snow made a blinding whiteness, but there was nothing to see anyway. Johannsen said, "I think she got away."

I wanted to agree, to banish the image of my sister lying dead on the trail. "Then we'll get help soon."

Johannsen answered with brusque honesty. "Darrow's right. They won't wait around for help to arrive." Glancing out the window he added, "We should take our shot while there are only two out there."

I pictured men with guns creeping downhill from an angle outside our view. He was correct. Retta had drawn one of them away. We needed to act before they returned to full strength.

"They want Darrow," I said aloud.

Johannsen turned toward me. "Yeah?"

"What if they thought they were getting what they came for?"

Johannsen frowned. "What are you thinking?"

When I told him, his frown deepened. "Too dangerous."

"Are we better off waiting for them to come down and set fire to this place?"

"No," he admitted. "But I should go."

"Look at you." I raised one hand to his height. "Who'd be fooled into thinking you were Darrow?"

After a long pause, Johannsen sighed. "Can you look a man in the eye and shoot him?"

I thought about how these men had murdered Stacy, hurt Rory, and might by now have killed my sister. "I can."

A few minutes later I was in disguise and fighting to keep my nerve. Wearing a ski mask, gloves, and boots, I was shapeless and featureless. "Almost perfect," Johannsen said. Taking sunglasses from his coat pocket, he put them on me. "Your eyes give you away." He pulled the mask over my face, hiding my chin and cheeks. "That's better."

I gave a thumbs up. He moved to the window, calling, "We send the guy out and you leave. Is that the deal?"

George replied, "We just want the husband."

"Okay. He's coming." Johannsen opened the door, and, taking a deep breath, I stepped out and started uphill, trying to walk like a man and hide the fact that my right arm was not in the sleeve of the snowmobile suit. We'd stuffed it with Johannsen's hat and my scarf, and he'd attached a rag-stuffed mitten to the cuff with electrical tape I found in the cabin.

Inside the suit, my arm hugged my body and my hand gripped the butt of Johannsen's 9 millimeter. It felt heavy, and my armpits were sweaty despite the cold. "I'll be right behind you," he'd said as he worked on me. "When you reach the top, go as far forward as you can. That will pull their attention away from the cabin. Get between the snowmobiles Retta and I left up there, then stop. Count to ten, shoot whoever's on your left, and take cover. Be ready to give me the gun when I reach you."

I went over the instructions again as I forced my feet forward, struggling to remain upright. If I fell it would be obvious I was using only one arm, and they'd know something was up.

Luckily, our many trips up and down the slope had made a fairly solid track, and I reached the top without incident. On my right George crouched, training his gun on me with a smug expression. On my left Carlos held a gun that looked too small for his oversized hand.

My feet felt like there were anchors attached to them, but I kept moving forward. When I reached the road I stepped between the snowmobiles. They weren't a lot of protection, but I felt less exposed with solid metal on either side of me.

"Stop!" George ordered, but I took a few more steps, forcing them to turn away from the cabin below. I'd planned to shoot George, the decision maker, but he was behind me. I'd have to work with what I had.

When George repeated, "Stop!" a second time, I obeyed. They were both turned toward me, and I pictured Johannsen sliding out the cabin door and heading up the rise. Maybe I wouldn't have to shoot anyone. Maybe Johannsen would—

That was the wrong way to think. I had to take the shot while it was unexpected. George and Carlos were on opposite sides of me, which would make it hard for them to shoot at me without the danger of hitting each other. Taking a deep breath, I acted before my courage leaked away. Raising the muzzle of Johannsen's gun inside the suit, I braced it against my hipbone, aimed at Carlos' chest, and shot through the fabric. Immediately I dropped to a crouch, peering over the snowmobile seat to see the result of my action.

The shot didn't fell Carlos, but both men ducked for cover, Carlos over the bank and George into some trees lining the road. I couldn't see where Carlos landed, but I hoped he was dead, wounded, or at least floundering in waist-deep snow.

"Who fired that shot, Carlos?" George called. "Carlos?" There was no answer.

The downside of Carlos' disappearance was that George no longer had to worry about hitting his buddy. He fired and the bullet hit the sled, making a sharp *ping!* that hurt my ears. I crouched even lower, my heart pounding in my chest. Air flowed through the bullet hole I'd made in the suit, cooling my ribs on the right side.

Where was Johannsen? It wouldn't be long before George maneuvered to a position where he could get a clear shot at me. I had no place to go.

"Carlos!" George called out. "If you get a shot, aim for his leg. We need him alive." That told me two things: George didn't know where Carlos was either, and he still thought I was Darrow. That was a tiny advantage. They didn't want to lose the person they thought could give them the book.

Remembering Johannsen's instruction that I be ready to hand him the gun, I set about getting my right arm into the sleeve. In seconds, I realized we'd made a terrible mistake. I couldn't do it. The fabric we'd used to fill stayed right where it was, and from my awkward position, I couldn't force my arm downward. I'd have to open the zipper and get my arm free that way.

Except that wasn't as easy as it sounded. My left hand was inside an extra-long mitten, and I had no way to pull it off. Johannsen had covered my mouth to hide the fact that I wasn't Darrow, so I couldn't use my teeth. I wriggled my fingers inside the mitt, trying to work it off, but elastic around the wrist— great for keeping out drafts—made it difficult to slide off.

After several feverish seconds of struggle, I shed the mitten by clamping it between my knees and pulling my hand out. That was something.

When I tried to unzip the suit, I encountered another problem. Johannsen had tucked the ski mask in at the neck and zipped the suit tightly to conceal my face, but in the process he'd caught the nylon fabric of the mask in the zipper. I couldn't see it, of course, but it felt well and truly jammed. I was sealed like tuna in a can.

I gave in to a moment of despair. Johannsen was counting on me handing him his gun, and I was unable to do that. Retta had done better, I told myself. She'd reduced the number of enemies we faced from three to two. Some detective I was— helpless, pinned down and unable to warn Johannsen, who would enter the scene with at least one gun aimed at him, maybe two, and no way to defend himself.

CHAPTER THIRTY-EIGHT

Retta

I made it back to the trail without too much trouble, and it was a relief to be able to open the sled up on a familiar, prepared surface. Still, I'd been gone from the cabin for some time. George and Carlos might have made their move by now. Worse, I had a long way to go if my calls for help hadn't gone through. Even if they had, it might be hours before they found the cabin. I prayed that somehow, Barbara and Lars could hold out that long.

My worries didn't last, because the law—at least a single entity of the law—came chugging down the trail toward me. It took a few seconds to register what I was seeing. The groomer driver was unfamiliar, but behind him, something furry rode. As I got closer, the furry thing looked more and more familiar.

Then the other passenger caught my attention, giving me one of those gut-wrenching moments when you're reminded of a loved one who has left this world. The guy's tattered overalls looked like the ones Don used to wear to work outside during the winter. Blinking the past away, I looked again. Two familiar shapes pressed their way past my other concerns, and I identified them. Rory and Styx!

"Retta!" Rory called, waving wildly. I stopped, leaving the sled idling as I ran to where the groomer rattled and hummed. Styx met me with a joyful yip, putting his paws on my shoulders. I staggered back, keeping my balance with difficulty as I patted his head and scratched his ears.

"It's okay, baby," I crooned, comforted by his solidity and warmth.

"Where are they?" Rory had come up behind Styx, his anxious face incongruous in the outlandish outfit he wore. "Are they all right?"

"They're pinned down at the cabin," I shouted over the noise of both engines. "Two men with guns." I looked back the way I'd come. "There were three, but one chased me and I managed to dunk him in the river."

"Barb?"

"She's okay. So are Winston and Agent Johannsen."

Rory's eyes unfocused for a second as he pictured the scene. "Gabe," he told the driver, "Take Mrs. Stilson back to my truck so she can get the sheriff out here."

The guy nodded, but I said, "He can show them the way. I'm going back with you."

CHAPTER THIRTY-NINE

Barb

Crouched between the snowmobiles I waited, but Johannsen didn't appear. It seemed like forever, but forever wasn't enough time to conquer the zipper that wouldn't unzip. I pushed at the fabric with my fingers, hoping to free it from the teeth. I yanked on the pull, trying to force it down. I extended my neck in an attempt to stretch the nylon mask thin and slide it out of the jammed spot. Nothing worked.

As I tried, failed, and muttered some pretty bad words, scenarios flitted through my mind. If Carlos was unhurt, he might have forced Johannsen back into the cabin. The agent might be caught somewhere, pinned down. If his wound was more serious than he'd admitted, he might have passed out from loss of blood. Even if he was still mobile, an unusable arm presented problems, as I could attest.

Had Carlos shot him as he fought his way toward me? I couldn't recall how many shots had been fired. Worst case scenario was that Carlos had killed Johannsen while I ducked the bullets George had sent my way. In that case, I was on my own. Well, there was Darrow, but I knew I couldn't count on him.

What should I do, or more precisely, what could I do?

First, I needed better cover. Sooner or later, George would take his chance. From my current position I couldn't aim the gun at him. Any shot I fired was likely to hit one or the other of the snowmobiles and ricochet back at me.

Releasing the gun, I went back to clearing the sleeve. I pulled the empty right-hand mitten off and tried to pull the stuffing out that way, but the cuff narrowed the opening, and my fingers just slipped off the fabric, which stayed wedged in place. When I gave up and reached for the gun again, I couldn't find it. I almost panicked. Why had I let go of it?

There it was, in my pant leg. I pulled it slowly toward me, aware that the safety was off and I might shoot myself in the thigh if I wasn't careful.

Once I got my hand and the gun back up to my waistline, I felt a little better. If George did come at me, I could wait until he was directly above me and shoot through the fabric again.

If only Johannsen would get here! He'd unzip the suit and retrieve the gun—

Movement caught my eye and I looked up. George had moved to where he could see me clearly. He pointed the gun at me, its barrel low. My legs tensed in anticipation of a bullet through my thigh, my calf, my foot. Frantically I yanked at the zipper. I had only a few seconds.

A noise—a roar—interrupted my thought, and I turned to see something out of a nightmare—or in this case, a surreal-but-wonderful dream. A snowmobile bore down on George at full throttle. On it sat a figure whose professionally high-lighted hair streamed behind her. Retta! Behind her was someone wearing a bright red hat with earflaps, a tattered, faded orange jumpsuit, and blue-and-yellow-striped, University of Michigan stretch gloves. As the sled neared, he leaned out to peer around Retta's shoulder. Rory!

George froze, unsure if he should stay or run. The machine kept coming. As George's head swiveled between me and the oncoming sled, his courage wavered. At the last second, he jumped sideways, diving back into the trees with neither grace nor caution.

Unable to turn aside, the snowmobile continued past me, left the road, and took to the air, narrowly missing the trees George sheltered in. The engine whined to a higher note as the track left the ground. Rory and Retta floated briefly like oversized swallows before dropping out of sight. Somewhere below me the machine growled again, roared briefly, and stopped with a choking groan.

I fired a shot in George's direction, hoping to give them time to reach cover. The smell of singed fabric rose from the second hole in my suit, but George didn't fall. As the echoes died away, he slid over the rim of the hill, heading to where Rory and Retta had disappeared.

A few seconds later, a shot rang out. On one hand that was good, because it meant someone had survived the landing. Still, Rory and Retta were sitting ducks with George above them and possibly Carlos somewhere below. Rising briefly I fired again, worried about wasting bullets but desperate to help. I waited. There were no more shots.

What I did hear were sounds of blows being struck: dull thuds, widely spaced, and grunts of exertion.

Skittering to the rim, I slid into the clump of trees where George had been a short while before. Below me was a tableaux that seemed to move in slow motion. On one side of the cabin, Johannsen traded blows with Carlos, and though he fought fiercely, his wounded arm clearly hampered him. The deep snow was another problem, though in that both men were similarly handicapped. Each time one landed a blow both staggered backward. Determined, each man waded back toward the other in order to re-engage.

Standing upright, I tried again to unzip my suit and free the hand that held the gun. I straightened the zipper as much as I could, but the pull stopped at the knot of fabric under my chin. If I fired at Carlos from inside the suit, my chances of hitting Johannsen were equally likely.

Johannsen was hurt, but he was focused. I got the sense he was figuring Carlos out, watching his moves and measuring his cadence. Though I know little about such things, I guessed the agent was letting his opponent wear himself out and waiting for a chance to do some damage.

At the other side of the cabin, Rory crouched behind the generator shed, apparently watching Johannsen and Carlos. Twenty yards away, George wallowed toward him, circling in an attempt to get a shot off. Rory seemed unaware, and I almost shouted a warning, but he glanced up, saw me, and made a quick gesture of caution. I realized I was completely exposed on the ridge. If George turned and spotted me, he'd easily pick me off.

I ducked, and Rory returned to what I saw now was a ploy. He was actually waiting for George, but why? He had no weapon, and George was, as they say, armed and dangerous. Whatever his strategy was, it didn't seem likely to be successful.

Then I saw something else. As George closed on Rory, Retta stole out from behind the outhouse, holding a chunk of firewood like a softball bat. Intent on Rory, George didn't see her, and she swung her improvised weapon sharply, catching him on the upper arm. Roaring with pain, he dropped to one knee. When he stood again, the gun was still in his hand. Retta struck again, whacking his wrist this time. The gun dropped into the snow. As George dived after it, she hit him a third time across the back.

He still didn't stay down, but rose and punched at Retta with his fist. When she backed away, he immediately returned to searching for the gun. But Rory had left the shelter of the shed and started toward George. He left one boot behind, but he fought his way forward. He had to reach George before he retrieved his gun.

Though I was mesmerized by what was going on below me, I hadn't stopped fighting the suit. I pulled at the neckline until I half choked myself in an attempt to tear the fabric. I stuck my fingers up the stuffed arm and tried frantically to pull the wadded fabric out. I even jerked at the sleeve itself, trying to break the stitching at the shoulder. None of those things worked.

I had to get my arm free! Although I couldn't fire at George or Carlos without endangering Rory or Johannsen, a warning shot might be convincing—if our attackers could see that I really did have a gun.

If I could show the gun. If I could aim it. If I could get my arm out of the stupid suit.

Something bumped past me, almost knocking me down. With a mighty leap, Styx landed in the snow a few yards downhill, his whole body a-quiver with anticipation. Someone unfamiliar with the dog might think he was determined to subdue the bad guy and rescue his mommy. To me it looked like he wanted a hug.

Either way, Styx was a formidable sight as, using his webbed paws like paddles, he swam through the snow toward Retta. "Styx!" She called as George dug frantically through the snow. "Stay back, Baby!"

In a desperate attempt to help, I stood, tilted the gun muzzle away from the scene and myself, and fired another shot. When it echoed over the ridge, everyone, even Styx, looked up, but they couldn't tell where the sound came from. The holes in the suit weren't visible at a distance, so I appeared to be merely an observer of the events below. I thought about shouting, "I have a gun," but with no way to prove it (or point it), I'd be wasting my breath.

I might even have made things worse. Carlos took advantage of Johannsen's moment of distraction to hit him squarely in the face. The agent reeled briefly but remained standing, blood squirting from his nose.

With the approach of the big dog, George abandoned his search for the gun. Circling around Styx, he began fighting his way uphill, obviously headed for the snowmobiles and escape. With a burst of effort, Rory closed the distance between them, caught George by the collar, and spun him around. While George was still off-balance, Rory hit him with an uppercut that snapped his head back. It looked for a second like he would collapse, but calling on some reserve of energy, George delivered a return punch Rory just managed to avoid. Leaning in, Rory hit his opponent in the stomach, doubling him over. *That will do it,* I thought, but George remained on his feet. With vicious fury he went at Rory, no doubt aware of what he faced if he was arrested.

Styx was still heading toward Retta, but she moved away from him, toward the cabin's porch. He followed, tongue lolling with effort, as she reached her goal, an ice spud leaning against the side wall. Ordering Styx to stay, she took up the spud and turned, undecided. Who would she assist, Rory or Johannsen?

The agent and Carlos were still struggling, but it was clear they were both near exhaustion. Though he was the more intelligent fighter, Johannsen was weakened by his wound, and Carlos was his match in size and strength. Rory and George continued trading blows as well. Retta hesitated briefly, holding the long-handled spud. Tipped with a small, flat blade, it was a good weapon if she could get close enough to whack an enemy with it. Her problem was two-fold: the decision of who needed help more, and the distances between them.

I had to do something. Twisting my arm inside the suit, I tried again to free it. Nothing. Tears of frustration came to my eyes as I stood there, looking down. Two men who'd come to rescue me were in trouble and—

Men! I looked down, recalling something that had never meant much to me before. My suit, made for a man, had a convenience slit for urinating on the trail. Only a small patch of Velcro held it closed. Maneuvering the gun muzzle in that direction, I used it to pry the Velcro open and pushed the pistol and my hand out the hole. Pointing the gun at the sky, I fired.

"Stop!" Turning the gun toward Carlos' massive chest I added, "I won't miss at this range."

Carlos looked up at me, apparently dismissed my courage, and took another swing at Johannsen. "Duck, Lars!" I shouted. With quick understanding, he dropped to the ground. I fired twice from the groin position, one I'd never practiced on the pistol range.

To be truthful, I think I closed my eyes at the last second. The shot went wide, but not by much. Hearing a cry of pain, I opened my eyes to see Carlos holding his elbow and Johannsen rising to his feet. I felt simultaneous but opposite reactions: Joy that I'd hit the mark and shock that I'd actually put a hole in another human being.

Taking advantage of his opponent's confusion, Rory grabbed George's collar. "You're under arrest, jackass."

Johannsen turned Carlos, gave his arm a cursory glance, and said casually, "He'll live." As he pushed Carlos toward the path, Johannsen looked at Rory—the garish gloves, orange suit, and red, flop-eared hat—and turned to me questioningly.

"Agent Johannsen," I said, "meet Chief Neuencamp."

CHAPTER FORTY

Retta

If anything in this world was ever funny, scary, and miraculous at once, it was my sister Barbara standing on a snowy ridge with a Glock 9 millimeter sticking out of her fly. I didn't know whether to laugh or break down in tears. As always, my big sister came through, though not with her usual, over-developed sense of dignity this time. Barbara can think on her feet, and she does what's necessary, no matter what it takes.

I followed Johannsen and the prisoners uphill, carrying the spud in case someone needed swatting. George said nothing. Carlos whined about how much his elbow hurt. Lars claimed he was fine, though he held the wounded arm tightly to his side. He'd easily have defeated Carlos if he hadn't been wounded.

My Styx came through it all beautifully, scaring the bad man so Rory could deal with him, and once it was over, he visited everybody, willing to hug and be hugged.

When we reached the road, Lars took his gun from Barbara without even a glimmer of a smile. After some digging, Rory retrieved the weapon George had dropped, and when he joined us I stepped aside, letting the two law officers handle things. When Barbara explained her problem with the zipper, Rory handed me his pocket knife and I cut away the jammed fabric, opened the zipper, and un-stuffed her sleeve so she could use both hands again.

Lars had one set of handcuffs, which Rory put on George, tight enough to make him wince. Positioning him on a snowmobile facing backward, Rory tied his feet to the bumper bar at the back, using the drawstrings out of his jacket. When he finished he stood back to check his work. "Retta, if he moves, hit him with that spud."

"Not a problem, Chief."

Next Rory went to work on Carlos, splinting his arm with branches tied in place with more laces. While he worked, Barbara fetched Winston from the cabin, and Agent Johannsen went to examine the body of the man George had shot. "Hey!" he called. "This guy's still alive!"

Rory turned from tightening a knot. "Who is he?"

Johannsen turned to George, who shrugged. "Some guy we hired to help us get here."

"We have to get him to a hospital," I said.

"He's as stuck out here as the rest of us," Rory replied. "We have to wait for—"

Just then we heard a rumble, and soon a voice called, "Chief? Chief, are you okay?"

"Is that who I think it is?" Barbara asked.

Rory nodded. "I sent him to get help, but apparently he followed us." Cupping his hands to his mouth he called, "Gabe, can you bring your machine in here?"

"On my way!" We heard the engine shift into gear, and in a few minutes the groomer lumbered through the woods, knocking down small trees as it came. The driver wore one of those elf hats with a tassel hanging down the back and a grin that said he was feeling clever. On the back of the groomer was the guy who'd chased me through the woods, wet to the armpits, shivering with cold, and tied to the vehicle's frame with bungee cords.

"I called the sheriff on the radio," Gabe told us. "He's coming, but they had some kind of problem."

"And how did you do that?" Rory asked, gesturing at Gabe's prisoner.

With the eagerness of a true storyteller, Gabe said, "It was part capture and part rescue, if you ask me. He come staggering onto the trail, dripping wet and waving a gun. I stopped, and the dog there jumped off and went running at him." Gabe's grin got even bigger. "He freaked, but the dog was just bein' friendly." Turning to me, he asked, "What's his name, ma'am? If I heard you say it, I forgot."

"Styx."

Gabe nodded vaguely, and I guessed Greek mythology was foreign to him. "Anyway, Styx created a distraction, and that gave me time to arm myself." He patted a small chain saw carried for times when a driver needed to clear trees from the trail. "Soon as I fired 'er up, he started surrendering like mad."

We all looked at the glum-faced prisoner, whose expression showed disgust. "Bigfoot *and* a chainsaw-waving maniac," he mumbled. "It's like one big horror movie out here."

"Gabe, you did well," Rory said.

"Except the dog took off. I couldn't call him back."

"That's because he knew I was in danger," I said. "Styx is a very brave boy."

Though we hadn't been formally introduced, I'd heard about Gabe and his former life of crime from Faye. He seemed to me a Huck Finn type—not ill-intentioned, just ill-equipped in some areas. He was obviously pleased to have helped Rory, and when he spoke to Barbara, you'd have thought she was royalty.

Johannsen suggested Gabe take the unconscious guide out on the groomer. Rory agreed, having done what he could for him with the first aid kit I carried on my sled. He had a chest wound, but landing in the snow had stopped the bleeding, giving him a chance. While Gabe turned the groomer around, I went back to the cabin and got the two sleeping bags I'd brought. We wrapped the wounded man in one for warmth and padded the groomer with the other.

"Hey, I'm shot too!" Carlos complained.

"Shut up," Johannsen said, but Barbara went down and got the third sleeping bag for him. I suppose the first time you shoot someone, you feel a little guilty about it.

Johannsen handed Barbara Ann his gun so she could guard the prisoners while he, Gabe, and Rory lifted the wounded man onto the vehicle. Glancing at Winston, who didn't even offer to help, I wondered what I'd seen in him. Even as a casual date, he didn't look so good to me now.

Once they'd situated the guide, Rory led Carlos to the back of the groomer, sat him down, and tied his good arm to a sidebar. "Go ahead," he told Gabe. "We'll follow with the others."

With a jaunty wave, Gabe started off. Carlos huddled at the back, looking grim and hanging on for dear life.

That left Daniel—the guy who'd chased me—George, and Winston to ride with Rory, Johannsen, and me. There was one sled left. Barbara looked at it doubtfully.

"Wait here," Rory told her. "I'll come back for you."

I was proud of Barbara Ann when she said, "Start that thing up and show me how it works. If I can handle shooting a man, I suppose I can drive a snowmobile."

CHAPTER FORTY-ONE

It took so long that I was shaking for lack of a cigarette, but two Bonner County deputies arrived at Winston's house, found their way to the barn, and took Max "Basca" Santiago into custody. One of the officers had handled horses before, so the other took Max to the car in handcuffs while we set about soothing the horses' nerves with a lot of crooning and petting. As we worked I told the deputy, whose name was Bryce, about the book.

"If we lead them out one at a time, I could search the stalls while you keep them quiet," he suggested. That's what we did, though we only had to search one. Bryce slipped a rope over the red horse's neck and I led her out of the stall, telling her non-stop what a good girl she was. I kept her head turned away while he went in, sidestepping the worst of the mess, and searched. On the back wall an old canvas bag hung on a nail, and as soon as he touched it, Bryce caught my eye and grinned. Inside the ragged bag was a sealed pouch, and inside that was the book that had caused so much trouble.

The deputies took Max to jail, and I promised to come in and give a statement when the sheriff returned. I hurried home, hoping to find my sisters or at least hear that they were on their way. Neither had happened, and Dale and I spent a long two hours waiting for word.

When the call finally came, Sheriff Idalski said his men had found them safe. I learned later it was more the other way around. First Gabe, then the rest, had reached the spot where the sheriff's people were gathered. They'd trailered their sleds to the starting point, but no one had been able to locate their usual guide. Of course, that was because he was the man Gabe brought out on the back of his groomer. Idalski said he'd been stabilized and taken to the hospital for treatment.

An hour after the sheriff's call, five exhausted people showed up on our doorstep. Hearing the commotion, Buddy limped out to the office, barking furiously. When I picked him up his barks turned to growls. He was learning to tolerate others, but our conversation was underscored with muted sounds of his unhappiness at the presence of so many extra people. I thought it was kind of cute.

Barb told the story, with Retta interrupting to add details. Styx became the hero when she talked, because he'd courageously attacked both George and Daniel to save her, Gabe, and Rory. Barbara rolled her eyes and I guessed she thought Styx had been looking for someone to tell him what a great dog he is. I was in no position to say which of them was correct.

Dale stood behind me, listening to the account. When they wound down, he urged, "Tell them about your day."

All eyes turned to me, and I gave a brief version of my encounter with Santiago.

"You took down a drug lord?" Retta's voice rang with surprise.

I grinned. "Well, Buddy and I and a couple of horses."

Win had been talking on the phone since they walked in the door, but he'd heard parts of my story. "I told you," he said, pocketing his phone. "Those critters hate men. I'll have to find a woman buyer, I guess."

"You're going to sell them?" I asked.

"I'm going to sell everything," he replied. "The feds will take the money, but Mr. Glass thinks they'll let me keep the house. I mean, Stacy wasn't a drug dealer or anything. Once it sells, I can start over." Gesturing toward the window he added, "Somewhere warm."

"I kind of like the cold." We all turned to Agent Johannsen, who'd been quiet up to that point. "Now that I know someone who has snowmobiles—" He looked at Retta, "—and a cabin—" He turned to Rory, "—I wouldn't mind coming back for a few days' vacation."

"That sounds great," Retta said. Barb's gaze met mine, and her lips twitched.

"I'll have to clean the place up before you come." With a glance at Barb Rory added, "I might need help."

"It happens I have experience as a glazier," Barb said. "I replaced two windows in this place when I moved in, all by myself." It was the closest I'd ever heard my sister come to bragging, and Retta and I exchanged knowing looks. If Barb was willing to return to Rory's cabin in the woods, the reward she anticipated had to be pretty darned special.

CHAPTER FORTY-TWO

Barb

"I have to admit," I told Faye as we got into her car the next day, "Your sister was a welcome sight when she came roaring through on that snowmobile. Another few seconds and George would have shot me."

"Wish I could've seen her," she said with a grin.

The weather had turned mild, at least for January. Everything looked bright in the morning sun, and for once there was no biting wind. My house was encased in white, the cleared driveway wet-black against the piled banks on either side. Michigan really is a beautiful place, despite the long winters.

As she put her car into gear, Fay's her expression turned sober. "Barb, this is the third time you were nearly murdered on the job. Maybe we should stick to white-collar crime and deadbeat dads."

"Who'd have predicted this case would be dangerous?" I searched my pocket for a tissue for my drippy nose. "Besides, we saved our client from a murder charge and sent four criminals to jail. Doesn't that make you feel good?"

"Well, yes, but if you'd died, or Retta—" Turning into the parking lot of The Meadows, she squeezed her car into the last spot. A hand-lettered sign stapled to a light post proclaimed, "Musick this Sunday. Friends and family member's welcome."

We were in Faye's car, so I didn't have the tools to correct the errors, even if I'd been brave enough to attempt it in broad daylight. I turned sideways in the seat so I didn't have to look at it, but it felt like that misused apostrophe was tapping me on the shoulder while the misspelled word tittered in my ear.

Faye didn't appear to notice. "We'll talk after I straighten out Harriet's latest mess."

She went off, skirting slushy patches on the sidewalk with small, careful steps. I watched, wondering what it was like to deal with Harriet the Harrier on a daily basis. Today the old lady refused to participate in physical therapy, and they'd called Faye, hoping she could talk sense to her. A phone conversation had gone nowhere, so Faye had come to listen to Harriet's latest complaint.

Faye would handle it, like she handled everything else, with understanding, intelligence, and good humor. Now that we lived in the same house, I saw how often her boys came to her for advice and help, how much the nursing home depended on her to handle the irascible Harriet, and how much Dale relied on her. She responded lovingly and patiently to all those demands, but it had to be a drain.

Thoughts of Dale's clinginess diverted my mind to Rory. As we aged, would he drive me half crazy with his old-man ways? I wasn't nearly as patient as Faye. And what if he had a senile mother somewhere who'd demand I dance attendance on her, as Faye was doing for her mother-in-law at this moment?

The night before, after all the stories were told, Rory had tilted his head toward the back door, indicating we should go outside together. I left the others repeating their favorite bits and followed him onto the back porch. Taking a seat on the swing that was Faye's usual smoking spot, he patted the boards next to him.

I moved a coffee can of butts to a spot where I couldn't smell it. "How long before they come looking for us?"

He put an arm around my shoulders. "Not long, but I've wanted to hug you since I saw you scrunched behind that snowmobile," he replied. "You looked so scared."

"I *was* scared."

"We all were. Retta was shaking like a leaf, but she did what had to be done, and so did you." We were silent for a while as I enjoyed the feeling of his arm around my shoulders. "What's next for us, Barb?"

Having no answer, I changed the subject. "Did they call your daughter when you got hurt?"

His mouth quirked with humor at my avoidance of his question, but he said, "She's in Venezuela, doing research on their legal system. By the time they reached her, I was out of the hospital. I called and told her it was no big deal."

"She's a lawyer?"

He shrugged. "Almost. Two semesters, maybe three, and she'll be eligible for the bar."

"Excellent."

"It is. Now answer my question."

I sighed. "I really like you, Rory. You must know that."

"But—?" There was a question in his tone.

"I'm used to living alone, used to doing as I please."

"And you think I'd interfere with that?"

"Not you personally," I said miserably. "Anyone. I like my own schedule." Groping for an example, I said, "There are times when I resent that Faye wants me to share three meals a week with them. It shouldn't feel like a duty, but somehow it does."

He was quiet for a long time, and I thought about how weird I sounded. What kind of person doesn't look forward to daily contact with others?

As the silence stretched, I concluded there was no hope for a relationship between us. I'd go back to calling him Chief Neuencamp. We'd pretend we'd never kissed, never exchanged confidences, never felt tender feelings stirring. Maybe I really was as cold as Retta and several men in my past had called me.

When Rory spoke, I was ready for anything but what he said. "Well, then, that's perfect."

"Perfect?" I repeated.

Turning to me, he said, "I lost my wife because being a cop is the most important thing in the world to me. My hours are horrible. My mind is usually on something related to my job. I forget birthdays, anniversaries, dinner dates." He grinned. "Any woman would hate living with me, including you."

"I would?"

"Yes. But that doesn't mean we can't make this work."

"This?"

"Us." He touched my hand gently. "We like each other, right? We want to be together, just not all the time. What if we go with that?"

It was the kind of speech that bothered me: "be together," "go with it." Vague and imprecise. Still, I got the gist. "Don't they call that friends with benefits?"

Rory shook his head. "You know we're more than that, but we're also adults who can think independently. A lot of stuff people insist is necessary for a happy relationship is pure garbage. I don't need you to cook my breakfast or watch football with me on Sunday afternoons." A little embarrassed, he paused. "I like you, Barb. I don't care about the details if you and I get to be together when the time is right for us both."

I sat in silence for a moment. "You're saying we can have a relationship that nobody but us will understand."

"Exactly. I won't smother you with attention. You'll accept there'll be times when I'm not available, maybe physically, maybe emotionally." He grinned again. "I will try to show up when your job gets you into trouble."

We left it at that—well, except for some kissing.

When Faye came out of The Meadows, she lit a cigarette before reaching the twenty-foot limit decreed by a sign in the lobby window. "We struck a deal," she told me as I exited the car and joined her on the sidewalk.

"What did you promise the old bat?"

"Actually, I was on her side on this one. Physical therapy at ninety? Really?" She took a long drag. "I spoke to the doctor, who agreed to leave Harriet alone."

It made sense to me. "If you make it to ninety, you should have choices."

"And get to die on your own terms." Kay stubbed out the cigarette in a small metal ashtray she carried in her purse. "Know what she said when I told her?"

In a parody of Harriet's voice and increasing deafness I said, "What? What was that?"

Faye gave me her patient smile. "She said, 'Faye, you get it, and you're the only one.'"

"Wow! She acknowledged you by name and gave you a compliment, all in one sentence?"

"It was kind of sweet."

An old biddy like Harriet sweet? Only my sister Faye can think like that.

We started for the car, and she returned to our earlier conversation. "Are you sure you want to continue the agency?"

"Are you saying you might want to give it up?"

Faye tossed her purse onto the back seat. "You know I hate the prospect of ending up somewhere like this." She nodded toward the long, low building before us. "Life isn't worth it if you don't do something worthwhile."

"Like being private investigators?"

"It's worth it to me," she said firmly. "I just want to know if it's worth it to you."

Starting the agency had been Faye's idea. She'd imagined helping people in crisis, but she hadn't been able to imagine the risks. Now she was willing to give it up, but it was because of fears for me and Retta, not for herself.

"We don't need to close the agency, Faye. We'll just get serious about safety."

"How?"

I thought about that. "Well, we can hire some help. If you'd had someone with you at Darrow's house the other day, Santiago would probably have run."

"And who would we hire?"

"I told you we might be able to use Gabe."

"No, you didn't."

I realized it was Retta I'd mentioned it to. It was weird to think I'd mentioned something about the business to her before I told Faye.

Faye asked, "What possible use could Gabe be?"

I shrugged. "He could be trained to do some of the legwork, I think."

She rolled her eyes. "Gabe?" Softly she repeated in a disbelieving tone, "Gabe."

"And we've got Rory," I said to get her mind off Gabe.

"Who has a full-time job."

I floundered a little. "Well, there's Retta."

"Retta?"

"Maybe it's time we let her be part of the agency...as an auxiliary investigator."

"And what in the world is that?"

I grinned. "One who does what we say and has no vote on anything important."

Faye chuckled. "How long will she stand for that?"

"It's better than giving up the agency entirely."

With a sigh, Faye started back to the car. "I guess more staff might help, but—"

"Look." I waved a hand toward the nursing home. "I'd rather George had killed me than end up like poor old Harriet. How about you?"

"Well, yes."

"Then let's stop worrying about what might happen. We could get hit by a train on our way back home—at least we might if Allport had a train."

She grinned, and the worried look left her eyes. "I get it. We don't have to do this by ourselves."

"Right," I said. "I'll talk with Gabe. You can explain to Retta that she's—a tiny little part of the Smart Detective Agency. Tell her: No rearranging the office, no redesigning the letterhead, no telling us what to do." I added in a mutter, "Not that it will work."

"And Dale," Faye said.

"What?"

"We need to find something he can do."

Big sigh. I'd begun this enterprise in large part because I cared about Faye, who longed for adventure and the chance to help others. Now, it seemed, I'd be dealing with both my sisters, a sometime boyfriend, a petty criminal turned hero, a disabled brother-in-law, and even Buddy the dog. "Okay," I told Faye. "We'll get it all moving forward—somehow."

She smiled. "You and me against the world, right?"

I couldn't let that pass. "You and *I*, but yes, that's exactly it."

CHAPTER FORTY-THREE

Retta

If you ask me, things worked out really well. Basca and his men went to jail, and from there they would no doubt go on to prison. The detective agency was featured in the paper as a pivotal force in capturing several hardened criminals who invaded little Allport. I felt a tiny bit guilty for not calling in the state police when Faye wanted to, but if I had, the agency wouldn't have gotten such great publicity. In addition, I might never have met Lars, who is a very, very attractive man. These things have a way of working themselves out.

I'm more likely to be a real partner in the agency now that I've proven I can handle danger without going all freaky. I was really scared, I'll admit that, but it didn't keep me from doing what had to be done. Barbara said in front of Rory and everyone that she'd probably have died if I hadn't acted as I did.

On the minus side, I might have messed up my chances by moving too quickly. The three of us had lunch the day after Basca's arrest, following the taking of our statements at the sheriff's office. It was nice to be three sisters doing things together, and we chatted happily about our adventures. Faye made a big deal out of Buddy's part in her ordeal, and I was polite. Apparently no one had called in response to her ad, so he was now a permanent part of the household. I wondered how Barbara felt about that, but she, too, was polite.

In a situation like that one topic leads to another, and soon we were talking about the agency's future. Though I didn't mean to approach the subject so soon, the idea I'd had for some time just popped out. Right away I knew I'd slipped up.

Barbara's face got that hard look, and Faye said, "The Sleuth Sisters? You want to change the name of the agency to The Sleuth Sisters?"

"We're sleuths, and we're sisters. It makes sense, doesn't it?" Ignoring Barbara's tight lips I went on, "I made some sample logos up, so you can choose the one you like best." I made a little joke. "I already know which one Faye will like." They said nothing, so I went on, "It's important to have a brand nowadays, so people recognize right away who you are."

"No changes." The words came out of Barbara's mouth like bullets.

"But if you—"

A look from Faye, half warning, half plea, stopped me. Apparently Baby Sister isn't allowed to have opinions or input. I'm supposed to look cute and remain silent, like when we were kids.

They'll come around, though. I am exactly what the agency needs, though it's hard for them to admit it. I'll work on them, but I won't be pushy about it. I'm just not that kind of person.

ABOUT THE AUTHOR

Maggie Pill is also Peg Herring, but Maggie's much younger and cooler. Visit her website: http://maggiepill.com

Be on the lookout for Sleuth Sisters #3: *Murder in the Boonies* (Working Title) in 2015!

The abrupt disappearance of the renters at the Sleuth Sisters' family farm presents Faye with the chance to do something she's always dreamed of: start a draft horse rescue. The circumstances surrounding the move are strange, though, and Faye, Barb, and Retta begin to suspect that at least some of the family members didn't leave voluntarily.

Balancing a menagerie of animals with tracking down clues as to where the man, his wife, and her three daughters might have gone, the sleuths uncover a series of surprises that lead to dangers they never anticipated. As those dangers grow, the sisters—and ultimately everyone in the surrounding area—are plunged into deadly peril.

www.ingramcontent.com/pod-product-compliance
Lightning Source LLC
Chambersburg PA
CBHW060955120726
47910CB00002B/648